MW00711017

UNBROKEN

Jesse—
Love and Kisses
But keep your shirt on for
the memories. Enjoy the
Story.

xxx

Visit us at www.boldstrokesbooks.com

By the Author

Healing Hearts

No Boundaries

Love's Redemption

Unbroken

UNBROKEN

by
Donna K. Ford

2017

UNBROKEN

© 2017 BY DONNA K. FORD. ALL RIGHTS RESERVED.

ISBN 13: 978-1-62639-921-1

THIS TRADE PAPERBACK ORIGINAL IS PUBLISHED BY
BOLD STROKES BOOKS, INC.
P.O. BOX 249
VALLEY FALLS, NY 12185

FIRST EDITION: MAY 2017

THIS IS A WORK OF FICTION. NAMES, CHARACTERS, PLACES, AND
INCIDENTS ARE THE PRODUCT OF THE AUTHOR'S IMAGINATION OR
ARE USED FICTITIOUSLY. ANY RESEMBLANCE TO ACTUAL PERSONS,
LIVING OR DEAD, BUSINESS ESTABLISHMENTS, EVENTS, OR LOCALES
IS ENTIRELY COINCIDENTAL.

THIS BOOK, OR PARTS THEREOF, MAY NOT BE REPRODUCED IN ANY
FORM WITHOUT PERMISSION.

CREDITS
EDITOR: RUTH STERNGLANTZ
PRODUCTION DESIGN: SUSAN RAMUNDO
COVER DESIGN BY SHERI (GRAPHICARTIST2020@HOTMAIL.COM)

Acknowledgments

Writing *Unbroken* was a long undertaking. Although the story was mostly finished, these characters allowed me to take a year away from them to write *Love's Redemption*. The time away was well spent, and I can say this story was worth the wait.

I would like to offer a special thank you to my dear friend Kellie. Thank you for sharing your stories with me. I am so proud of your strength to overcome the past and the courage to build an amazing life with your own happily ever after.

This has been a very special year for me for many reasons. It has been marked with tragedy and joy, both of which have changed my life forever. I said good-bye to my dear daddy this year. That is a heartbreak that will never heal. But I know he was proud of me and this work, and I know he loved me. What more could I ask? This was also the year my girl and I said I do. She is my best friend and my forever person. Thank you, Keah, for being my world, my love, and my partner. I want to offer a special thank you to my dear friends D. Jackson Leigh and Sheila Causby for standing beside us as our best persons, and to Hilde Phipps for her unconditional love and beautiful words of union. It was wonderful to have the blessings of so many family and friends surrounding us.

So much more goes into writing a book than the hours spent plotting, writing, and editing. It takes the support and patience of those we love and those who work to get our stories to our readers. As always, I am grateful to Bold Strokes Books for making this dream possible. I am especially thankful to my editor, Ruth Sternglantz, for her amazing support, patience, and understanding. She is a great teacher. And last, I don't know what I would do without my beta reader Brianne. I hope she knows how special her friendship is to me and how thankful I am for her work.

Dedication

For Keah, forever is a good start.
In memory of Donald E. Ford, the strongest man
I've ever known. I miss you, Dad.

Chapter One

Jackie fell back against the bed breathing hard, her sweat-soaked hair clinging to her neck and cheeks.

"Oh my, you are something special," the woman beside her cooed.

Jackie rubbed her face. Despite the hours she'd just spent having sex, she was empty and detached. Normally when she felt this way she could blow off her tension with a beautiful woman for a night. And Heather was beautiful—she practically oozed sex. Everything about the way she talked and moved was designed for luring women to her bed. She was the kind of woman that made Jackie's fever boil. But tonight something was different. She hadn't wanted to be touched. Every time Heather tried to claim her, she had turned the attention around until Heather had collapsed, sated and physically exhausted.

"I don't think I can move another muscle after that. Whatever it is you needed to work out tonight, I hope it comes back. I'd love to do seconds sometime."

"Hmm." Jackie mumbled noncommittally, staring at the odd patterns on the ceiling. She leaned up on one elbow and looked at the clock. It was four in the morning.

Jackie pressed a quick kiss to Heather's lips. "I have to go."

"So soon?" Heather moaned and rolled onto her stomach.

"Heather?"

When there was no answer, Jackie climbed out of bed, gathered her clothes, and left. She didn't get it. Why hadn't she been able to get into things with Heather? She was attractive, willing, very responsive, and almost insatiable. What was the problem? Jackie sighed as she slipped her hands into the pockets of her jeans and hunched her shoulders under the weight of her unrest.

She wouldn't see Heather again. Maybe she needed to take a break from the one-night stands and the occasional couplings with a few acquaintances she sometimes met up with for short rendezvous.

Jackie was barely aware of the changing lights along the Henley Street Bridge as she crossed the Tennessee River on her way home. A light rain misted against the windshield as water slushed beneath the tires. The streets of Knoxville glistened as the lights of the city illuminated the wet roads with a kaleidoscope of color. The wipe-wash sound of the wiper blades stuttering across her windshield counted out time like a metronome, hammering the nail of disappointment deeper into her mind.

She opened the door to her apartment and tossed her keys on the small table by the door. She couldn't wait to get a shower and wash away the smell of sex and the feel of Heather's hands on her skin. She stood with her head bowed beneath the spray letting the water beat against her shoulders and stream down her face. But no matter how long she stood there, and no matter how hot the water, the emptiness seeped deeper into her bones.

She rubbed the towel back and forth over her head to soak up the water as she walked to her bedroom. She stopped in front of the dresser and stared at the framed black-and-white photo of a strikingly beautiful woman with windblown hair, her face turned to the sun, eyes closed, and a hint of a smile in the curve of her lips as if she were about to be kissed. Jackie never let a day go by without looking at this photo and wondering where her mother was. Every year since her mother had left was harder, not better. The old adage that time healed all wounds didn't apply to her. As time passed and the image and the photo faded further into the past, it was as if the color of her own life seeped away and she feared she would someday find herself a faded, empty image of herself.

Jackie rubbed her hand across her face and sighed in resignation. If she had to describe her feelings, she would say she was lonely. But that couldn't be right—she didn't get lonely. She didn't need anyone. It had been years since she had allowed anyone close enough to her to cause that kind of need. She touched her finger to the frame. Maybe this was what had her out of sorts. She always missed her mother this time of year.

Well, whatever it was needed to work itself out soon. She climbed into bed, letting the cool sheets and heavy comforter cradle her. She sighed. Friday night would be as good a time as any to shake things up a bit. Going out with the crew from work would settle her down and put things back on track. God, she hoped so, because this restlessness was beginning to wear her down.

She peered through the shadows and the glow of moonlight at the picture on the dresser. What happened to you? Where did you go?

The image of her mother smiled back at her as if she should know the answer. Jackie pulled the covers up under her chin and turned away from the memory of her mother and the loneliness that tethered her to the past.

The sound of the intercom was like an alarm blaring inside Kayla's head. She rubbed her already throbbing temples to soothe the incessant pain. She looked at the clock, thankful to see it was already six thirty. She blew out a sigh of relief that the torturous day was finally at an end and she had made it through another week of back-to-back clients. Miraculously, she had somehow kept up with all the paperwork that went along with the caseload. Kayla closed the last file on her desk, already looking forward to a long hot bath, a glass of wine, and some quality time with a good book. A gentle tap at her door drew her attention. She looked up, surprised to see her friend and colleague at her door.

"Hey, do you have a minute?" Jen asked.

Kayla took in the hollowed look in her friend's eyes and her heart sank with dread. She knew by the tremor in Jen's voice that something was wrong.

Kayla raised an eyebrow and cocked her head to one side. "Are you kidding?" she said sarcastically.

"Busy day, huh?"

"That's an understatement. I feel like my brain has been through a blender."

"Yeah. You kind of look like it too," Jen said with a teasing smile.

"Thanks." Kayla grimaced. "What's up, Jen? All kidding aside, you look like you need to talk."

Kayla had worked with Jen for two years. They had started out on a community project together and although their work had taken them in different directions, the bond between them was strong and they were each other's inner office voice of reason.

Jen cringed. "Is it that obvious?"

Kayla shrugged. "To me it is."

Jen smiled but dropped her gaze.

Kayla could see Jen was hurt and that could mean only one thing. "What did he do this time?"

Jen brought a trembling hand to her lips as she looked up at Kayla. All the worries of the day suddenly faded when Kayla saw her friend so fragile. She shut her office door and handed Jen the box of tissues she kept on the edge of her desk.

Jen took a deep breath and looked up at Kayla, her eyes glistening with unshed tears. "He stayed out again last night. I even went to the bar and tried to make him come home with me. He just laughed at me. He told me I was a buzzkill and he was going to go find someone who wanted to have a little fun. I found him passed out on the couch this morning, soaked in his own urine."

"Oh God, Jen, I'm so sorry."

Jen shook her head. "No, that's not even the worst of it. He called me this morning and said he wants me to leave. He wants a divorce." Jen closed her eyes as if she could shut out the pain. Her hand shook as she toyed with the tissue.

Kayla reached for her friend and tried to console her in the best way she could, but inside she was secretly jumping for joy. She never wanted to see Jen hurt, but she hoped that if Jen would finally divorce Mike, she could break free of his abuse and be happy.

"Can you believe it? *He* wants to divorce *me!*"

Kayla shook her head. "What a loser. You know, if he can't see what he has, he doesn't deserve you."

Jen sniffed. "I've cried all day. I just felt so hurt. Then he called a few minutes ago and wants me to put money into his bank account. Can you believe that?"

"Please tell me you didn't do it." Kayla said with a groan.

Jen sighed with resignation. "I did."

"Jen!"

"That's the last time, I swear. I just couldn't let him go all week at work without food."

Kayla clenched her teeth and tried not to growl. "Yeah, we both know that's not what he'll be spending the money on."

"I know." Jen sniffed again. "Maybe I should just go ahead and file for the divorce."

Normally Kayla would keep her opinion to herself, but this was not a client, this was her friend. "Yes. Yes, you should. Enough is enough."

"Where would I go? I just can't move back in with my parents—I already feel like a failure. I don't have enough money to start over. He's drained the bank account and what little I have saved just isn't enough."

Kayla considered her answer carefully before responding. "You could stay with me until you get your own place."

Jen looked up suddenly, her eyes wide with surprise. "Really?"

"Of course. What are friends for, if not to help you get out of a tough spot and help trash the guy who is…well…being an ass?"

Jen's smile was real this time. "So does that mean you'll also go out with me tonight?"

Before Kayla could protest, Jen put up her hand, effectively halting Kayla's words before they even left her mouth.

"I just can't sit around wondering where he is or what trouble he's getting himself into. I need a distraction. Come on, Kayla, it's Friday night, and Tennessee doesn't have any games going on so you can't use that as an excuse to avoid going downtown. Let's go out."

Kayla wanted to argue. She always felt weird when she went out with Jen. She felt out of place in the straight clubs. She just wasn't girly enough and the guys either gave her a hard time or she was ignored completely. She tried for a compromise. "How about we just hang out at my place? The beer and wine are cheaper and we don't have to worry about cab fare."

Jen shook her head. "Come on, Kayla. Please?" Jen pleaded.

"Oh, crap." How could she say no? Jen was just too damn cute and vulnerable and...well...cute. "Okay. Where are we going?" Jen threw her arms around Kayla. "Thank you."

Kayla sighed and hugged her friend. She knew it would be a long night, but if it helped Jen find a reprieve from her hurt, it would be worth it.

❖

The moment they walked into the bar, Kayla knew she had made a terrible mistake. It wasn't the painted-on Wrangler jeans everyone wore, or the crunch of peanut shells under her feet. It wasn't even the looks they got from the men lined up at the bar as they entered. It was the mechanical bull wildly bucking and thrashing in a small roped-off area to the left of the entrance that filled her with dread. To Kayla's amazement the bull cast off its rider, who flailed around like a rag doll flung into the air. Kayla jumped back as the rider landed at her feet with a sickening thud.

"*Oomph*," the rider grunted.

Cheers erupted from the crowd as Kayla reached down to help the stranger up, hoping no bones were broken.

"Thanks," the rider said, grasping Kayla's hand to pull herself up. "That's going to hurt tomorrow."

"It looks like it hurts now," Kayla said, shocked that the rider was a woman.

"Maybe a little bit, but don't tell anyone I said that." Out of nowhere she quickly leaned in and kissed Kayla on the mouth.

Cheers erupted again from a circle of men on the opposite side of the bull. "Excuse me," the woman said as she withdrew her lips from Kayla's. She flashed Kayla a devilish grin and rushed back to the bull.

Kayla stood rooted to the spot, stunned. Her eyes were riveted to the long lean body, taut muscles, and firm ass. What on earth just happened?

A fierce pinch on the back of her arm made her flinch. "Ouch." She spun around and glared at Jen with her best *What the hell?* look.

Jen had her hands on her hips and wore an incredulous expression. "I can't take you anywhere. We've only been here five minutes and you've already kissed a girl."

"I didn't kiss her," Kayla protested, still not believing what had happened. "She kissed me!"

"That's just a technicality. The point is, your lips were on hers."

"At no fault of my own. I didn't do anything, I swear. And why isn't anyone freaked out about it...besides you, of course?"

"Kayla, this is a *gay* bar. Haven't you noticed?"

Kayla looked around, seeing the men at the bar in an entirely new light. "You've got to be kidding me. You brought us to a gay bar?"

"Yeah. I know it can be hard on you when we go out to some of the straight clubs, and I'm not in the mood for the male drama tonight. So I decided to try things your way."

"My way?" Kayla said, arching her eyebrows.

"You know what I mean. I wanted us to have fun. That means going to a place where we can both relax and enjoy ourselves."

Kayla was amazed. She had never seen this side of Jen and she didn't quite know what to think of it. She smiled as the realization set in. If the welcome at the door was any indication of how the evening would go, this was going to be one hell of a night. "Come on then, let's get a drink."

They made their way through the throng of men and women to a tall bar-length table that doubled as a railing encircling the dance floor. The whole setup reminded Kayla of a rodeo arena. A rowdy group of young men made their way onto the dance floor, pairing off and gliding into each other's arms as seamlessly as a flock of starlings. The two-step had never looked so good. Their broad shoulders and muscles bulged as hands grasped possessively to the tight jeans stretched across firm buttocks.

Kayla smiled at Jen who was gaping at the men, her mouth half open and eyes wide. She knew Jen was comfortable with people who were gay, she just wasn't so sure she had much opportunity to see the real thing in action.

"Your mouth is hanging open."

Jen looked at Kayla, wide-eyed. "Those are the most beautiful men I've ever seen."

Kayla laughed.

"Seriously, look at them. I can't believe we haven't come here before. As of tonight, this is my new favorite bar."

Kayla worked to suppress her grin. "They're all gay, Jen."

"I know," Jen said cheerfully. "That's what's so great. I can look all I want and not have to worry about pickup lines, rude groping, or unwanted flirting. I love it."

"Is that how you usually feel when you go out?"

"Please," Jen scoffed. "Do you think I like putting up with all those guys pawing at me when we go out?"

Kayla furrowed her brow, confused. "Well, yeah," she said.

Jen shrugged and waved her hand in the air as if swiping the thought away. "Well, sometimes I do, but right now I just want to be around men without having to worry about what they'll do next. At least you don't have to worry about things like that, K."

At that moment an arm slid around Kayla's waist from behind. Without warning, a woman leaned over between Jen and Kayla and set a beer down on the bar in front of Kayla. As the woman withdrew she leaned in and kissed Kayla on the mouth. Her left hand pushed into Kayla's hair and held her gently as their lips met.

Kayla pressed her hand to the woman's chest and pushed her away.

"What the hell do you think you're doing?" Kayla said with irritation.

The woman took a step back and grinned. "I'm apologizing."

"What?" Kayla looked at the woman, staring into hazel eyes that looked like starbursts, the colors of brown and green stretching across her irises with subtle streaks of gold. Despite the sudden rise of anger, Kayla couldn't help but feel like she was falling into a sea of scattered light.

The woman flashed a crooked smile and took another step back, her arm still resting along the back of Kayla's stool. "I came over to apologize for my behavior earlier. I'm Jackie Phillips." She extended her hand to Jen.

Jen shook the offered hand. By the look on her face she was almost as confused as Kayla felt.

When Jackie then offered her hand to Kayla, Kayla stubbornly refused. "You mean you're apologizing for kissing me earlier by kissing me *again*?"

Jackie looked down at Kayla and shook her head. "No. I'm not apologizing for kissing you. I'm apologizing for leaving without introducing myself. The second kiss was because I enjoyed the first one so much I wanted to make sure I got to do it again."

Kayla scowled. Her pulse raced as shock and annoyance threatened to ignite her anger. "Are you always so sure of yourself?"

"Pretty much," Jackie said, smiling.

Kayla felt the heat rise in her face as her temper flared. She was embarrassed at having been treated so carelessly in front of everyone. Jackie had no right to put her hands or her lips on anyone without their permission. "Well, I hope you enjoyed yourself, because that's the last time it's going to happen."

Jackie studied her for a moment. She cocked her head to the side and trailed her eyes across Kayla's face. When Jackie looked into her eyes, the intensity of her gaze took Kayla's breath.

"Okay. You're right," Jackie said, putting both hands up in a sign of surrender. Her eyes softened and her brow furrowed slightly, forming a small crease between her eyes. "I was out of line. I'm sorry if I offended you."

Kayla wasn't ready to let the issue go, but all her bravado seemed to evaporate when she saw the softness enter Jackie's eyes. She tried to be angry, but the truth was that Jackie was hot, very hot. Kayla hadn't been out with a woman in six months, and if she was being completely honest with herself, the kiss had been nice…shocking and rude, yes, but nice.

"So, what are your names?" Jackie asked.

When Kayla didn't respond, Jen answered. "I'm Jennifer Harris but you can call me Jen, and this is my friend, Kayla McCormick."

"Well, Jen and Kayla, let me buy you a drink to make up for my forwardness."

Kayla was about to say no, when Jen spoke for them both. "That would be wonderful, thanks."

As Jackie walked toward the bar to get the drinks, Kayla glared at Jen. "Why did you do that? She's rude and presumptuous—"

"And cute," Jen added. "Besides, it's nice to see the gay world isn't all that different after all. This way I get to watch you figure out what to do with the pickup lines, rude groping, and unwanted flirting." Jen smiled. "This is fun."

"Great," Kayla grumbled. "I'm glad you're amused."

Jackie returned with the drinks and pulled up a stool.

Jen immediately jumped into conversation. "So, what was the bull like? Do you do that a lot?" Jen laughed into her drink and winked at Kayla.

"No. This is the first time I've been here. I'm here with some guys from work and we had a couple of bets running. They bet I couldn't stay on the bull for five seconds."

"How long did you last?" Jen asked.

"Eight. I could have made it longer, but when you two walked in, I couldn't pass up the opportunity to meet you." With the last statement, she met Kayla's eyes.

Kayla wasn't buying it. "So you threw yourself at my feet deliberately?" she said in disbelief.

"Well, I wasn't supposed to land on my face, but yes."

"Right. And what was the other bet exactly?"

Jackie grimaced and shook her head. "I better not say."

"Come on," Jen pleaded. "Out with it."

Jackie looked away this time and shifted uncomfortably in her chair. "The guys bet me I wouldn't be able to get a girl to kiss me tonight."

Kayla's face burned. "So not only were you rude, you used me as the butt of a joke. Nice." Kayla scowled at Jackie.

"Well, I just acted on impulse. As soon as I realized what I'd done, I wanted to make it up to you."

"By humiliating me? *Twice!*" Kayla had had just about enough of this charade and rose from her chair to leave. A firm but gentle hand caught hers before she could step away.

"No. I swear the second kiss was real. The more I watched you, the more I realized you were someone I wanted to know. I'm not even really sure why I kissed you again. It just felt nice. I'm really sorry. I know I'm not explaining myself very well, but I didn't mean to embarrass you. Can we start over? Please."

Jen laughed. "Come on, Kayla, it wasn't that bad." Then with mock surprise she covered her mouth with her fingers. "Or was it?"

Kayla couldn't help but laugh a little. She rolled her eyes. She might have been able to hold on to her anger if she was just dealing with Jackie, but the two of them together were impossible.

"I'll live."

❖

Three drinks later, Kayla found herself on the dance floor trying to learn the latest line dance. Jen and Jackie seemed to pick up the moves easily, but she continued to struggle. After she almost tumbled into the man in front of her, she felt a hand brush along her back and grasp her hip. Jackie moved so close to Kayla the sides of their thighs brushed. Jackie guided her through a complicated series of stomps and kicks, their bodies swaying seamlessly to the music. Kayla had to admit, Jackie felt good. It was nice to have someone pay attention to her, a very sexy someone.

Jackie took Kayla's left hand and stood slightly behind her, then wrapped her right arm around Kayla's waist and pressed her right hip just to the back of Kayla's left. Kayla could feel Jackie's breast brush her back as they moved, and the press of Jackie's hand against her side was gentle but firm. The slightest movement of her hand and shift of her body made her feel as if they were joined and their movements had become one. A wave of heat ignited in her belly and spread through her body. A light sheen of sweat broke out on her skin and her stomach fluttered with arousal.

Kayla laughed out loud when Jackie spun her around. With one quick twist they were face to face, and Jackie's strong hands were holding her, guiding her, driving her. Jackie moved her hands to Kayla's waist, pulled her close, and began to sway in a slow dance as the music changed. In an instant the playful energy between them shifted to something much more alluring. The hypnotic rhythm of the music coupled with the press of Jackie's body against hers was intoxicating. Kayla felt a twitch between her legs. She was aroused, and as they moved, she imagined Jackie's naked skin pressed against hers. Every step, every turn on the dance floor was like free-falling, and Kayla had the urge to press her lips against the sweat dampened skin of Jackie's neck.

Jackie was silent as she held Kayla in her arms. Kayla's breath against her cheek was like a caress, and every cell in her body pulsed in time with the rhythm of Kayla's breathing. Normally she would use the closeness to suggest a more intimate joining, but just holding Kayla was more satisfying than anything she had experienced in the last few weeks, and she wanted to hold on to that feeling as long as she could.

The music ended and Kayla pulled away. "I need to go to the bathroom. Dance with Jen for a while—I'll be right back."

Kayla's withdrawal was like having the air swept out of the room, and Jackie wanted to grasp on to her, anything to push away the emptiness she knew was waiting for her outside Kayla's embrace. Jackie held her breath as Kayla's hand slipped from hers. She didn't understand what was happening, but she knew she wanted more.

Jen claimed her arm. "Hey, tiger, my turn."

Jackie nodded, thankful for the distraction. She let out her breath and took Jen's hand, hoping to chase away the emptiness of Kayla's absence. "Good idea, come on."

Jackie worked to clear her head as they danced and quickly slid back into her usual playful flirtations. She teased Jen about her missed steps and who had the better hip thrust. Jen laughed and countered every jab with a jest of her own. Jackie enjoyed the banter and wondered at the easy flow of conversation and the pleasure she felt not pursuing sex with a woman.

Kayla watched Jen and Jackie dance. She laughed when Jackie picked Jen up and spun her around until Jen's laughter rang out over the crowd. Kayla was amused by Jackie's antics, and despite her inner warnings, was intrigued by the attractive, confident woman. Kayla felt a stirring in her middle and shifted uncomfortably. The last thing she needed was to be attracted to someone so impulsive. Kayla knew she was just reacting to the physical lure of Jackie's flirtations, but since when did she even entertain flirting back? She'd had enough warnings about the carefree lifestyle, growing up with constant reminders about her parents, that she knew that kind of life wasn't for her. She preferred predictable and stable.

Kayla saw Jackie watching her and looked away. She recognized the look of interest that had settled into Jackie's eyes, and she didn't want to admit how much she wanted that attention. Jackie gestured to Jen to take a break, and a minute later they plopped down into their chairs beside her. A light sheen of sweat coated Jen's skin and her eyes were bright with playful energy.

"You two looked pretty good out there," Kayla said smiling at Jen. She was pleased to see her friend having a good time. It had been a hard day for Jen and she needed this diversion.

Jen laughed. "Casanova here kept stepping on my heels, but otherwise I guess she was all right."

"Hey"—Jackie was quick to jump to the defense—"that was only because your steps were too small."

The sound of cheers got their attention, and they looked over to see a new crowd had gathered around the mechanical bull.

"Oh, let's go see," Jen said grabbing Kayla's hand and pulling her out of her chair. Jackie followed so close she could have been Kayla's shadow, allowing only a step or two between them. A small thrill tingled across Kayla's skin at the slightest touch of Jackie's hand on her back. Damn it, why did she have to like her?

A throng of men and women stood watching as people took turns trying to ride the bull. Each time a rider was thrown or simply fell off the machine, the crowd roared with laughter and cheers. Jen laughed too and cheered and jumped up and down when one man managed to stay upright through a series of wicked twists and turns and bucks. Jen's laughter was contagious, and soon Kayla was laughing too.

"Do you want to try it?" Jackie asked, leaning across Kayla to get Jen's attention.

Kayla caught her breath as Jackie's breast brushed lightly against her shoulder, and she shuddered at the jolt of electricity that surged through her. She glanced at Jackie, quickly sneaking a peek at the line of muscle at the base of her neck. The pulsing beat of Jackie's heart was instantly echoed between Kayla's legs. Kayla shut her eyes and looked away. *God, what's happening to me?* She had to get her mind off the feel of Jackie's body and back on the reason she was here.

Excitement blazed in Jen's eyes. "Oh yes!"

"Come on," Jackie said, taking Jen by the hand and leading her to the man at the controls.

Kayla watched with anxious amusement. This ought to be good.

A few minutes later the crowd roared with laughter as Jen attempted to get astride the contraption. She managed to get her body up onto the bull by bouncing on the mat before jumping onto the slick leather back, but the momentum carried her over the other side, and she hit the mat with a sharp smack. Jen lay on the mat for a moment laughing before gathering herself for another try.

Kayla laughed as she watched her friend try helplessly to hang on to the unpredictable machine, her left arm and both legs flapping like a rag doll as she was tossed willy-nilly from side to side.

Jackie came back to stand next to Kayla and pressed her hand lightly against Kayla's back. Kayla was acutely aware of the suggestion in Jackie's touch and the heat of Jackie's palm warming her through the thin fabric of her shirt. When Jackie leaned over the railing and cheered for Jen to hang on, her hand slid to Kayla's waist and rested against her hip. Kayla knew she should move away but was mesmerized by the rightness of Jackie's touch. The pressure of Jackie's hand on her sent chills up her spine. Despite her better judgment, she allowed this one indulgence. Despite how the evening had started, Kayla had enjoyed Jackie's company and found her mind wandering to places she knew could only mean trouble.

Jen fell from the bull again in what seemed like slow motion. Her laughter rang through the crowd with a high-pitched squeal punctuated with a snort just as she came to rest on the mat. Kayla and Jackie ran to Jen and helped guide her back to her seat.

Jen raked her fingers through her hair to smooth the unruly strands. She was still laughing. "That was great!"

Kayla laughed. "You were pretty good. I've never seen that technique before. You definitely fall like a pro."

"Ha-ha." Jen tried to swat Kayla's shoulder as she slid her chair closer with a grimace. "Ouch, I think I'm going to have a bruise."

"Oh yeah, more than one, I'd say," Jackie said as she slid her arm casually around the back of Kayla's chair.

A voice over the loudspeaker announced last call. "Seriously," Kayla said pulling out her cell phone to check the time, "I can't believe we've been here all night." She was a bit disappointed that the night was coming to an end. Although she didn't exactly know what to make of her interest in Jackie, she wasn't ready to break the connection. She knew that once she walked out the door, she would come to her senses and playtime would be over.

"Hey, I'm going to the little girls' room before we go. I'll be right back," Jen said, pushing back her chair. She swayed a little and grimaced before heading to the back of the bar to the restrooms.

Jackie reached for Kayla's hand, wrapped her long fingers around Kayla's more delicate hand, and extricated Kayla's cell phone. She quickly manipulated the buttons on the screen.

"What are you doing?" Kayla asked incredulously.

"I'm putting in my contact information so you can call me."

Kayla leaned back in her chair and raised her eyebrows. "What makes you think I'm going to call you?"

Jackie looked up and met Kayla's gaze with such intensity Kayla felt like she had been touched. Jackie's voice was smooth as silk and she answered seriously. "It isn't that I expect you to call me, Kayla, but I hope that you will. I'd like to see you. You know, like a real date, not just a meeting in a bar. I haven't been able to think of anything except you all night."

Kayla was surprised by the sincerity and tenderness in Jackie's voice. In that moment all Jackie's bravado was gone. Kayla felt Jackie's gaze, as intimate as a touch that sent a shiver up her spine.

Jackie slid a hand along Kayla's jaw and caressed her face. Kayla looked up into Jackie's eyes as Jackie leaned in and kissed her. The kiss wasn't like the others. This kiss was soft and tender, like the gentlest glide of satin against her lips, and the faintest brush of tongue teased her flesh with the promise of a deeper, more sensual passion.

Jackie pulled away, her lips hovering only a breath away from Kayla's mouth.

"Will you call me?" she whispered.

The heat of the question was like a flame on Kayla's lips. Her pulse raced as she fought the urge to claim Jackie's mouth again. She could feel Jackie's fingertips like tiny points of promise against the tender skin of her neck. Hazel eyes held her captive, pleading for her to say yes. But Kayla knew better. The night had been fun, but it wasn't her, and Jackie Phillips was the last thing she needed in her life right now.

"No," she breathed huskily, her voice coated with desire. Her body was saying yes, but Kayla knew better than to listen. The spark between them might be hot tonight, but that kind of heat would quickly burn itself out.

Jackie smiled and nodded. She trailed her fingers along Kayla's neck, across her shoulder, and down her arm until her fingers molded into Kayla's hand. "I hope you change your mind."

Kayla pulled her hand away. Every second she touched Jackie made it harder to walk away, and she was not an impulsive person. She didn't give in to reckless desires or fall for women in bars. The more space she put between them, the safer she would be.

Kayla looked around for Jen. She wanted to get out of there as soon as possible. She didn't want Jackie to see her true feelings. She didn't want Jackie to see she was getting to her. It was time to get her feet back on the ground and her head out of the clouds. It was time to go home.

Chapter Two

Kayla sauntered into the kitchen, taking in the familiar sign of a hangover. Jen sat at the kitchen table nursing a cup of coffee as if she could will the pain in her head to stop pounding against her skull. She looked like she hadn't slept well and the coffee didn't seem to be doing much to help. Jen was wearing a pair of light blue cotton sleep pants and an oversized sweatshirt that had seen better days. Despite her swollen red-rimmed eyes and messed-up hair, she was beautiful. Kayla's heart warmed. She imagined Jen as the little sister she'd always wanted. Kayla cleared her throat and took a coffee cup from the cupboard. She filled her cup before turning to face her friend.

"How are you feeling?"

Jen groaned. "My whole body hurts."

Kayla grinned, understanding that after the events of the evening, Jen probably wasn't exaggerating.

"Can I get you anything?"

Jen opened her eyes into slits and surveyed Kayla as she slid her coffee cup across the counter. "How can you sound so cheerful this morning? Aren't you the least bit hungover?"

Kayla shrugged and shook her head. She didn't get hangovers. "Sorry. Want breakfast?"

Jen grimaced and clasped her hand over her mouth as if she might be sick. "Do you mind if I just sleep it off?"

"Sure. Like I said, you can stay here as long as you want."

Jen sighed. "Thanks, K." She got up from her chair and added sugar to her cup. Before turning away, she put her arms around Kayla and pulled her into a hug. "Thanks for going out with me last night and for letting me stay with you. You're the best."

Jen's lips brushed Kayla's cheek. Hesitantly she put her arms around Jen, and wondered how Mike could be so blind to how wonderful Jen was. She would never understand how Mike could treat Jen the way he did.

"I had fun too," she whispered, giving Jen a squeeze before releasing her. She smiled at Jen, hoping she couldn't see how concerned she was, and her worry had nothing to do with Jen's hangover.

Jen smiled at her thoughtfully as if she was about to say more, but the moment passed and she moved away. She picked up her cup and disappeared down the hall.

Kayla watched Jen go and thought back on their evening. It had been good to see Jen laugh and have a good time, and she hoped that it was only the beginning for Jen. She had been through a lot with Mike in the two years they had been married. The thought of Jen laughing and dancing instantly brought up the image of Jackie, and a tingling sensation danced along her skin. *What are you doing, K? You know better than this.* She shook herself to rid the memory of Jackie's lips from her mind. She didn't need to think any more about Jackie Phillips or the dream she'd had of her last night. At a loss for what else to do with herself, she decided to head out to the gym. A good workout would help clear her mind. She was just overreacting. She didn't want to be attracted to Jackie—she didn't need that kind of trouble in her life. Kayla picked up her keys and headed for the door to escape the memory of Jackie's kiss.

All through her workout as Kayla pushed her body, she did everything to release the relentless tension evoked by her attraction to Jackie. Soon her mind calmed, but her body still hummed with sexual energy, and she hadn't been completely successful in ridding her thoughts of Jackie. Kayla sighed and increased the pace on the treadmill. It really had been too long. As the sweat trickled down her chest into the swell of her breasts, a new thought began to penetrate her mind. She licked her lips, recalling the delicate taste of Jackie's mouth during that last kiss. She allowed her thoughts to play out the memory of each touch. She groaned. No amount of running could make her forget that kiss.

What would her grandmother say if she were there right now? Kayla cringed. This was just the kind of thing her grandmother always warned her about. She was just feeling lonely lately. That didn't mean she had to go losing her head. This was the kind of thing that would get her hurt.

Kayla felt a little more together by the time she returned home. Jen's car wasn't in the garage and the house was quiet.

Kayla groaned when she saw a note lying on the counter. *Thanks for everything. I'm going back home. I'll figure out what I need to do next. See you Monday. Love, Jen.*

Kayla let out an exasperated sigh. Jen had gone back to Mike. She knew this wouldn't be the last time Jen would need her. As long as Mike was in the picture, Jen couldn't be happy. She crumpled the note and tossed it in the trash. She didn't understand why Jen couldn't break away from such an abusive relationship, and she worried that things would only become more unstable as Mike's drug use escalated. But for now, all she could do was to be there for her friend and wait.

Kayla sat at her desk, thumbing through her calendar. Six weeks stood between her and the annual conference on behavioral health and addictive disorders she would be attending. It was the biggest training she'd attend all year, allowing her to meet counselors from all over the United States presenting on the latest research in her field. Although she would spend seemingly endless hours in lectures each day, she looked forward to a break from the usual office routine. She had managed to book an extra week at the beach resort following the conference for a long-overdue vacation. That would at least make her travel free and help out her budget a bit. It was times like these that she really did love her job.

Of course the first week she would pine for the warm rays of the sun as she listened to the latest studies in brain research, therapy techniques, emerging problems in the world of psychology, and endless talk of the barrage of books touting the latest treatments for all sorts of disorders. But her evenings would be free to explore the beach, eat all the oysters her little heart desired, and maybe even explore the local nightlife.

Just thinking about the getaway was exciting. She wouldn't know a soul and could do anything she wanted without worrying about running into a client. It would be nice to get away.

Kayla's phone buzzed and Jen's name flashed across the screen.

"Hey, Jen, what's up?" Kayla said cradling the phone against her shoulder as she flipped through her schedule.

"Are you busy?"

"Not at the moment."

"Are you going to that conference in Florida in May?"

Kayla had a sinking feeling in the pit of her stomach. "Yeah, I'm already registered, why?"

"Well, the board has decided I should go to represent the coalition. It looks like we'll be going together. Isn't that great?"

"Wow," Kayla said trying to sound excited. "That is great." Kayla imagined a balloon bursting over her head and mentally kissed her worry-free trip good-bye.

"They also want me to consider taking a transfer to the Nashville office. They need someone who already knows the grants we work under to help restructure the program."

Jen paused, and the silence on the line bore into Kayla's brain as she took in the information. She experienced shock, dismay, and happiness in quick succession. Luckily, she was used to keeping her feelings and reactions to herself until she knew where things were going.

"What do you think?" Jen added nervously.

Kayla struggled to think. "Um…what did you tell them?" she asked as her mouth went dry.

"I said I needed to think about it. I know Mike won't go for it, but maybe it's time for me to think about making some real changes for myself."

"Okay." Kayla still wasn't sure what she should say, so she waited for Jen to continue.

"I'm not sure what I should do. It's a great opportunity and it will make me make some decisions about my life."

"What are you going to tell Mike?"

Kayla heard Jen sigh and could imagine her slumped forward, her elbows on her desk, her forehead cradled in the palm of her hand. "I'm not sure yet. With his job, he could live anywhere. But he thinks my job is stupid, and I know he won't want to go to Nashville. If I decide to do this, it'll mean going alone. Right now he doesn't have to know anything. I've been staying at my mother's since I left your place."

Kayla was surprised by the news. She'd been certain Jen had gone back to Mike. "That's tough. Want to come over tonight and talk about it over dinner? We can break open a bottle of wine and celebrate."

"Thanks, K, but I'm still at the Nashville office. I won't be heading home until tomorrow morning."

"I understand. We'll do lunch when you get back." Kayla tried to sound upbeat, but her emotions were in turmoil. Her long-awaited getaway was now going to include Jen, her best friend was thinking of moving three hours away, and she was worried about what Mike would do to Jen if or when he found out about her plans to move, especially if those plans didn't include him.

"I've got to run, K. I just wanted to share the good news."

"Sure. Be safe, and congratulations."

Kayla rubbed the bridge of her nose between her thumb and finger and mumbled to herself. "Not good, not good, not good." She sighed and looked at the clock. Suddenly the thought of going home to her empty house was depressing. She would miss Jen if she moved, but she was happy that Jen was beginning to think of herself and her own future instead of letting Mike hold her back.

She sighed. She thought of her grandmother. She'd had her quilting club and church groups until she died, and despite her age and limitations she'd led a fulfilling life. Kayla realized she hadn't done much to build a life of her own outside of work, and now that her grandmother was gone, the emptiness had started to show. She needed to change that, but how? Where did she start?

Kayla toyed with her phone, scrolling through her contacts. She stopped when a new number grabbed her attention. Jackie Phillips was not the answer she was looking for. She'd done her best to forget the tall, beautiful dark-haired woman, but the memory of that last kiss continued to make her heart race.

An hour later Kayla still hadn't moved. She picked up the phone and found the number Jackie had programmed into her cell. She stared at the phone, her finger hovering over the call button. She drew in a deep breath and put the phone down. No. She wouldn't call Jackie. She liked her orderly, predictable life. Going out with Jackie would be inviting trouble. Her parents had lived the fast and furious lifestyle and she knew there was no room for her in that world. Maybe she should consider getting a cat.

The sound of a disembodied voice rang out over the intercom. "Kayla, could you come to the front please, code Charley."

Kayla froze. She glanced at the code sheet next to her phone. Code Charley was an alert that someone was potentially hostile. Kayla grabbed her keys and locked her office on the way out. As she made her way down the hall, she tried to ready herself for what she was about to face. Her heart raced and she tried to maintain an outward appearance of calm.

She could see Martha at the front desk through the glass partition that divided the reception office from the waiting area. Martha was pale and her eyes were wide. She looked scared to death. Kayla turned the corner toward the waiting area. A tall gangly man paced the small lobby like a lion in a cage. His head was bowed and he rubbed his hand over his close-cropped hair in an anxious gesture. Kayla's stomach lurched. Although she had never met Mike in person, she recognized him instantly from the photos in Jen's office.

Kayla stepped into the room making sure to keep her distance. She cleared her throat. "Hello, can I help you?"

Mike turned toward her so fast, Kayla took an involuntary step back. His eyes were wild and there was a noticeable tremor in his hands. The shimmer of sweat on his pale skin and dark circles under his eyes made him look ill.

"Who are you?" He asked.

"I'm Kayla McCormick. I'm one of the therapists here."

He narrowed his eyes and scrutinized her. "You're Jen's friend. She talks about you."

"Yes, I know Jen."

"Where is she? I want to see my wife."

Kayla extended her hand. "Then you must be Mike—I'm glad to finally meet you." Kayla hoped her open and friendly demeanor would help Mike relax.

Mike stared at her hand a moment before taking it. His palm was clammy and Kayla felt the tremor in his hand. She was certain he was experiencing withdrawal symptoms, and that could be a game changer.

Kayla released his hand and moved away so that she could see beyond his shoulder to Martha.

"I'm sorry, Mike, but Jen's out of town right now. We aren't expecting her back today."

"I don't believe you. Where is she? I want to see her, now."

"Would you like to sit down and talk about it? Maybe I can help."

"I don't need your help. I need my wife."

It was apparent Mike was growing desperate and more unpredictable.

"I'm really sorry. Jen didn't mention she was expecting you before she left. I really would like to help. Would you like to tell me what has you so upset?"

For a moment Kayla thought Mike was going to give in. He looked confused and swayed slightly on his feet. Then his eyes widened and he jerked as if he'd been struck.

"You're keeping her from me. I'll get her myself."

Mike tried to pass to the hall but Kayla stepped in front of him. She held up her hands with open palms in a gesture to stop his progress while trying to be nonthreatening.

"I'm sorry, you can't go back to the offices. I need you to think for just a minute, Mike. Did you see Jen's car in the parking lot when you came in? I promise you I am not trying to keep you from her, she's simply not here. I'd love to talk if you like, but otherwise I'll have to ask you to leave."

Kayla glanced over Mike's shoulder and was relieved to see Martha signal that the police were on the way.

"Think about it, Mike. No one is keeping you from your wife. She really isn't here."

Mike glared at her. Everything about him seethed distrust and desperation. Mike tried to step by her again, and Kayla took a step to the side blocking his path. This time she put her hand on his arm to change his focus. She knew this was a gamble, but she couldn't allow him into the back offices where clients might be at risk.

He stopped and stared at her as if he didn't know what to do next. The scream of sirens broke through the silence. Mike jerked his head around as if he didn't know where to run. He slammed his hands into Kayla's chest and shoved her away from him. Kayla flew backward. She crashed to the ground and slid backward on the slick floors, her head and shoulders hitting the wall behind her.

Kayla was more stunned than hurt. She hadn't really expected Mike to strike her, and everything happened so fast she didn't have time to defend herself.

Mike ran out of the building the instant Kayla hit the floor. Martha was by her side an instant later.

"Oh God, Kayla, are you all right?"

"I'm okay." Kayla straightened and took stock of her body. To her surprise there was no pain except maybe some minor bruises, and her neck was a little stiff. She really was okay.

Once she was standing again, Kayla took Martha's hand. "Call Jen. We need to warn her."

Martha nodded and ran to the phone just as the police came through the door.

Chapter Three

The next morning Kayla couldn't get out of bed. Every time she moved, searing pain streaked down her neck and back like she was being stabbed with an ice pick hooked to a live wire. She managed to shift herself around so she could reach her phone, but it took her a while to decide who she could call. She called work and canceled her appointments for the day and then went through her very short list of options for getting medical attention. She could call an ambulance, but that seemed a bit dramatic and she didn't want them breaking down her door to get into her house. Now that her grandmother was gone, she didn't have any family left. Kayla finally called her neighbor. They weren't close but he had always been nice and always offered to help if she needed anything.

Three hours later she was home from the doctor and was tucked back in bed with prescriptions for muscle relaxers and pain medication, which she hated. But at least she could sleep awhile, and maybe when she woke up this time, she would be better.

The next time she opened her eyes the clock said eight o'clock but it was light outside. Kayla frowned. Surely she hadn't slept an entire day. She checked the date on her phone to be sure and saw that she had missed six calls, and indeed, a day had passed.

Kayla tested her range of motion and found if she drew her knees up to her chest and moved slowly, she could bring herself to a sitting position. It didn't take long for her to figure out that the medication was not the way to go if she was going to get better.

She checked her missed calls. Two were from work and the other four were from Jen. After a much needed adventure to the bathroom, Kayla called the office. She could kill two birds with one stone by catching Jen at work. After a brief chat to reassure Martha that she was okay, she was put through to Jen.

"Oh my God, K. Are you all right? I'm so sorry. I don't know what he was thinking."

"Don't worry about it, Jen. I'm okay. How about you? Are you all right?"

Jen sighed. "Yeah. I just can't believe he did this."

"That's not your fault."

"I guess. But I still feel terrible."

Kayla took a deep breath and grimaced as pain stabbed beneath her shoulder blade. "I need a favor."

"Okay."

"I'm going to try to get in to see a physical therapist today. Can you take me?"

"Of course. I'll cancel the rest of my day and be right over."

"Thanks."

Kayla let out a sigh of relief. She wasn't used to asking for help and the situation made her realize just how alone she was. If Jen hadn't been there, she had no idea who she would have called. The neighbor was working today, she had no family nearby she could call, and her list of friends were mostly the people at work. Maybe she should rethink her introverted ways and get out more.

Kayla was still struggling to get dressed when Jen arrived twenty minutes later.

Jen took one look at Kayla and panicked. "What's wrong? Should we go to the hospital? Should I call an ambulance?"

Kayla rested her hand on the back of the sofa to steady herself as she slid on a pair of flip flops. "I think I just have a few kinks to work out. I'll see what the physical therapist has to say, but I'm sure it's fine."

"You don't look fine. You can barely walk."

Kayla sighed. She didn't have the strength to argue and didn't want to snap at Jen when she was just worried.

"Please. Let's just try this first. I saw my doctor yesterday, but I don't think meds alone are going to help."

Jen conceded. "Okay, just tell me what to do."

When they arrived at the physical therapist's office, Kayla found it even harder to get out of the car than it had been to get in and she was getting a little scared. What if this was something serious?

The waiting room was small and offered a clear view onto the treatment floor where several people were doing strange exercises targeting different injured body parts. Kayla spotted one man with a neck brace and cringed at the thought of having her head immobilized. That was the last thing she needed.

Her attention was drawn to a young woman who approached the desk and picked up a chart. Every cell in Kayla's body was at full attention as her eyes trailed up and down the tall, lean figure. There was no mistaking the taut muscles, dark hair, and confident swagger. Kayla stopped breathing when Jackie turned toward her, a cocky grin on her face.

"Kayla?"

Oh God, this can't be happening. "Hello, Jackie." Kayla almost choked. "You work here?"

Jackie laughed. "Yes, I'm one of the owners." She kneeled down next to Kayla and looked at the file, frowning. "What happened to your neck?"

Kayla was taken off guard. What was she supposed to do now? She grimaced. "I fell a couple of days ago and jammed my shoulders and neck up against a wall. My doctor gave me some muscle relaxers and pain medication, but they just make me sleep and the pain isn't getting any better."

Jackie glanced to Jen, who had been sitting quietly observing the interaction. Kayla followed her glance. Jen looked stricken. Kayla didn't know how to make her feel better and convince her to stop blaming herself. She patted Jen's knee. "I think I scared Jen half to death this morning."

"Hey, Jen," Jackie said with a smile. "Good to see you again."

Jen nodded. "You too."

Jackie stood and held out her hand to Kayla. "Why don't we go back and see what's going on with your neck. You're welcome to come too, Jen."

"Thanks, but I think I'll wait out here."

Jackie nodded. "Okay, we'll be just around the corner there if you change your mind."

Jackie helped Kayla to her feet and held on to her hand to steady her. Kayla was surprised when Jackie didn't let go of her hand as they walked through the room.

"Have a seat on the table," Jackie said patting the table with her hand. She held both hands in front of Kayla as if she was ready to catch her if she fell. Jackie stood so close, Kayla's thigh brushed Jackie's arm. The instant they touched, warmth spread through Kayla as if she had been wrapped in an embrace. Kayla pulled away and scolded herself for the thoughts about Jackie's body that sprang into her mind the moment they made contact.

"I need to check your neck. Is that okay?"

"Yes."

Jackie stood in front of Kayla and gently wrapped her hands around Kayla's neck. Kayla was boneless as Jackie began gently working her fingers up and down her spine. Jackie asked a multitude of questions about the injury, level of pain, and positioning. The shock of seeing Jackie had almost worn off when she began her tender ministrations at the back of Kayla's neck and down her shoulders. Now all Kayla could think of was how good Jackie's fingers felt against her skin. If it hadn't been for the pain, she would have been completely lost in Jackie's hands.

"You know, if you wanted to see me, all you had to do was call," Jackie teased.

"Trust me, if I wanted to see a woman, I wouldn't be this dramatic about it."

Jackie smiled. "Well that's good, because you had my attention the moment I laid eyes on you."

Jackie brushed her thumb across Kayla's cheek.

"Do you flirt with all your patients like this?"

Jackie shrugged. "Only the beautiful ones."

Kayla could hardly choke back a gasp as Jackie placed her fingers at the back of her neck and her thumbs at the base of her jaw and lifted slightly on her head. The pain vanished.

"Oh my God, that's wonderful. How did you do that?"

Jackie smiled. "Hmm, I like a woman who's easy to please. Just imagine what else I can do."

"My neck feels better. That doesn't mean I want to sleep with you," Kayla admonished. "Seriously, how did you make the pain stop like that?"

Jackie gently released the pressure on Kayla's neck. "Hang on a second and I'll show you."

Jackie stepped away from the table, happy for a moment to get herself together. She'd tried to play it cool from the moment she'd seen Kayla's name on the client list, but she was unable to deny the surge of excitement and worry that had knotted in her gut when she thought Kayla was hurt. She was relieved that the problem was something manageable. But even an injury like this had the potential to cause Kayla problems for the rest of her life.

Jackie returned with a replica of the human cervical spine. She settled onto a stool next to Kayla and pointed to the areas between the vertebrae.

"You have a slight bulge in a disk." Jackie pointed to the model. "The soft tissue between your vertebrae right here is putting pressure on the surrounding nerves. We need to reduce the swelling and try to coax the tissue back into alignment as much as we can, if we can."

Kayla looked worried. Anytime the spine was involved it was scary, and she could imagine what might be going through Kayla's mind at that moment.

"You can do that?" Kayla asked.

Jackie smiled her most reassuring smile. "I think so. It'll take a few weeks though. That means you'll have to see me again."

"I'll do anything to make this pain go away."

Jackie smiled. "Really? Anything?"

Kayla's face reddened at the suggestion. "Well, almost."

"Hmm…then we'll have to work on that too."

"Jackie," Kayla said with a warning tone.

"No worries, nothing big to start, just some exercises. For now, I want you to rest and take the meds like the doctor told you to. If you don't want to take the pain pills, at least take an anti-inflammatory. Reducing the swelling is the key we need to make this work."

Kayla sighed. "Okay. I'll do it."

"Good." I want to see you again in two days. Can you come back in by the end of the week?"

"I'll make it happen. I just want this to get better."

Jackie smiled and placed her hand over Kayla's. She heard the fear in Kayla's voice. "Well, although that will technically be our third date, I promise to take things slow."

Kayla sighed. Jackie caught the slight grin curve at the corner of her lips. That was a start.

❖

Jackie picked up the file on her way to the waiting area. Kayla and Jen were seated close to the door. They looked anxious.

"Kayla."

Kayla looked up.

"You can come on back now." Jackie motioned with the chart.

Kayla stood and walked slowly toward Jackie, her steps measured and cautious.

"How are you feeling?"

"I feel better than the last time I saw you, but I'd really like to get this ice pick out of my back."

Jackie nodded. "Let's see what we can do about that." Jackie placed her hand on Kayla's back and guided her into a treatment room. "We'll work in here today to give you some privacy."

Kayla looked nervous. She looked around the room, registering every detail.

"Have a seat."

Kayla sat on the treatment table without a word.

"You're quiet today. Are you okay?"

"I've been better, but I think I'm just nervous."

"Hmm, good to know I have that effect on you."

Kayla was quiet. Wow, she must really be scared.

"Okay, sit up straight and square your shoulders. Here's what I want you to do." Jackie demonstrated the movement to retract her neck and had Kayla put her fingers to her chin and thrust her head in a backward motion while keeping her shoulders square and her neck straight.

"Now, you try." Jackie placed her hands around Kayla's neck so she could feel if the maneuver was right.

Kayla imitated the move.

"Very good. Now, do that ten times and rest."

Jackie watched Kayla repeat the move. It was a common technique, but she wanted to make sure Kayla didn't experience any additional pain that might signal a bigger problem.

"That feels better already," Kayla said after she'd repeated two more sets of the maneuver.

Jackie smiled. "Good. Have you been taking your medication?"

Kayla grimaced. "I took some Mobic I had for my knees. But I really don't like the muscle relaxers, and the pain pills are just out of the question."

Jackie pulled up a chair and sat in front of Kayla, placing her hands on either side of Kayla's legs. "Look, I know you don't like taking the muscle relaxers, but you really need them right now, at least at night. They'll help you rest better and release some of the tension that's just going to keep the area inflamed. You really need this for a little while, maybe just a couple more days."

Kayla sighed. "Okay, I promise to take them over the weekend."

"Good. I'll see you Monday then."

Kayla touched Jackie's arm. "Thank you."

Jackie's skin tingled as if she had stepped into the rays of the sun. Kayla's voice was soft and sincere, and Jackie was grateful for the relief she saw in Kayla's eyes. She was proud she had been able to ease Kayla's pain.

"You're more than welcome. I'm glad I could help." Jackie wrapped her fingers around Kayla's wrist and squeezed. She replayed the night at the bar over in her head and lingered on the memory of Kayla's lips as soft as flower petals and just as sweet. Disappointment crowded her already jumbled emotions when she thought of Kayla's promise not to call...and she *hadn't* called.

The message was loud and clear. Kayla wasn't interested in her. Jackie grinned to herself. Maybe that was what was so alluring about Kayla—she was hard to get. She frowned. No, that wasn't it. There was something real about Kayla, something wholesome and honest that Jackie admired. Kayla was the kind of woman who wouldn't settle for what Jackie had to offer. But Kayla had been so vulnerable and trusting as Jackie cradled her head in her hands. Jackie shivered. The moment she'd looked into Kayla's eyes and had seen her unguarded trust had been the most rewarding moment of her day. The whole interaction had her unsettled. For the first time, Jackie questioned herself, her life, and the emptiness that had been plaguing her. She was attracted to Kayla. That was no surprise—Kayla was beautiful. Maybe she just needed to shake things up a bit. Maybe Kayla was the challenge she needed to get out of the rut she'd been in.

Jen was waiting for them in the lobby. "How did it go? Are you okay? I'm so sorry, K."

Jen was close to panic and Jackie wondered what had her so worried. Jen's reaction seemed guilty.

"I'm okay, Jen. Stop worrying."

Jen looked to Jackie, her eyes imploring and desperate.

"She really is going to be okay. With a little work, we'll have her dancing again in no time. What happened anyway? You act like you pushed her down a flight of stairs or something."

Jen paled and looked away. "I might as well have."

Jackie was confused. "What do you mean? I thought she fell at work."

"Not exactly, my husband pushed her down."

Jackie looked to Kayla, her confusion growing. "Why did he do that?"

"It's nothing really," Kayla interrupted.

Jen's eyes were brimming with tears now and the words poured out of her as if she was confessing a crime. "He was in drug withdrawal and showed up looking for me. When he didn't get his way, he freaked and pushed Kayla down." Jen's voice was shaky and held an edge of anger.

There was a sudden roar in Jackie's ears. *Withdrawal. Drugs.* Jackie heard the words echo in her mind and her blood ran cold.

"There's no reason to worry about that now. I'm okay." Kayla wrapped her arm around Jen and rubbed her back. "Jackie took very good care of me and I'm feeling better already."

Kayla smiled at Jackie, but Jackie couldn't bring herself to smile back. The thought of someone deliberately hurting Kayla was terrible enough, but drugs made it worse. It was a good thing she'd learned this now.

Kayla's smile faltered and Jackie quickly changed the subject. Her brain was on overload and she had moved into defense mode.

"I'll get your appointment card if you'll wait here a minute."

"Sure," Kayla answered.

When Kayla and Jen were safely out the door, Jackie took a deep breath. There was no way she was getting mixed up in any way with anyone who had anything to do with drugs. Kayla was beautiful, but no one was worth that kind of hell.

CHAPTER FOUR

Jackie pulled in to her office ten minutes late despite getting up an hour earlier than usual. She'd had a night of fitful sleep and disturbing dreams and was in a bad mood. She tried to put the night out of her mind by driving around town for what seemed like forever as she took in the ornamental cherry and redbud trees that were competing for most spectacular blooms of the year. She hoped the time and change of focus would settle the unease that had plagued her all night, but as she walked into the office, her stomach clenched as if she had been punched. *Jesus, what the hell is wrong with me?*

She ran through the client list and tried to get a handle on her day. If she could just throw herself into her work, she could put the past back into the past. She scanned the list and stopped when her eyes fell on Kayla's name. Her stomach fluttered with anticipation. She had known Kayla was coming in today, but just seeing her name stirred her up and she didn't like it.

Jackie replayed Kayla's last visit in her mind and realized she had been out of sorts since last seeing her. The circumstances behind Kayla's injury had caught her off guard. She'd heard the warning loud and clear. Reluctantly Jackie admitted Kayla's confrontation with Jen's husband was probably what had stirred her memories of the past. She should listen to what her big brain was telling her and back off where Kayla was concerned. She had spent too many years getting her life together to let the past derail her now.

Jackie looked up as the door opened and Kayla walked in. She looked windblown and tense and beautiful. Jackie took a deep breath as every fiber in her body tingled and hummed with anticipation. Her *brain* might know seeing Kayla was a bad idea, but her body had other plans.

"Good morning," Kayla said.

"Good morning," Jackie answered. "It looks like you're moving pretty good today."

"I've been better, but yes, I can at least move around now without feeling like someone is stabbing me in the back."

Jackie smiled. "That's progress, I guess, but let's see if we can do a little better." Jackie motioned for Kayla to follow.

Kayla followed Jackie into the treatment room she'd been in just days before but this time there was a small portable machine in the corner with wires and dials that looked like something out of a science fiction show.

Kayla hesitated just inside the door as Jackie stepped in behind her and closed the door.

"How was your week?" Jackie asked casually.

"Aside from the stabbing pain that has taken up residence under my shoulder blade, things have been good."

Jackie laughed at Kayla's sarcastic tone. "Have a seat on the table."

Kayla did as she was instructed. Jackie faced her and rested her hand gently on Kayla's shoulder. "I'm going to start you off with some heat and light stimulation to loosen up the muscles."

"Okay."

Jackie attached small patches of electrodes to Kayla's neck.

"Can you loosen your shirt a little?"

Kayla stiffened, momentarily insecure in the small space and vulnerable to Jackie's tenderness. Reluctantly, she opened a button on her shirt and felt the fabric pull back from her shoulders as Jackie continued to attach the electrodes down her back.

When Jackie finished, she pulled Kayla's shirt back into place and draped a steaming towel across Kayla's neck and shoulders. She picked up another towel and rolled it into the shape of a tube.

"Lie back." Jackie gently guided Kayla back onto the table and placed the towel beneath her neck.

Jackie's hands were soft and warm as she touched her, and Kayla held her breath for fear a sigh might escape her lips. She had expected Jackie to be flirtatious and teasing, but she had been sweet and tender in a professional way. Perhaps there was more to Jackie than the reckless, impulsive woman she had seemed to be when they met. Yeah, right. That was probably just wishful thinking.

Jackie adjusted some dials on a machine next to the treatment table. "Let me know when this starts to feel too strong for you."

"Okay."

A tingling sensation started in her neck and grew more intense as Jackie manipulated the dials.

"Does that feel okay?"

"It feels good actually." Kayla was surprised by how relaxing the combination of heat and stimulation was. Everyone always talked about physical therapy being painful, but this was pleasant.

Jackie smiled down at her. "I'll let you rest here for a while and I'll be back to check on you in a bit. Do you need anything? Do you feel okay?"

"I'm fine." Kayla smiled despite her unease about being left alone. She wasn't prepared for this professional, gentle side of Jackie. She had spent the last three days preparing to put up boundaries with Jackie, to resist her undeniable charm, but now Kayla found herself drawn to Jackie for entirely new reasons.

"You're leaving?"

Jackie slid her hand into Kayla's and squeezed. "I'll be right outside. I just want you to relax awhile. I'll be back, I promise."

Kayla felt silly for being such a baby, but she was scared and vulnerable and Jackie was a comfort to her.

"Okay."

"Good. See you in a few."

When Jackie left the room, Kayla let out a long sigh and closed her eyes. She knew she was acting like a child pining over a crush. It was unlike her to let anyone get under her skin like this, but she had to admit it was nice to have a woman pay attention to her. And although Jackie was just doing her job, it felt good to have someone take care of *her* for a change.

❖

Kayla opened her eyes at the gentle rap at the door just as Jackie stepped into the room. She wasn't sure how long Jackie had been gone. To her surprise, she'd fallen asleep.

"How are you feeling?"

"Good. I could get spoiled by this," she admitted.

"Is that so bad?" Jackie said as she helped Kayla sit up and began removing the electrodes from her skin.

"No." Kayla admitted. "I think I rather like it."

Jackie's hands stilled and Kayla thought she detected a slight catch in her breathing. Jackie didn't respond with her usual flirtation, and that surprised Kayla. Jackie had been completely professional with her throughout the entire session. What had changed?

"How about you? How have you been?" Kayla asked.

Jackie smiled, but there was no light in her eyes when she spoke. "I'm good. It's been a busy week, but other than that, I have no complaints." Jackie removed the towels and pads from the treatment table. "Okay, I need you to sit up straight and tall and do the movements I showed you last week." Jackie demonstrated again and watched intently as Kayla repeated the maneuver.

Kayla did as she was asked but her eyes never left Jackie. "You seem different today. Is something bothering you?"

Jackie placed her hands against Kayla's neck and danced her fingers along her spine. "Very good. Do that ten times and rest a minute."

"Is there?" Kayla asked again.

"Is there what?"

"Something wrong?"

"No." Jackie frowned and seemed to consider something. "So, Jen's husband has a drug problem? You don't strike me as the kind of person who would be mixed up in drugs."

Kayla understood Jackie's curiosity but she also detected something personal in the question. "I'm not mixed up in anything. It isn't even the kind of thing I deal with often. I'm a mental health counselor, and in my line of work I encounter a little bit of everything." Kayla studied Jackie as she spoke. "Why do you ask?"

Jackie shrugged. "Just curious. The story last week had me confused and I couldn't help but wonder about it."

Kayla stopped her exercises and met Jackie's gaze. She understood that something significant was happening for her with Jackie. In her professional life, she was used to asking questions of others, but suddenly she found herself wanting to share with Jackie. For some reason, it was important that she explain. "It was a very unusual situation. Jen is more a victim than I am. Mike has never come to the office before and I got in the way."

"So you don't usually have drug addicts attacking you?"

Kayla smiled. "Of course not. I care about all of my clients, and I can't imagine any of them harming anyone intentionally. But Mike isn't a client. This was the first time anything like this has ever happened."

Jackie brushed her fingers along Kayla's neck and shoulders, needing the physical connection to ground her to the moment. She was unusually tense and guarded and she wasn't sure why. Kayla was being very pleasant and there was no reason for the unease making her skin itch. She wasn't sure what she was looking for, but something told her Kayla was holding back.

"Well, this guy didn't do you any favors." Jackie's anger simmered too close to the surface, making her tone harsher than she intended. The incident with Kayla had made her defensive. "This kind of injury is likely to be a long-term problem. Even if we get you through this episode, it's very likely you'll have recurrences. These exercises you're learning now will be your best defense to keep the pain at bay."

"Oh." Kayla looked stunned as she considered the information. "I guess I didn't realize it was that serious."

"Anytime someone hurts you, it's serious," Jackie snapped and immediately regretted the remark. "I'm sorry. It's none of my business." Jackie tapped her finger on the end of Kayla's chin. "Ten more. I just hope you're careful from now on."

"Trust me. I don't want to experience anything like that ever again. Like I said, it was a very unusual situation. I'm perfectly safe now."

Jackie forced a smile. "Good." She busied herself around the room while Kayla went through the exercises. She hoped Kayla was right. Maybe it was a fluke incident. She'd overreacted and was thankful Kayla hadn't called her on her rudeness. At least now she understood things a little better. It wasn't like Kayla was mixed up in drugs herself. She'd just been in the wrong place at the wrong time. Jackie relaxed a little as some of the tension melted away.

She continued her instructions, determined to keep her mind on her work. Kayla was just another client. She had no right to get into her personal business. This was work and she would handle this situation like all the others. She could do that, right? Sure, she could tell herself that all day, but it didn't change the way she felt.

"I want you to do that exercise again, but this time when you retract your head, I want you to turn your head to the left, like this." Jackie demonstrated again and took Kayla's chin between her fingers and thumb while she cradled her neck with the other to make sure Kayla had the movement right.

Kayla felt the heat of Jackie's body as she cradled her face in her hands. She knew Jackie was only doing her job, but the touch sent a rush of heat through her skin. She thought of her relationships with her clients and shuddered at her behavior. This must be what transference feels like. She was clearly confusing Jackie's caring with attraction.

Jackie nodded and smiled. "Perfect. Now do ten more of those."

"Okay." Kayla was relieved when Jackie stepped away. She took a deep breath and tried to rein in her traitorous emotions. This was a professional relationship, nothing more.

Jackie smiled when Kayla finished. "That's it for today. I want you to do those exercises three times a day for the next week, and more often if you feel your neck or shoulders begin to stiffen up or hurt."

"Got it." As Jackie drew away, Kayla grabbed her hand, not ready to let her go. "Thank you. This really helps."

Jackie smiled and took a step back. Kayla felt the withdrawal as if a door had closed between them. Jackie had been tender with her, her touch caring and gentle, but there had been a distance between them that Kayla didn't understand, and the absence of Jackie's flirtations and cheerful disposition had left her confused and disappointed. When had she started wanting Jackie's affections? *This is silly.* This was Jackie's work. The Jackie she knew here was not the same as the Jackie she had encountered at the bar. *I wonder what the real Jackie is like?*

"Practice." Jackie feigned a stern look. "I'll see you next week."

Kayla smiled. "Of course."

She had at least one more week to figure Jackie out. Maybe next week she would get some answers about this contradictory woman. Her curiosity was piqued and when she wanted to know something she could be relentless. She wasn't usually wrong about people, but something told her there was more to Jackie Phillips than she knew, and despite her first impression, or maybe even because of it, she wanted to know more.

Jackie looked at the appointment calendar and was relieved to see there were no new names on the list. She looked at the clock, shocked she had managed to end a day on time for once.

"Hey, Jack."

Peter, her coworker and business partner, closed the door to his office. He smiled broadly and threw his backpack over his left shoulder. He had showered and changed and looked ready for a night on the town.

"Well look at you. Who knew you had anything in your wardrobe besides gym clothes? Hot date tonight?"

Peter grinned. "Not yet. How about you? Do you have any big plans for the night?"

"Nope," Jackie answered.

"Want to grab a decent dinner for a change and see what kind of trouble we can find?"

Jackie wasn't sure why she hesitated, but for a moment the idea of being surrounded by strangers felt like too much work. But the thought of going home to her apartment alone and the relentless silence and loneliness was even worse.

"Sure. You call it."

Peter clasped Jackie by the shoulder. "I've got just the place."

Jackie groaned. "Why do I have the feeling I'm going to regret this?"

Peter laughed. "Nonsense, you'll be fine. Now get your gear and let's get out of here—I'm starved."

Jackie followed Peter to a small building on the outskirts of the city. What was he up to? She groaned when she pulled into the parking lot of the Purple Pig. She was going to kill him. The Purple Pig was a leather bar that catered to men and their motorcycles. Jackie looked down the row of bikes parked in front and did a double take when she spotted a horse tied to the post at the corner.

"Ah, hell, this I've got to see."

She climbed out and met Peter at the front of her car. "When you said decent dinner, this isn't exactly what I had in mind," she said as she nodded her head toward the bar.

Peter shrugged. "You haven't had the smoked wings and the sweet potato pie."

"You're kidding, right?"

"Nope. Don't worry, I know the guys here tonight and you're safe."

Jackie sighed. "Fine, but I don't fight, I don't do men, and I'm not bailing anyone out of jail."

Peter laughed. "Good Lord. First of all, there won't be any fights, the men are all mine, and no one's going to go to jail. Trust me. It isn't as bad as it looks. If it makes you feel any better, my aunt owns this place and no one here is brave enough to take her on."

Jackie considered the revelation. "Your aunt owns the Purple Pig?"

"Yep, and she's expecting me for dinner and I'm going to tell her it's your fault if we're late. Now, come on." Peter put his arm around Jackie's shoulders and tugged.

"Oh, what the hell."

The crack of pool balls pierced through the roar of voices that filled the small space as they pushed through the door. Jackie looked around the room and noted the handful of men crowded around the pool tables didn't seem fazed by their entrance. She followed Peter through to the back. Instead of a door leading out to the patio there was an open garage door. Outside, fifty or more people mingled around a large fire pit and a group of men and women were playing Cornhole to their right.

Peter stepped up to the outdoor bar, leaned over, and kissed the tall broad-shouldered brunette on the cheek. Jackie was stunned. This couldn't possibly be Peter's aunt. This woman couldn't be more than five years older than Jackie and looked like Terri Clark.

"You're late," she growled.

"It's her fault." Peter pointed to Jackie.

Jackie smiled apologetically and held out her hand. "Sorry, ma'am."

The woman took Jackie's hand and held it as her eyes trailed up and down Jackie's body. "Hmm. You're forgiven."

"Jackie, this is my aunt, Adele. Adele, this is Jackie, a friend from work."

Adele hadn't taken her eyes off Jackie. "Well, Jackie, welcome to the Purple Pig. If you're hungry, I'm sure I've got something you'll like."

Jackie smiled. "I'm sure of it, ma'am."

Adele stepped back, her expression suddenly serious when loud voices signaled a problem at the Cornhole game. Adele picked up an air horn, and everyone stopped what they were doing when the blaring sound burst through the raised voices.

"Hollace. Murley. Cut out the macho bullshit or I'll see your asses outside!"

The two men turned and waved her off. "Sorry, Adie," they called in unison. The shorter man in black leather chaps and black muscle shirt shoved the beanbags into the chest of the larger man with an American flag bandana wrapped around his head.

Jackie's ears were still ringing from the air horn when Adele turned back to her.

"What would you like to drink?"

"A Bud Light will be fine. Thank you."

Adele turned to Peter. "What about you, sweetie? And don't say one of those pansy fruity drinks. It's beer or whiskey or soda. I'm not hauling ice for these lugs when you get them started on those damn daiquiris again."

"Come on, Adie, let's put a little sweet in your tart."

Peter ducked when Adele tried to swat him. "Okay, okay. I'll have a Jack and Coke."

Adele quickly produced their drinks and disappeared into the back.

"Is she really your aunt?" Jackie asked.

Peter sipped his drink. "Yep. My grandmother said she was a change-of-life baby. I figured that was appropriate since she changed everybody's lives." Peter grinned. "We pretty much grew up together since we're so close in age. She's more like a sister than an aunt, but she still likes to pretend she's the boss. But I know all her secrets and I can get my way when I want it."

Jackie was intrigued to see this side of Peter. They had worked together for three years now, but this was the first time she had met anyone from his family.

"I think she likes you," Peter said with a wry grin.

Jackie gave his shoulder a shove. "Why haven't you mentioned her before?"

He shrugged. "I don't know. You know how it is, work is work, and family is family. I guess this makes you a little of both."

Heat rose in Jackie's cheeks as warmth spread through her. She didn't know what to say. She didn't even know if she really understood what family meant. But she knew this was a really big deal and her heart swelled with gratitude and ached with loss. "That's nice. Thanks."

Peter laughed. "You say that now, but wait till Adele gets her hands on you. You might change your mind."

"I'm going to tell her you said that."

"Tell me what?" Adele said as she pushed through the swinging doors and placed two heaping plates of pulled pork, potato salad, green beans, and corn bread in front of them.

"I was telling Jackie how sweet you are."

Jackie started to say something, but Peter stuffed her corn bread into her mouth.

"Yeah, I'm feeling the love," Adele said and rolled her eyes. "Just stay out of trouble and let me know if you need anything." Adele brushed her fingers across the back of Jackie's hand before she disappeared into the crowd.

Jackie admired her body as she walked away. She was a beautiful woman, and Jackie considered accepting the subtle invitation that had been offered. Then again, she had to work with Peter every day and the last thing she wanted to do was to mess up that relationship. She might not have a family of her own, but she knew it was something sacred. Peter trusted her enough to share his with her and she wouldn't cross that line. She wasn't family. That was something she could never have. But having Peter accept her and trust her with those important to him was a gift.

"Hello, beautiful," a deep voice said behind them.

Jackie turned as a tall, well-built man in worn jeans, a white button-up shirt, and a black cowboy hat leaned against the bar and clasped his hand possessively around Peter's knee.

Peter made a show of chewing his food and wiping his mouth before he answered.

"Hello, Calvin. I thought I saw your horse outside. What's wrong, couldn't find a barn to roll around in tonight?"

"Oh, come on now, sugar, let's not be like that. I've been here every night for a month looking for you. I've missed you."

"You have my phone number. You know where I live and where I work. If you really wanted to talk to me, you wouldn't have to look in a bar."

"Hmm, you've got me there. Let me make it up to you."

"Go away, Calvin." Peter said. But his voice wasn't angry—he sounded hurt.

Jackie pushed close to Peter and extended her hand. "Hi, I'm Jackie."

The cowboy took her hand and smiled. His grip was firm but not challenging and his eyes were glacial pools of blue surrounded by a boyishly handsome face with dimples punctuating his glowing smile. *Oh, boy, Peter's in trouble here. This guy is heartbreak material.*

"I'm Calvin. It's a pleasure to meet you, Jackie."

Jackie nodded. "The thing is, Calvin, I'm not sure my friend here is up for company right now. Would you mind giving us a minute to chat?"

Calvin pursed his lips and studied Jackie as if he were sizing her up. She held his gaze with a smile of her own. Finally, Calvin stood and shook his head. "No problem at all, ma'am."

He placed his big hand on the back of Peter's neck, leaned down, and whispered something Jackie couldn't hear. Peter glanced at Calvin and watched him walk away.

"Want to tell me what that was about?"

Peter downed the rest of his drink. "I've known Calvin since we were kids. I've been in love with him since we were sixteen, and he knows it. Sometimes he likes to pretend he loves me back."

"I'm sorry."

Peter shrugged. "Old story. Nothing we need to worry over tonight." He set his glass down on the bar and played the glass back and forth between his fingers. "What about you? Anyone special?"

An image of Kayla instantly flashed in Jackie's mind. She shook her head. "No. I don't think that's in the cards for me."

Peter turned his head to the side and looked at her. "What does that mean?"

Jackie shrugged. "Nothing."

"Well, if she does find you someday, do me a favor and don't be an ass and blow her off."

Jackie knew Peter wasn't really talking about her. She could see the pain etched in his eyes, and she knew it came from loving someone who didn't love him back. That was a pain she was familiar with and it was exactly why she had closed that door to her heart.

"No worries." She bumped her beer bottle against his empty glass with a loud clink. "How about I buy the next round?"

Peter smiled. "Are you trying to get me drunk so you can take advantage of me?"

Jackie laughed. "Uh, no way, partner. But you could use a little loosening up and I don't want your aunt to think I'm bringing you down."

Peter signaled for two more drinks and went back to his food. Jackie glanced around the room and saw Calvin watching from the fire pit. By the hungry look in his eyes she doubted he had to pretend about loving Peter, but something obviously stood in the way. She wondered what Calvin was afraid of since he clearly wanted to be with Peter. She understood that sometimes the thing you ran from the hardest was the thing you needed the most.

Jackie downed the rest of her beer to chase away her musings. She didn't like to think about her past and she certainly didn't want to think about the things she couldn't have. Peter was a good friend. Tonight, that was enough.

Kayla lay on her back and relaxed as the heat of the towels warmed her skin and relaxed her tense muscles. Jackie had been quiet as she worked, and Kayla missed their friendly conversation. She noticed that each time she saw Jackie, she was more and more detached and somber, and Kayla was determined to learn why.

The faint knock at the door sent her heart racing. She followed Jackie with her eyes as she moved around the room.

"How are you feeling?" Jackie asked without looking at her.

"I feel good. Every day seems to get a little better thanks to you."

Jackie smiled. "That means you've been doing your homework."

Kayla smiled in return. "Religiously, I don't want a repeat of what happened."

Jackie didn't respond but Kayla felt her fingers stiffen and still as they moved along her neck.

"Have I done something to upset you?" Kayla asked.

Jackie went back to the task of removing the pads from Kayla's shoulder. "No, of course not. Why do you ask?"

"You seem distant. Quiet. I get the feeling that you're a million miles away this morning. And the last two weeks you've seemed, I don't know, angry with me or something."

Jackie stopped what she was doing and stepped in front of Kayla. She placed her hands against the treatment table at Kayla's sides and met her eyes. "I'm not angry with you." She sighed. "I just thought it best if we kept things between us professional. I'm a little sensitive about the addiction thing and I let that show. I'm sorry."

Kayla placed her hand over Jackie's and ran her thumb along the inside of Jackie's wrist. "You shouldn't have to apologize for your feelings. I take it you've had to deal with addiction before?"

Jackie looked away. Kayla's touch was soft and her voice was comforting, and Jackie couldn't stop the storm of memories that flooded her mind.

"You could say that. My father was an alcoholic and not a very nice man." Jackie wasn't sure why she told Kayla about her father, but she needed Kayla to know. Her nerve endings felt raw and exposed and Kayla had somehow reached inside her and pulled out her truth.

"I'm sorry. That must have been very hard for you."

Kayla's voice was little more than a whisper. Jackie closed her eyes and pulled away. The gentleness of Kayla's touch and the sympathy she heard in her voice were too much, and she felt as if she might fly apart if she didn't put some distance between them. She didn't want Kayla to see her weakness…her pain.

"It was. I'm sorry I made you feel uncomfortable."

Kayla clasped her hands in her lap. "You didn't. I mean, I was just concerned."

Jackie needed to regain control. She didn't like to think about her past and she never talked about it to anyone, and this was not the place to start. "Okay, back to work. I need you to stand and face this corner. Place your hands on the adjacent walls and lean in as far as you can, like you're trying to put your nose in the corner."

Kayla raised one eyebrow. "Seriously?"

Jackie smiled. "I'm afraid so. Go on."

Kayla sighed. "I know you're changing the subject, but thank you for telling me about your father."

Jackie scrambled to regain control of her defenses. She didn't understand this sudden need to share her secrets with Kayla, a client, a woman who was little more than a stranger. But she had been drawn to Kayla the instant she saw her walk into the bar that first night. Kayla shook her up, confused her, and made her feel things she didn't want to feel, but craved.

"Try to do three sets of ten for now and then rest."

Kayla did as she was asked.

Jackie was relieved to be back on safe ground. What was she thinking, telling Kayla about her father? She never talked about him. She didn't even like thinking about him. No one in her life knew about her past, and the more distance she put between her and those memories, the less she had to admit to her failures.

"Jackie?"

Jackie jumped, startled out of her thoughts. "Sorry, you caught me daydreaming." Jackie handed Kayla a small length of latex tubing. "Now I want you to put this behind your head and pull, like this." Jackie demonstrated the movement.

When Kayla raised her hands and tried the maneuver, Jackie closed her hands around Kayla's and guided her until she was certain Kayla had it right. Kayla's hands were soft and smooth, and Jackie held on longer than necessary just to have an excuse to touch her.

Kayla grimaced and Jackie's stomach flipped in a rush of fear. She paused, her face only inches from Kayla's. "Did that hurt? Where's the pain?"

Kayla's breath caught as her body warmed at the contact of Jackie's touch. Jackie was so close she could feel the heat mingle between their bodies. She shook her head. "It's nothing. It's just a little stab between my shoulders. I'm okay."

Kayla averted her eyes but she could feel Jackie's gaze on her. The moment Jackie placed her hands over hers, her entire body had responded. Jackie smelled like fresh rain and summer flowers, and it had been all Kayla could do not to breathe in the tantalizing scent. The last thing she needed was for Jackie to see the arousal that had caught her off guard.

Jackie loosened her grip on Kayla's hands and lengthened the tube. "Try again."

Jackie's voice was husky and it grated across Kayla's already frayed control like blunt fingernails scraping across her skin. If she didn't put some distance between them soon, she was going to do something that would be a clear violation of Jackie's professional boundaries.

As if reading her mind, Jackie let go of her hands and stepped away.

Kayla wrapped the latex tube around her hand to keep from reaching out to touch Jackie. Jackie's eyes were dark as if a storm was brewing in their depths. Kayla recognized the vulnerability in Jackie's withdrawal after her revelation about her father, but now a new emotion had surfaced, and Kayla was as drawn to the feral look of desire as she had been to Jackie's willingness to share her pain.

"Take that band home with you and add it to your daily exercises along with the corner stretches. You should see a significant reduction in the pressure behind your shoulder blades with these moves. I'll see you again in a week, but we can only continue these sessions for a couple of more weeks without a doctor's referral. You'll need to see your physician to see if she wants you to continue."

Kayla was stunned. She had expected the treatments to end, but hadn't been prepared for it to happen so soon. "I don't know. What do you suggest?"

Jackie took her hand and smiled reassuringly. "You're progressing well and there haven't been any new symptoms. It wouldn't hurt to see your doctor, but as long as you keep up your exercises, I think you'll be okay. If you experience any worsening of the symptoms, you can always see your doctor and get the referral to come back to see me."

Kayla was relieved to know she could still reach out to Jackie if she needed her. The thought surprised her and she realized how much she had grown to rely on Jackie in the short amount of time she had been in therapy. Kayla felt a sense of security wash over her when she saw Jackie or felt her reassuring and confident hands working to heal her.

"To be honest, I'm a little afraid. This whole mess rocked me more than I thought it did, and I'm not used to people taking care of me." Kayla focused on the comforting warmth of Jackie's hand holding hers. It felt nice. And in two short weeks Jackie would be gone and the wild stirring in her blood, her body, her dreams, would quiet again, and her life would return to its normal routine. "But I think I'll be okay on my own."

Jackie smiled and squeezed Kayla's hand. "All right then, I'll see you next week."

Kayla nodded. She followed Jackie to the front desk and took the appointment card.

"Thank you." Kayla wanted to say something, anything to keep Jackie talking…anything to prolong the contact between them. She knew Jackie had work to do and she needed to get to work herself, but she felt rooted to the spot, unable to make the separation. She opened her mouth to say something, but just as she was about to speak, her cell phone rang interrupting her before she could add anything more.

"See you next week," Jackie said, turning and picking up another file.

Kayla reached for her phone. She was being ridiculous. She would see Jackie next week, and when their sessions ended, perhaps they could be friends. Kayla glanced back and watched Jackie disappear into an office. She had seen Jackie's vulnerability, her fierce desire to protect, and her caring tenderness, and she had experienced Jackie's impulsive, carefree, flirtatious side too. She had never been more attracted to a woman in her life.

Chapter Five

It had been three weeks since her last session with Jackie. Kayla had remained professional with Jackie through the final visit at her office and told herself it was best if she didn't pursue anything personal with her. She thought that time would diminish her infatuation and allow her to return to her normal, orderly, predictable life. But what had once been comfortable and secure had become dull and lonely.

Kayla stared at the numbers on her phone. After an eternity she closed her eyes and pressed call. Just as she was about to hang up, she heard the line connect and Jackie's silky voice answered.

"Hello, Jackie Phillips speaking."

Kayla panicked and thought about hanging up. In a rush she just started talking. "Hi, Jackie, this is Kayla McCormick—"

"Kayla?" Jackie interrupted. "Is everything okay? Is your neck giving you trouble again?"

"No. No, I'm fine. I just…" Kayla had no idea what to say next. "Uh, well…" Kayla felt foolish and embarrassed. "That's not the reason for my call. When we first met you asked me to call you."

"And you didn't," Jackie said pointedly.

"Yeah, well, a lot was going on then. I think I know you a little better now. Is it okay that I called?" Kayla was glad Jackie couldn't see her. She was pretty sure her face was about to burst into flames and her stomach was about to revolt.

"No. I mean, yes. I'm not sure actually. Things have changed."

"I know." Kayla paused. "Am I too late?"

Jackie laughed. "I guess that depends on why you're calling. I was under the impression that I'm not exactly your type."

Kayla couldn't think of what to say. She cleared her throat and stammered a moment before managing to regain the power of speech. "This was a mistake. I'm sorry I bothered you."

"Wait, don't hang up." There was a moment of silence before Jackie continued as if she was listening to see if Kayla was still there. "There was obviously a reason for your call. What was it?"

Kayla scrunched her eyes closed and shook her head, mentally kicking herself. There was no turning back now. She had come this far, so she might as well go through with it. "I thought maybe you would like to have dinner with me tonight."

"You want to have dinner...with me...tonight?"

"Well, yes. I know this is short notice—if you can't make it, that's fine."

"I guess I could do dinner. What did you have in mind?"

Kayla was happy at first, but her relief was quickly replaced by panic. Part of her had expected Jackie to have other plans or to have some polite excuse to say no. She wasn't prepared for her to say yes. "Do you like Italian food?"

"Sure, but I don't get off work until six. Is that too late?"

"That'll be fine," Kayla said with a slight squeak in her voice.

"Give me your address and I'll pick you up. Is seven okay?"

Jackie didn't answer right away. "I look forward to it."

Kayla was oddly pleased with herself. Did that just happen? Had she just asked a woman for a date? She shook her head in disbelief. *I have a date.* Her skin tingled, her heart pounded against her rib cage, and she was both excited and terrified at the same time. It would be a miracle if she got through dinner without having a heart attack.

As the workday drew to a close Kayla's excitement grew. She had just enough time to rush home, shower, and get through the ritual of going through everything in her closet and having nothing to wear, and still get to Jackie's on time.

Her palms were sweating, her heart was racing, and she couldn't take a deep breath without coughing. She was breaking all of her own rules. She didn't do casual dating. And if her first impression was right, Jackie was the casual type. But she wanted to believe there was more to Jackie than that. She had to find out. She pulled on her favorite pair of jeans and a red button-down that was cut to show just the right amount of neckline leading down to reveal the subtle roundness of her cleavage. She checked herself in the mirror and brushed a wayward strand of hair away from her cheek. That should do it. Satisfied, she smiled to her reflection. "I'm ready."

Jackie ran her hand through her hair. A broad smile crept across her face as she stared at the phone. She had been certain she would never hear from Kayla McCormick after her behavior at the bar the night they met. It wasn't unusual for her to be playful with women when she was out, but she hadn't expected to like Kayla as much as she did. Then the weeks working with Kayla in therapy had allowed her a chance to get to know her on a deeper level than she was used to, and the idea of going on a date was new to her. She saw a lot of women, but she couldn't say she dated them. Who cared how they started as long as the destination was the same?

She liked the way Kayla put her in her place and hadn't put up with her antics. But by the time she realized there was something different about Kayla it was too late to take back the way she had come on to her. Maybe she just needed someone like Kayla to shake her up a bit. Kayla wasn't the type of woman she usually hooked up with, but there was something about Kayla that sent her pulse racing in a way no one else had. Kayla was intelligent, beautiful, funny, and serious. She was a challenge.

Jackie could tell Kayla was hesitant about seeing her. She was certain there had been one point in the conversation when Kayla almost backed out. She still wasn't sure why she had agreed to dinner, and she certainly couldn't believe she had agreed to have Kayla pick her up at her apartment. She usually preferred to meet a woman in a neutral location, and then if things worked out she preferred to go to their place. It made it easier for her to make a quick exit instead of risking someone wanting to stay the night and getting the wrong idea there was a relationship in their future.

This was going to be a first. She cleared away her equipment and still needed to wipe down all the machines before leaving.

"Hey, Jack, can you come give this hand X-ray a look?" Peter called from one of the treatment rooms.

Jackie cringed but couldn't say no.

"Sure."

By the time she was finished, she was cutting things close. She took a quick shower and had managed to slide on a pair of jeans when the doorbell rang. She pulled a T-shirt over her head on her way to the door. She looked at the clock. It was exactly seven. She blew out her breath. Her hands were shaking. What was up with that? She took another deep breath. Even if she didn't feel confident at that moment, there was no reason to advertise it.

Jackie's apartment was across town near the University Hospital. Kayla pulled into a space and studied the modern brick building with large windows and balconies overlooking the Tennessee River. The place was nice. She could imagine sitting on the balcony watching the fog roll across the cool flowing water. It was a warm evening and the air caressed her skin, raising the small hairs on her arms and face. Her skin tingled but it was more than just the breeze exciting her.

Kayla focused on her breathing in an effort to calm her racing pulse as she raised a shaking hand and rang the doorbell. In moments she heard rustling on the other side of the door and then the click of the lock. When the door swung open her heart jumped. Jackie stood in front of her smiling broadly, her hair still wet from her shower. She was dressed in jeans and a T-shirt and her feet were bare. The sight of her was enough to take Kayla's breath away and her blood quickened with excitement. Jackie was even more beautiful in this raw exposure.

"Hi. Come on in while I finish getting ready."

Jackie's voice sounded unsteady and her words were rushed. Was she nervous? Kayla liked the idea that she could make Jackie nervous.

"My shift ran over and I'm running a little late. Sorry."

Kayla stepped inside and glanced around the neatly furnished apartment. "There's no rush. Take your time."

Jackie paused and her eyes roamed the length of Kayla's body in a quick assessment. She smiled warmly and leaned in and kissed Kayla on the cheek. "You look beautiful."

Kayla could feel the heat creep into her cheeks and she looked away to hide her blush. "Thank you."

"Make yourself at home," Jackie said with a wave of her hand toward the open room. "There's beer and soda and other stuff in the fridge in the kitchen. Feel free to help yourself. I'll only be few minutes."

"I'll be fine."

Kayla looked around nervously. She couldn't believe she was standing in Jackie's apartment. *What the hell am I doing?* She could hear Jackie moving around in one of the rooms down the hall and she couldn't help but take a sweeping gaze around the apartment to see what she could learn about Jackie by the things she surrounded herself with in her home. So far she appeared to be tidy, minimalistic, and an avid reader. There were books on almost every surface in the room, although tastefully arranged. Kayla peered at the titles, finding that each pile was arranged by subject. There were books on physiology on the desk by the window. A pile of books by the sofa were related to history. A shelf that encased the television was full of lesbian romance novels, and finally a smaller shelf in one corner housed science fiction and fantasy titles. It wasn't what Kayla had expected, but she was pleasantly surprised. It appeared there was a lot more to Jackie than she had originally thought.

Kayla went to the fridge and took out a soda. The refrigerator appeared even more minimalist than the living room. There were sodas but nothing diet, beer, and fruit juice, a carton of milk, and various vegetables and fruits. No condiments, no junk food, and no meat. Kayla wondered if Jackie was a vegetarian. The surface of the counter was completely bare. At first glance the kitchen looked like it had been staged. Kayla reprimanded herself for being intrusive and acting like a voyeur, looking into Jackie's private world, and decided to wait outside.

She took one last glance around the room and sipped her soda as she made her way out onto the balcony to watch the never-ending flow of water and a family of ducks playing on along the water's edge. She had never seen the city from this side of the river bluff, and as she looked out over the cityscape, she was touched by the welcoming beauty of the modest buildings bathed in the fading light of the sun. Everything looked magical in this light. The sound of the door sliding open pulled her from her thoughts.

Jackie stepped out onto the balcony. "Ah. There you are. What do you think of the view?"

"It's very nice. If I had a view like this, I'd be out here all the time."

"I am, when I'm home, that is."

Kayla turned and leaned one arm on the railing and looked at Jackie. She had changed her shirt and was now wearing a blue pullover with the university logo embroidered over the left breast.

Kayla gestured toward the logo. "I take it you're a fan."

Jackie shrugged. "Who isn't?"

Kayla smiled, taking in the warmth of Jackie's eyes.

"How's your neck?" Jackie brushed her fingers against a spot on Kayla's neck just below her ear. Kayla's skin was warm and the blood rose beneath her skin at the touch.

"Better. I still do the exercises and I can tell when it's getting stiff now, so I stay just ahead of it."

"That's good. You're a good patient."

Kayla grimaced.

"What? Did I say something wrong?" Jackie held her breath. She had never spent time getting to know a woman like this and she was sure she was blowing it.

"No, you didn't do anything wrong. It's just that tonight I don't want to think of us as patient and therapist. I hoped this could be... less professional."

Jackie smiled. She liked the idea. Normally this would be the opening she looked for to make her move on a woman, but that didn't feel right with Kayla. Kayla was gorgeous and sexy as hell, and Jackie was turned on by just the sound of Kayla's voice. But something kept warning her not to go there.

"You must have some pretty strict boundaries with clients in your work."

"Yes, I do," Kayla said before taking a sip of her soda.

"Well, technically you're not my patient anymore and I'm not breaking any rules."

Kayla smiled. "That's good to know."

Jackie shifted so that she looked out over the river and rested her elbows on the balcony railing. She could feel Kayla watching her and wondered what Kayla saw when she looked at her. "Speaking of work, you said you're a therapist, right?"

"That's right."

"What kind of therapist? I mean, what kind of problems do you treat?"

Kayla's expression became more serious. "Well, mostly I see people who have suffered some trauma or abuse. I help with things like anxiety, PTSD, phobias, depression, and a lot of other problems."

Jackie thought for a moment before responding. "I guess that explains why you always seem to be studying everything. You must see a lot of sadness in your work."

Kayla sucked in her breath. "Yes. It's an emotionally heavy job. But I like helping people, and at some point we all need someone to talk to."

Jackie watched Kayla's pupils expand and contract in response to her emotions as she spoke. Kayla shifted uncomfortably.

Jackie smiled, breaking the spell. "I suppose you're right. I know I like talking to you."

Kayla blushed and cleared her throat as she turned away. "Are you hungry?"

Jackie laughed. "I'm starving. I can't remember if I actually had a meal today."

"In that case, let's get going. I have a nice little place picked out for us."

Kayla followed Jackie inside and watched her move around the room, admiring Jackie's body while she wasn't looking. Her jeans hugged her slender hips and thighs, hinting of strong athletic legs. The cotton pullover had short sleeves that gripped the round biceps of Jackie's arms and her muscles flexed when she moved. Kayla liked the way Jackie moved. Her long limbs seemed purposefully controlled, as if she had spent years perfecting how to move her tall, lean frame to demonstrate just the right amount of grace.

Kayla led the way to the car and used the short walk to clear her head. But once inside the car, the space seemed too small. She was acutely aware of Jackie sitting next to her. She drew in a deep breath, pulling in the clean fresh scent of soap and something vaguely masculine that she couldn't quite identify, but knew was unique to Jackie.

Naples, the restaurant Kayla had chosen, was a favorite and she was excited to have someone to share it with. Once inside, she chose a table in the bar. She liked the small two-person tabletops with the dim lighting that seemed more intimate than the bright light and large tables in the main dining area. She liked the way the flickering gold flame of the candle in the center of the table danced and played with the colors of Jackie's eyes.

Kayla ordered wine and a plate of fried ravioli. Jackie decided on a beer and calamari.

Jackie grinned mischievously. "Want to share?"

Kayla bit down on her tongue and nodded. "Sure." Did Jackie mean the sexual innuendo or was she making that up? She was letting her imagination get the better of her.

"So, I couldn't help but notice you have a lot of books in your apartment," Kayla said before lifting her wineglass. "Very impressive," she said peering over the rim of her glass.

Jackie smirked. "Guess you didn't expect me to be the intellectual type, huh?"

Kayla grinned. "I admit it didn't fit my first impression of you, but so far the surprises have been good ones."

Jackie raised her eyebrows in question. "Really? What other surprises have there been?"

Kayla shrugged. "You came across impulsive and arrogant that first night. But since then you seem more…"

"Civilized?" Jackie interjected.

"Ha. Not quite that extreme, but in a way, yes. You seem more serious, thoughtful—I don't know how to explain it exactly."

"Well, I hope you like what you see."

Kayla studied Jackie for a moment, contemplating her answer. She liked what she saw very much, maybe too much. "Hmm, I guess you're all right."

Jackie laughed.

The waiter appeared with the meal and Kayla watched Jackie's expression as she took the first bite of her sea bass. Kayla knew it was the best in town, and she waited for the bliss to flood across Jackie's face. She wasn't disappointed. Jackie's eyes closed for a whole three seconds as she worked the flavors across her tongue. When she opened her eyes, they were bright and alive with pleasure.

"This is amazing," Jackie said pointing to her plate with her fork.

Kayla smiled, pleased by Jackie's enjoyment.

Jackie laughed and reached across the table to brush away a dribble of sauce that had fallen onto Kayla's chin.

The touch was tender and Kayla's skin burned as Jackie brushed her finger lightly across her lower lip. When Jackie withdrew her hand and rested it on the table, Kayla watched her long fingers stroke the rim of her glass.

The waiter came to clear the table. "Can I get you anything else, another drink perhaps or dessert?"

"No dessert for me," Jackie answered. "But I'd love another drink. Do you mind staying a while longer?"

"No. That sounds good to me." She turned back to the waiter. "I'll have another glass of wine too, thank you."

Jackie studied Kayla as she talked, memorizing the shape of her lips and the hollow at the base of her throat. And the way she toyed nervously with the stem of her glass. Jackie studied the unusual color of Kayla's eyes. They were a light milky brown, not the usual deep brown that made Jackie think of darkness. Kayla's eyes were warm and Jackie liked the way they seemed to brighten and glow in the flickering candlelight. She enjoyed Kayla. She liked how Kayla didn't let her by with anything and how Kayla paid attention as if what she thought mattered to her. That was new for Jackie, and she liked it. She didn't really let people know her, but Kayla made it easy to talk and relax.

Jackie reached a hand across the table and stroked her fingers across Kayla's hand, taking only the tips of her fingers in her own. She brushed lightly across the smooth skin, never taking her eyes from Kayla's gaze.

"I'm glad you called today. I admit I wasn't sure it was a good idea at first, but I'm enjoying this very much."

"Me too," Kayla said with a faint smile, slowly withdrawing her fingers and lifting her glass to take a drink of her wine. Kayla looked at her watch. "I guess we should be going. It's getting late."

Jackie's attraction to Kayla had her body on overload. She had no doubt sex with Kayla would be amazing. As they walked out of the restaurant she took Kayla's hand again. To her surprise Kayla didn't pull away this time, but laced their fingers firmly together. Emboldened by the contact, Jackie snaked her arm behind Kayla's elbow and rested her hand on Kayla's thigh as soon as she settled into the seat of the car.

Kayla's hands shook as she reached for the ignition. She was very aware of Jackie's hand on her thigh as she drove. The heat from Jackie's hand warmed her skin, a pulse of arousal beat between her legs, and she ached for a more intimate touch. Kayla was suddenly unsure what she should do. She tried to convince herself that she could have a casual sexual affair with Jackie, but she already wanted to see Jackie again. Why couldn't she just let go for once and go after what she wanted?

Kayla mentally kicked herself. How did she always manage to guilt herself into taking the moral high road? What was so wrong with fulfilling her needs? What was so bad about just having sex? She knew the answer. She was looking for forever. She didn't want a casual pass-in-the-night relationship. She wanted to wake up with the woman of her dreams. She wanted someone she could build a lifetime with, even if part of her didn't believe that would ever happen for her.

Jackie stroked Kayla's thigh. "Will you come up and talk for a while?"

Kayla took a deep breath. "I'm not sure that's such a good idea," she answered.

Jackie chuckled. "I promise to be on my best behavior. I just want you to see the view at night, and I'm afraid you'll disappear again once you leave."

Kayla glanced at Jackie, who had turned sideways in her seat and was looking intently at her. She looked at the clock display on the dash. It was already nine thirty. "I have to work tomorrow."

"One hour," Jackie countered.

Kayla smiled wryly. "You're very persistent."

"Only when I see something I want."

Kayla's breath caught and she was thankful it was dark so Jackie couldn't see her blushing. She had been doing that a lot tonight.

"I'm sorry. Was that too forward?"

Kayla was silent for a while as she struggled with her answer. What did it say about her if she said yes? Better yet, what did it say if she said no?

"One hour, Kayla. Say yes," Jackie whispered.

Kayla nodded. "One hour," she answered, letting out a long shaky breath.

Jackie smiled and pressed her fingers into Kayla's hand.

Kayla tried to take her mind off the feel of Jackie's skin. She focused on the road ahead and how she was going to get through this evening without losing her mind.

Jackie's voice broke through the stillness. "So tell me, what made you decide to call me tonight? I was afraid I scared you off."

Kayla chuckled. "I toyed with the idea after we met, and you did scare me. Then I ended up being your patient. Getting to know you a little over the past few weeks help me get over some of my first impression of you."

"What were you afraid of?"

Kayla thought about her answer. She didn't want to admit that the intensity of Jackie's kiss had haunted her.

"You're very intense," she finally said. "I guess I needed to prepare myself."

Jackie stroked Kayla's hand. "I know I came on a little strong the night we met, but I promise I'm not usually so obnoxious."

Kayla smiled, relaxing into the seat of her car. "I admit I was pretty annoyed with you, but I think what upset me most was feeling like you were playing me."

"Ouch. That's even worse." Jackie pretended to be wounded.

"You mean you weren't trying to play me?"

"No. I was just having a good time. I was caught up in kidding around with my friends and came on a little strong. But all I really wanted was to talk to you."

"Spoken like a true player."

Jackie grinned. "Okay. Tell me what you think a player is like."

Jackie was getting a little annoyed but it wasn't because Kayla was wrong, it was because so much of what Kayla was saying was true about her life.

Kayla laughed. "She's someone who will say and do almost anything to gain someone's interest so she can get laid."

"That's what I thought you'd say. Now tell me how I fit that description."

"Ha," Kayla scoffed. "The very first thing you did was kiss me and walk away, an act clearly designed to get my attention. Then you came up to me with an insincere apology and kissed me again, all a play to get an emotional reaction."

"So I was too forward."

Kayla laughed. "You came out with the confidence of someone who's used to getting exactly what she wants."

Jackie appeared thoughtful for a few moments. "And by your description that means sex. Is that right?"

"Yes."

Jackie raised one eyebrow and looked pointedly at Kayla. "Then why did *you* call me?"

There it was, the question of the hour. Kayla knew her face had to be scarlet at this point. She was certain she would spontaneously combust at any moment. She couldn't admit that the kiss had melted her defenses, leaving her hungry and wanting, and that Jackie's caring over the last few weeks was more attention or affection than she had had in years. She had seen Jackie's tenderness and her vulnerability along with her carefree lifestyle. The combination was like a spell that made Kayla want to break her own rules.

Jackie leaned close enough that her breath brushed Kayla's ear when she spoke. "Is that what tonight was really about, Kayla? Were you looking for—"

"No." Kayla interrupted before Jackie could say the words. She was shaking now and her voice was sharp and defensive. "I admit your kiss had me contemplating things I've never done before, but after spending time with you these past few weeks and then tonight, I can see there's more to you than the pickup game." Kayla's voice softened. "That's the person I wanted to know."

"And?" Jackie asked.

Kayla shook her head. "I don't know. I'm still trying to figure that out." Kayla was shocked by her answer, and even more surprised to realize it was true.

❖

The soft glow of moonlight spilled in through the windows, bathing the room in soft white light as they entered Jackie's apartment. Jackie poured Kayla a glass of wine and opened a beer for herself.

"Shall we?" Jackie motioned to the balcony.

The view was beautiful. The city lights cast against the night sky gave the feel of floating in space, each star a window opening to tiny private worlds. Kayla was mesmerized.

"I hope you haven't been disappointed tonight," Jackie said. "You were right about me before. I admit my relationships have been mostly of the sexual nature, but I've always been honest and the situation was always mutual. Maybe I need to work on my social skills. I really am sorry if I offended you."

Kayla was surprised by the openness of Jackie's admission. Jackie was a complex, beautiful woman. Kayla moved closer to Jackie, who leaned on the rail of the balcony, her elbows propped on the edge and her hands clasped in front of her. Kayla brushed her hand along the back of Jackie's arm.

"You haven't offended me," Kayla whispered tracing her fingers along Jackie's cheek and gently caressing her face. "There *is* one thing I would like to know though."

Jackie's voice rasped when she spoke. "What's that?"

"This." Kayla's lips brushed the soft perfect swell of Jackie's mouth. Jackie's lips were warm and supple and they parted slightly at the faint brush of Kayla's tongue. Kayla felt the warmth spread from the tips of her fingers up her arms and into her breasts. The tenderness she remembered consumed her senses, and she felt she would melt with the longing that coursed through her like the rushing waves of the ocean.

Jackie's arms slid around her waist and up her back. Firm fingers brushed through her hair and traced from her ear along her jaw and finally across the swollen fullness of her lips as their mouths parted.

Kayla kept her eyes closed. She wanted to savor the pleasure that lingered on her lips and in her body. Something stirred within her that threatened to break down all her walls of protection. It was like standing on the edge of a cliff feeling the wind whip past her, threatening to push her over the edge. One wrong step and she would fall, but the rush was too intoxicating to step away.

Kayla slowly opened her eyes and met Jackie's molten gaze, the colors of her eyes shifting from green to brown, beckoning Kayla into them with the promise of passion.

Kayla cleared her throat and took a step back. She placed her hand at the hollow of Jackie's throat and let her fingers brush the line of her collarbone. "I've wanted to feel your lips again ever since you kissed me good-bye at the bar."

Jackie stood very still. "I'm glad you weren't disappointed," she said in a whisper.

Kayla smiled before turning to look out over the city.

Jackie followed her gaze. Glistening lights reflected off the water in a kaleidoscope of color. She moved her hand across Kayla's shoulder and down her back and felt Kayla shudder under the touch.

"Are you cold?"

Kayla glanced up at Jackie. "No. I'm just enjoying your touch."

Jackie smiled and moved closer. She brushed her hand along the cool silk of Kayla's shirt, feeling the heat radiate from her body.

Kayla shuddered again. "I think I should go," she said in a shaky voice.

Jackie paused. She took her hand from Kayla's back and brushed her fingers along Kayla's arm until her fingers slipped into Kayla's hand. "Or you could stay."

Kayla met Jackie's gaze, her eyes glistening with the flames of desire. "Very tempting, but I can't. I don't want my time with you tonight to be about sex."

"What's so wrong with sex?"

"I just can't. I thought I could, but I can't. I'm looking for something more."

"So you aren't just after my body?" Jackie teased.

Kayla chuckled and traveled her eyes across Jackie's frame. "Hmm. Your body is very beautiful, but no."

Jackie smiled. "That means you like me."

Kayla tilted her head to the side, a faint smile playing across her lips.

"Maybe a little," she said before stepping back into the apartment. Jackie followed close behind. Her heart pounding against her ribcage as a shimmer of fear skittered through her. She feared that if Kayla walked out of her apartment it would be the last time she saw her.

"Can I call you? I'd like to call you. I'd like to see you again."

"You have my number in your file at work."

Jackie shrugged. "That's work. I want your permission."

Kayla hesitated before pulling out a business card from her wallet and writing her personal number on the back. She handed it to Jackie, eyeing the small card with uncertainty.

"It's okay, Kayla, I'm not some crazy stalker. Relax."

Kayla smiled. "It's not that. I just don't do this very often. I'm a little out of practice."

Jackie took the card, wrapping her hand around Kayla's fingers as she did.

Kayla held her breath as Jackie wrapped her arms around her and pulled her close. Jackie's breast brushed against her own and her nipples tightened. Kayla gasped as Jackie's lips claimed her. Jackie kissed her more confidently this time, a deep and penetrating exploration that filled her with longing until her heart was near to bursting.

Kayla's legs were weak as pleasure surged through her. Jackie's tongue swept through her mouth, releasing waves of desire that made her tremble. Firm hands held her upright and the strength in the embrace offered safety. Without conscious thought, Kayla wrapped her arms around Jackie's shoulders and surrendered. All her hesitation and confusion burned away beneath the fire of Jackie's touch like paper against embers. She moaned as Jackie's hands moved into her hair, deepening the kiss that already had her spinning out of control. Too soon the kiss slowed, and Kayla relished the feel of lighter kisses along her jaw and down her neck, before Jackie's lips returned to her mouth.

Jackie stroked the swollen flesh of her mouth with her tongue and nipped at her lower lip. Kayla gasped. Her breath was heavy and her heartbeat was a steady roar against her eardrums. Her body was consumed with desire and need. God, had she ever wanted a woman this badly before? She couldn't think.

Jackie brushed her lips against Kayla's ear, her hot breath sending shivers down Kayla's spine. "Stay."

Kayla struggled to regain the ability to think. She was ready to do anything Jackie asked. Her reasoning was overcome by her desire. Her thoughts were jumbled and disjointed. She brushed her hand along Jackie's cheek. "I would like that very much, but I can't."

Jackie moaned her disappointment but never stopped the play of her lips against Kayla's neck. Her hands found Kayla's breasts, and she played the tender flesh between her fingers, making Kayla melt inside, and she pressed her body harder into Jackie's hands. Her words said no, but her body said yes.

Kayla heard a moan escape her lips, but there was nothing she could do now to stop this exquisite pleasure. She didn't want Jackie to stop, damn the consequences.

It was Jackie who pulled away this time. "When can I see you again? Are you free Friday?"

Kayla fought to regain control over her thoughts and her body. She was overcome with disappointment and relief that Jackie had given her a reprieve. Her body began a slow recovery from the rush of adrenaline, but her legs were unsteady and the throbbing between her legs made her weak. "Friday is good," she said breathily, as she fought the urge to beg Jackie to make love to her.

"Okay then, I'll call you." Jackie pulled back, allowing a slight separation between their bodies.

Kayla found it difficult to distance herself from Jackie—her body cried out for her touch. With one last surge of effort she pulled away, straightened her shirt, and brushed her hands through her hair. At the door she stopped and turned back to Jackie, confused. "You had me just now. I would have gone to bed with you."

"I know," Jackie answered, her tone low and gentle.

Kayla's brow furrowed with confusion. "Why did you stop?" she asked, her voice thick with uncertainty.

"You said you didn't want tonight to be about sex. I have to respect that. What you see is what you get with me. No strings, no commitments."

Kayla smiled, her hand resting on the half-open door. She studied Jackie and saw honesty and desire and, perhaps, vulnerability in her eyes. She nodded. "Good night, Jackie."

"Good night, Kayla."

The sound of the door shutting behind Kayla was like shutting off the air. Jackie fought to take a breath and thought her lungs would explode. She let out a long sigh. She couldn't believe she had just let Kayla walk out when she could have had her in her arms and in her bed at that very moment. *What am I doing?* Jackie ran her hands through her hair. Her body was tense with want. It would have been easy to just take Kayla to bed, to sate the desire coursing through her. But she couldn't stomach the thought of taking Kayla for simple pleasure. She couldn't bear the thought of the emptiness that waited for her at the end of the night. She ran her hand across her chest and tried to quiet her racing pulse. What she had said was true. She never slept with a woman unless they both agreed on the rules. No strings, no commitments, just sex. Kayla might have wanted to sleep with her, but that wasn't enough. She would want more. And more wasn't something Jackie had to give.

Jackie went to the fridge and pulled out a beer, popped the top, and drank deeply. She settled on the couch, too wound up for sleep. She let her thoughts wonder. It had been eleven years since she'd left home and she hadn't looked back once. She didn't need anyone. She knew how to keep people at a distance, only taking what she needed when she needed it. That had always been enough. Why were things different now? What had changed?

Jackie studied the name engraved on the front of Kayla's card before flipping it over to the hastily scrawled number on the back. She took a deep breath and sighed. Should she see Kayla again? Probably not. She ran her hand between her legs and pressed against her swollen flesh. She was so aroused it would only take a couple of strokes to get her off. She groaned and pulled her hand away. Friday lingered in the distance like a forbidden fruit that she couldn't wait to taste.

Chapter Six

Kayla was late getting to the Mexican restaurant. She spotted Jen across the room and tried to read her expression to get a feel for Jen's mood before sitting down across from her. She could usually tell what kind of day it would be just by reading Jen's expression and body language, but today Jen seemed subdued. There was no hint of puffy eyes, her brow was smooth, and she managed a half smile when she looked up to see Kayla approaching.

"Hey, you made it."

"Yeah. I was beginning to wonder myself. Sorry I'm late. The good news is my one o'clock canceled today, so I don't have to be in a rush to get back." Kayla placed her hands on the table in front of her and waited for Jen to fill her in on the latest drama. When Jen didn't say anything, Kayla plunged right in.

"So, tell me what's going on with you. Are you still thinking about the Nashville transfer?"

Jen sighed. "Yes. I mentioned it to Mike. He doesn't want to move of course. He says there's no reason to move. He says things are fine here. He says I need to get that crap out of my head and stop trying to act like I'm better than him." Jen dropped her head at the final statement.

"I'm sorry. What do you think about it?"

Jen shrugged. "I don't know. I feel so confused all the time."

"So you feel like you have to choose between your professional goals and Mike. Is that it?"

Jen looked up from the napkin she had been toying with. "That's exactly it."

"Maybe it would be good for Mike to see you make a decision without him. Maybe he'd realize he could lose you."

Jen looked pained. "Yeah, and what if he doesn't care?"

Kayla reached out and took Jen's hand. "Oh, Jen, if he's that thick let him get lost. You deserve so much better than that."

Jen's eyes glistened with tears. "I'm afraid I'll spend the rest of my life alone. Who'll want me?"

Kayla couldn't believe what she'd just heard. "You're kidding me, right? There are lots of beautiful, wonderful people out there who would fall over themselves to be with you. I promise you, you are someone who can choose who you want to be with."

Jen sniffed. "You're my friend—you're supposed to say stuff like that."

Kayla laughed. "Yes, but in your case it's true. I've never sugarcoated anything for you before, and I'm telling you, you can have whoever you want."

Jen swiped a tear off her cheek and returned to playing with her napkin.

"How much time do you have before you have to give the board an answer?"

Jen sighed. "They gave me a month to think it over, but they would like an answer as soon as possible."

"Well, take your time. It's good to know you have options. I'm glad they've noticed all the hard work you've put in. You deserve this opportunity."

Jen looked up, her eyes a little brighter this time. "You know, that's one of the reasons I love you. No matter what, you're always on my side."

Kayla sat back in the booth and smiled. "What are friends for, if not to point out all the reasons why you're so wonderful?"

Jen smiled her first real smile and blushed.

. "I'm hungry," Kayla said, taking advantage of the change in Jen's mood. She grabbed the menu. "Let's eat."

She didn't want to say so, but she was worried about Jen. She couldn't imagine what it would be like if Jen moved away. Jen was her only real friend, and she would miss her. The thought made her feel selfish. Jen was important to her, and more than anything she wanted her to be happy.

Still smiling, Jen glanced up from her menu. "Enough about me, what's been going on with you?"

Kayla was taken off guard by the question and immediately thought of Jackie. She felt a little uncomfortable telling Jen about her dinner with Jackie, but she wasn't sure why. She shrugged and pretended to study the menu. "Nothing really, same old stuff, I guess."

It was Jen's turn to play the supportive friend. "You know, K, you really should get out more."

Kayla avoided making eye contact with Jen. She knew she should tell her about going out with Jackie, but she just wasn't ready for all the questions. She wasn't even sure how she felt about Jackie and she didn't want any pressure to explain. She rarely talked to Jen about the women she went out with, not that there was much to talk about. She had dated a couple of women since meeting Jen, but it hadn't gotten serious and it was embarrassing to explain all the reasons women gave her as to why they didn't want to see her anymore. Just to be safe, she would keep things to herself. But inside she was dying to talk to someone about it. If she could talk it out, it would make more sense than it did bouncing around inside her head.

"I know. I guess we both have some changes to consider," Kayla answered.

Jen grumbled. "Yeah. You know, sometimes being a grown-up really sucks."

Kayla laughed. "I know, but it sure beats having other people telling us what to do all the time. Would you really go back to being a kid if you had a choice?"

Jen pretended to contemplate the question. "Well, let's see…no bills, someone to cook for me every day, dance recitals, and playing dress up. In a heartbeat, I would."

Kayla laughed again. That was one of the things she loved about Jen. She could always find the simple innocence in everything.

Kayla fumbled with her phone, trying to answer the call and drive. "Hello, Kayla McCormick speaking."

"Hmm, I like the professional voice, very sexy."

Kayla smiled, recognizing Jackie's voice. Jackie had told her she would call, but Kayla was still surprised. She just couldn't accept that Jackie really wanted to see her. To be honest she had been praying Jackie would call, if only to have a chance at a repeat of that bone-melting kiss. Jackie made her feel things that made her lose her reasoning ability, made her want to throw caution to the wind, and scared her to death. But it was the exciting, edge of your seat, can't wait to see what happens next kind of scared.

"Hi. Sorry about that, I didn't recognize your number," Kayla answered trying to sound casual.

"That works for me. I liked it."

Kayla was glad she was alone in the car so no one could see the eager smile on her face. "What are you up to?"

"Oh, nothing, I just had a few minutes and wanted to call. I was hoping you took lunch at the same time as most offices do. Do you have a minute?"

"Sure. I'm just on my way back to the office now."

"Great, about tomorrow…"

Kayla held her breath. *Here we go, she's canceling.*

"What would be a good time for you? I was thinking sometime around six. Does that work?"

Kayla was shocked. She'd been certain Jackie was going to give her some excuse why she had to back out. Kayla thought about her schedule. "That sounds good. Would you like me to pick you up at your apartment or meet you somewhere?"

"Actually, I thought I would pick you up."

Kayla hesitated. She didn't like to bring people to her house until there was a more substantial relationship involved. She didn't want bad memories following her around her house if things didn't work out. "Umm…I'd rather pick you up."

"What's the matter, don't trust me?" Jackie teased.

"No, I would just feel better if I came there."

"Okay, we'll do it your way for now. You'll want to wear shorts and a light shirt. Maybe bring a light jacket just in case there's an unexpected chill. We'll be outside and it's supposed to be a warm night."

Kayla's curiosity was piqued. "Where are we going?"

"You'll see."

"Come on, Jackie. Where are we going?"

"Nope, you'll just have to trust me."

Kayla bit her lip to hold back her laugh. "Well, I guess I'll compromise this once."

"Good. Hey, I have to run. I'll see you tomorrow at six."

"Okay. See you tomorrow."

Kayla felt the sudden distance as the call disconnected. It was kind of disorienting, as if the sun had been eclipsed by clouds. She shook her head in stunned amazement that Jackie could so easily get to her. Just hearing Jackie's voice had been enough to start her heart racing. The absence of that simple connection was like being thrown off a merry-go-round and her head was still spinning. If she was this mixed-up now, what kind of trouble would she be in if she let things continue? She shook her head, trying to shake off the warning.

She sat in the parking lot outside her office lost in thought, memories of Jackie's warm arms around her making her smile. She had replayed the heated kiss over in her mind so many times she could almost taste Jackie on her lips. She shivered. God, what was it about this woman that had her daydreaming like a lovesick little girl? She couldn't remember anyone ever getting to her this way. She smiled. Whatever it was felt really, really good. She could hear her grandmother's voice in her head warning her away. *You better watch yourself. You get mixed up in a woman like that and you'll end up just like your parents.*

Kayla was startled when her phone rang again, jolting her out of her daydream. She was embarrassed to see it was the office calling.

"This is Kayla."

"I'm sorry to bother you, Kayla, but your next appointment is here. He's a little early. Do you want me to tell him you'll be running late?"

Kayla checked the time. "No, Martha. I'm just outside. I'll be right in, thanks." Kayla ended the call quickly and gathered her things. She couldn't believe she had been so distracted that she'd forgotten to get out of the car. Maybe her grandmother was right. Maybe she was asking for trouble. But for the first time in forever she had plans on a Friday night. A thrill ran through her making her shiver. Friday night couldn't come fast enough.

❖

Jackie leaned casually against her apartment building as Kayla drove up. Every cell in Kayla's body was on high alert when she took in Jackie's lean athletic legs, bare arms, and slim hips. She wore a pair of tan shorts and a dark blue tank top that hugged her body and showed off the broad muscled curves of her shoulders and arms. She wore a sporty pair of black sunglasses pushed up on her head that pulled her collar-length hair back from her face, revealing her strong jawline, and the perfect symmetry of her cheekbones.

Kayla was breathless. She reached over and pushed the door open as Jackie approached the car. Jackie poked her head inside, her arm draped casually against the roof of the car.

"Hello, beautiful," Jackie said cheerfully as she leaned into the car.

"Hi."

"I think you should let me drive since I'm the only one who knows where we're going."

Kayla considered for a moment as she gripped the steering wheel of her silver Nissan 370Z. It was her one indulgence. It was her way of spoiling herself on her meager salary. She felt slightly uneasy at the thought of turning it over to someone she hardly knew, and there was no way she would be without her car just in case she needed to leave on her own. She wouldn't be left stranded somewhere. She decided to trust Jackie with the car rather than ride with Jackie in hers.

"Okay, but we have to take my car."

Jackie smiled and ran around the car to open Kayla's door. "See now, that wasn't so hard, was it?" She teased. "I promise to take good care of you and your shiny little sports car."

Kayla's cheeks burned from the heat of her embarrassment at having her insecurity called out. But Jackie made her want to push the boundaries of her comfort zones. Jackie's playful, adventurous nature was contagious, and Kayla had an uncharacteristic desire to throw caution to the wind and see where Jackie might lead her.

She handed Jackie the keys and took advantage of her role as passenger to observe Jackie, and to take in their surroundings during the thirty-minute drive into the mountains. Kayla was vaguely familiar with the area but was surprised when they pulled up outside a marina. Music spilled out over the water and more cars streamed in behind them.

"Do you have a boat?" Kayla asked, still trying to figure out what they were doing.

"No, but we won't need one."

Kayla studied Jackie curiously. She could see that Jackie wasn't going to give her any more information, so she followed.

They walked the long pier to a two-story building where a steady stream of boats pulled up to the dock. A band was set up at one end of a long floating deck, playing Jimmy Buffett tunes that echoed off the surrounding mountains.

Jackie chose a table away from the band, making it easier to enjoy the music, but still hear each other talk. Kayla looked around, taking in the breathtaking view. Norris Lake stretched out in front of them surrounded by rolling mountains, lush green forests, and brilliant blue skies.

"This is beautiful." Kayla beamed.

"I thought you might like it. They just have bar food, but the beer is cold. Wait till you see the sunset—it's the best ever."

The crowd steadily grew as boaters came in from a day on the water. Kayla was impressed by the variety of individuals streaming in. There were young, old, male, female, singles, couples, children, and even a few other gay couples all enjoying each other. Kayla was impressed with the interactions and wondered why people couldn't be more tolerant in other areas of their lives.

Jackie casually laid her arm on the back of Kayla's chair as the sun spilled vibrant colors of red, orange, yellow, and pink across the sky, mirrored by the still water. Kayla sank into the feel of Jackie's arm as she absorbed the view. She was speechless. She had never seen anything so beautiful.

Kayla turned her attention to Jackie to make a comment on the view and met Jackie's piercing gaze. Her breath caught as she watched the lights of the fading sun dance like liquid heat in Jackie's eyes. She thrilled at the pleasure and peacefulness she saw as Jackie's expression softened.

"What are you thinking?" Kayla asked, breaking the spell. When Jackie spoke Kayla noticed they had drifted closer together.

Jackie smiled and her gaze shifted to Kayla's lips. "I was thinking how sad it is that you carry so much worry and tension in your eyes all the time. It makes me happy to do something to give you a temporary refuge from the stress of your life."

That wasn't what Kayla was expecting to hear. "Am I that transparent?"

Jackie shrugged. "I wouldn't say transparent. You're too guarded for that, but it's easy to recognize, if you take the time to look." Jackie drew another Corona from the bucket of ice and set it in front of Kayla. "Have another?"

"Thank you." Kayla was vaguely aware of the people around her now. The beauty of the sunset and the lure of the water only intensified her feeling of connection with Jackie. She was intrigued by Jackie's assessment and more than flattered by her attention. Normally she would withdraw from such attention, but instead she felt drawn to Jackie in a way that pushed everything around her into the background. At that moment they could have been the only people left in the world.

The drive home was a blur. Kayla watched Jackie drive and listened as she talked about her life. She learned that Jackie was from Florida and that she was an only child. Her passion for sports was the inspiration for her career choice after a shoulder injury forced her to give up her dream of making the Olympic swim team.

"What drew you to Tennessee?" Kayla asked to keep Jackie talking. She enjoyed the sound of Jackie's voice and it was second nature for her to listen. She wanted to know more about Jackie—she wanted to explore and uncover the complex layers that made up such an intriguing woman.

"I lived near here when I was much younger and I think it got into my blood. So I couldn't pass it up when I got an opportunity to work with the university athletics department while I worked on my doctorate. I was thrilled to be involved in the action again. After that, I managed to start a local practice that helps me pay the bills and I get to do what I love most."

Kayla cocked her head to the side and studied Jackie, trying to reconcile the differences between the woman she was with and the woman she first met.

Jackie glanced over at Kayla. "What?"

"You're a very fascinating woman."

Jackie looked doubtful. Kayla could see she had made her feel self-conscious.

Jackie cleared her throat. "I can't believe I've been talking so much about myself. I'm sorry, I've been rambling. I don't usually talk this much."

"It's okay. I like learning about you."

"I guess you get that a lot, people telling you everything."

"Sometimes," Kayla admitted. "But not like this. I've really enjoyed listening. It's nice to hear good things for a change."

They pulled into the apartment complex and Jackie sighed. She cut the engine and handed Kayla the keys. "Here you go, safe and sound as promised."

Kayla took the keys as Jackie leaned in for a kiss. She brushed her fingers through Kayla's hair and pulled her face toward her. Their lips brushed lightly at first, and then Jackie deepened the kiss. Kayla was falling and all she could do was hold on to Jackie. She pulled away gasping.

"Jackie...wait."

Jackie froze, her hands now motionless against Kayla's waist, her forehead pressed against Kayla's.

"We need to stop. I'm not having sex with you in my car like a couple of out of control teenagers."

It was Jackie's turn to laugh. "Yeah, I guess you're right, but it would be fun." Jackie pulled away and settled back into her seat. "I guess I got a little carried away."

"We both did. I seem to forget myself when I'm with you."

Jackie smiled. "I'm glad you do." She slipped her hand into Kayla's. "Will you come inside?"

Kayla struggled with her answer. Her body screamed yes, but her head warned no. "I better not. I can't trust myself right now."

Jackie's eyes closed for a moment and she drew in a deep breath. "Maybe this is one of those times when you should turn off that head of yours and just go with what you feel. Have a good time."

Warning bells clamored in Kayla's mind. "I'm afraid I'm not wired that way."

"Hmm, pity. I was looking forward to it, myself."

Kayla smiled. "Persistent as usual, I see."

"Like I said before, I'm not afraid to go after what I want."

Kayla was very still. She wasn't ready. As much as she wanted Jackie, she couldn't sleep with her. They wanted different things and she was kidding herself if she thought for a second she could have a sexual relationship with Jackie without getting emotionally involved.

"Jackie…"

"Hey, I get it. You're immune to my charms. I respect that. But you can't fault me for trying."

Kayla smiled.

Jackie sat back against her seat. She smiled faintly and rubbed her fingers over her lips as if she could still feel Kayla's touch there. "What are you doing tomorrow?"

Kayla shook her head. "Nothing much. Why?"

"I'm rowing in a local regatta tomorrow at Melton Lake. You should come. We could hang out and watch some of the races together. It's supposed to be a beautiful day and I can promise, you won't be bored. Besides, it'll give me another chance to convince you to take a walk on the wild side for a change."

Kayla was pleased and a bit surprised that Jackie wanted to see her again. She loved the regattas and she would love to see Jackie's muscular body flexing and straining in fluid motion with the water. Her mind was made up. "I'd love to go. But that doesn't mean I'm going to sleep with you."

Jackie smiled. "We'll see what tomorrow brings." Jackie stole another quick kiss before getting out of the car. "Besides, you can't say no forever." Jackie shut the door.

Chapter Seven

A sea of people crowded the shore along the river while teams of rowers glided across the water in needle-thin boats. The sun was bright and warm against Kayla's skin as she watched a team of eight heft their scull up over their heads and carry it from their trailer to the shore. The scull was bright yellow and blue, and Kayla liked the way the colors stood out in contrast to the blue-green water. She heard someone call her name and looked around just in time to see Jackie jogging toward her.

"Hey. There you are," Jackie said. "I'm glad you're here. Come on, I'll show you where my crew is and you can hang out with us. I only have one race left and I can watch the others with you."

Jackie confidently took her hand, lacing their fingers together as if it was natural for them to connect in this way.

"What have I missed?" Kayla asked.

"Nothing much. I sat in on a doubles race. One of the guys couldn't make it at the last minute."

"How did you do?" Kayla asked as Jackie pulled her through the crowd.

"Not too bad. We placed third."

"Oh. Well, that's good, right?"

Jackie smiled. "Better than expected since it was a coed race and our teammate that's out was a guy. We were lucky they let me stand in, even luckier to place."

"You must be really good."

Jackie laughed. "We're okay for a recreational team. We all do it for fun and no one has time to be really serious."

"How long have you been rowing?"

Jackie glowed with excitement as she explained everything.

"Oh, I just got into it a couple of years ago, but nothing team oriented until I joined the community rowing club. The water here at Melton is the best ever."

Jackie explained how the water level was controlled by the TVA through a dam system upstream, resulting in some of the smoothest water in the region. Today there was no wind and the water looked like glass as the sun sparkled across the smooth surface. These conditions made the area perfect for rowing, and Oak Ridge hosted regattas for teams from all over the world.

Kayla watched Jackie's expressions, registering the excitement in her voice as she talked about the sport. She also enjoyed watching Jackie's body. The tight spandex shorts and sleeveless tank hugged the contours of her body leaving little to the imagination. And Kayla's imagination was on overdrive.

Jackie led Kayla over to a line of boats on the grass and began to explain the different elements of the scull, and demonstrated how the boat worked.

Kayla laughed when Jackie playfully tried to get her to sit in a display model that some corporate sponsors were trying to promote. They joked and laughed together until a small woman came running up to them eager for Jackie's attention. She was so excited she almost vibrated.

"Hey, Jack. We really need you to come down to the lanes. We're getting ready to line up for the start and we need you. Come on!" The girl stood in front of them panting, her bright green eyes beaming with excitement. Her pixie haircut clung to the side of her face where sweat trickled down her jaw. She gestured wildly with her hands as if she could pull Jackie along with the energy she produced.

Jackie laughed. "Okay, okay, I'm coming."

The girl took off like a bolt of lightning, weaving her slight bird-like frame effortlessly through the crowd.

"That was Peanut. Her real name is Jane, but we all just call her Peanut."

"I bet I can guess why," Kayla said with a grin.

Jackie smiled back. She took Kayla's hand again. "Come on."

Kayla enjoyed Jackie's playful energy. Jackie's hand was warm and gentle and the pressure made Kayla feel welcome and wanted. It had been a long time since she had spent any significant amount of time with a woman she was interested in. The change was refreshing. Jackie shook everything up. Maybe she needed to lighten up more in her life. Maybe she didn't have to control everything all the time. But how long would it be before Jackie got bored with her homebody ways?

Kayla almost smacked into Jackie as they came to an abrupt halt. Jackie looked around for a moment before leading Kayla to a vacant spot on a small hill overlooking the dock.

"You should have a good view of the start from here." Jackie squeezed Kayla's hand slightly before letting go and sprinting off to the starting lanes. "I'll be back," Jackie called as she jogged away.

Kayla watched, mesmerized as the teams positioned their boats in the lanes. She was amazed how they kept the long thin boats from turning over. The teams deftly maneuvered the long oars through the water, lining the boats up in their designated lanes. Kayla spotted Jackie in lane four, standing on the small platform as she waited to help her team line up. Jackie was playful with the other women on the dock, and she received more than one look of interest. Kayla shifted and looked away, uncomfortable with seeing how other women reacted to Jackie.

Kayla grew very still when Jackie lay down on her stomach and leaned out over the water to steady the boat. She knew the race was about to start and her blood hummed with anticipation. She could hear someone speaking through a megaphone from a small tower but couldn't quite understand the commands. Suddenly she heard the shot that signaled the start, and the teams began the long arduous fight to the finish.

For the first few hundred yards, Kayla could see the synchronized movements of the crew rocking back and forth, the oars entering and leaving the water in perfect time with each other. With each stroke, the boats appeared to shoot forward in the water only to rock back a pace before starting the whole movement again. Kayla was mesmerized by the motion. It was like a dance where the partners moved in patterned rhythm together, flowing with the controlled beat of the music produced by the commands of the coxswain and the lapping of the oars through the water.

The boats passed from view and all she could make out was the flicker of the sun hitting the spoons of the oars. She waited with bated breath for the announcement of the winner. She trained her gaze back on Jackie, watching her anxious movements as she stood with a hand on one hip, the other cast over her eyes peering through the dazzling sun.

Announcements were made and Kayla saw the disappointment in Jackie's posture as she registered the loss. Her head dropped for a moment as she stared at the ground. She lifted her head toward Kayla and shrugged as if to say, *You can't win them all.*

Kayla smiled vaguely in answer.

"What happened?" Kayla asked as Jackie approached.

Jackie plopped down on the grass beside her and leisurely lay back on her elbows. "I'm not sure yet. It sounds like they lost momentum in the last fifty meters and couldn't keep up. I'm not sure why. We'll know more when Peanut gets back."

"When do you go out again?"

"I'll have to get to the boat soon. We'll go out for a bit before the race to loosen up, get into form, and swing around for our starting position. I'll leave you here so you can watch the start if that's okay. It'll be difficult for you to know who's who at the finish."

Kayla frowned. "Maybe you could explain what I should look for. Watching the start was fun, but it was hard not knowing what was happening at the end. I think I'd like to see you finish."

Jackie smiled up at Kayla. "Okay. Let's go then."

They made their way down the long path that ran along the river. Jackie showed Kayla the boats they were using and where she would need to be positioned for the finish.

Kayla watched Jackie and the rest of the crew settle into the shell and maneuver the boat into the water.

Kayla opened the small backpack she had brought with her and drew out her camera. The view was breathtaking and the rowing lanes and boats only added to the beauty. Kayla took several shots of Jackie in the boat before moving to her position in the crowd.

She enjoyed several other races before it was time for Jackie to race. She listened in on the conversations of the people around her and picked up on some of the terminology. Slowly she began to understand the announcements being broadcast from the giant tower.

She listened intently to the progress of Jackie's team when the race started. She shielded her eyes with her hand and peered into the distance, trying to make out the boats that at first only appeared like moving dots. The closer they came the more her excitement grew.

Kayla trained her camera on the finish trying to capture the teams as they crossed the line. The crowd grew more enthusiastic as the boats drew closer and closer. She had a surge of excitement when she finally recognized Jackie's team, causing her pulse to race as adrenaline flooded her system. They were neck and neck with the blue and yellow boat she had admired on her way in. She could see the broad shoulders of the rowers straining with effort as the teams tried to propel their fragile crafts across the still water. Kayla drew her camera and began snapping frame after frame, cataloging the battle. She zoomed in for the final frames hoping to catch the precise moment when the craft would cross the finish.

She could hardly process the flow of information with the thrill surging through her body. In the last second Jackie's team gave a final burst of effort, just managing to shoot the tip of the boat over the finish a fraction of a second ahead of the other team, winning the race by a nose.

Cheers erupted all around Kayla as the crowd celebrated the win. Kayla watched the faces around her sharing their happiness. She was proud of Jackie and her team.

When Jackie returned after storing the scull, she was all smiles as she walked proudly across the grass to where Kayla waited.

"That was beautiful," Kayla said when Jackie was only a few paces away. "Congratulations on your win."

Jackie surprised Kayla by wrapping her arms around her, picking her up, and swinging her around in circles. They were both laughing when Jackie finally released her.

"That was such a rush. It was totally unexpected and we weren't favored to win."

Jackie's eyes glowed with excitement and Kayla could feel the energy pouring off her. She had to be pumping out enough pheromones to attract every woman in the park. There was something disarming about seeing Jackie so playful and open.

The rest of the day went by quickly as they watched the races and talked. Kayla was disappointed when they had to leave so Jackie could help the rest of the team store and transport the gear back to the clubhouse.

"Thanks for being here today."

Kayla smiled. "It was fun. I had a great time."

Jackie's smile could have melted snow with its warmth. "Sorry I can't do dinner."

"That's okay. Duty calls." Kayla smiled up at Jackie through the car window wishing the day didn't have to end.

Someone called Jackie's name. Jackie waved. "I'll be right there."

Kayla saw a tall brunette waiting by a row of boats. She was one of the women from the start lanes she had seen Jackie with earlier. Was that someone Jackie was seeing?

"I better let you go. Your friends are waiting."

Jackie smiled. "Yeah, I better run. I'll call you." She kissed Kayla on the cheek. "Good night."

"Good night."

Kayla was disappointed. She didn't know what she had expected or hoped would happen, but this wasn't it. The day had been magical and she'd been swept up in Jackie's enthusiasm and playfulness. Jackie had a way of making her feel like the only woman in the world, and she'd hoped they'd have more time alone to talk and explore their connection. Kayla glared at the woman obviously waiting for Jackie, as if she had some claim on her. Kayla's face burned with the sudden heat of jealousy. *What are you doing, Kayla?* She knew she didn't have a claim on Jackie either, but no matter how much she might try to deny it, she wanted Jackie's attention to be hers.

❖

The familiar car parked outside Kayla's house was the first warning that something was wrong. Kayla pulled her car into the garage as a million scenarios flooded her mind. It wasn't unusual for her to come home to find Jen seeking refuge at her house, but it always meant that Jen was hurting and that was almost unbearable. It tied Kayla's stomach in knots.

Kayla grabbed her bag and hurriedly made her way into the house. "I'm home."

"Hey. Where've you been?" Jen asked from the living room. "I thought about sending out search and rescue."

Kayla let her bag drop onto the table by the door and leaned over the sofa to kiss Jen on the cheek. "Well, had I known I'd have company, I would have been sure to be here, but as I didn't, I kind of had a date."

Kayla looked around the room, taking in the subtle cues of Jen's mood. There was a half-empty bottle of wine on the table, Jen's eyes were red rimmed from crying, and dark circles hung like storm clouds beneath her swollen lids. Jen's eyes lit up with curiosity at the news that Kayla had been on a date.

"No way!" Jen sat up suddenly and peered at her.

"Yep. Second one this weekend." Kayla waggled her eyebrows up and down playfully for effect.

"You're kidding. You never go out. Who is she?"

Kayla could see the wheels turning as Jen seemed to think over the information she knew about Kayla before venturing a guess.

Jen drew in a sharp breath. "It's Jackie," Jen exclaimed excitedly. "Am I right?"

Kayla smiled and sat down on the sofa next to Jen. She took the glass of wine from Jen's hand and took a sip as she casually draped her arm around Jen's shoulders.

Jen eyed her expectantly, the surprise still registering on her face. "Come on, Kayla, spill it."

Kayla smirked. "There's nothing to tell really. We hung out last night at a marina on Norris Lake and then I went to see her today at a rowing competition. That's it."

"What about the good stuff? Did you stay over last night?"

"No, I did not stay over. Come on, Jen, you know me better than that."

"So you haven't…you know."

"No. We haven't." Kayla hesitated a second before adding in a husky tone. "But, oh God, I wanted to."

A smile burst across Jen's face and she turned and pulled her legs up onto the sofa to face Kayla. "You mean you guys made out?"

"I guess you could say that. We kissed…a lot. And wow."

Jen hit Kayla with one of the bolsters. "I can't believe you didn't tell me you were going to go out with her. How did this happen?"

Kayla's cheeks warmed. "Well, actually, I called her last week and we had dinner Wednesday night."

Jen's brow furrowed. "Hold it. Wednesday? So you mean this was your third date in a week? We had lunch Thursday and you didn't say a word to me about this."

"I'm sorry," Kayla said guiltily. "You just had so much going on and I wanted to talk about you. I didn't want to make it about me. And to be honest, I wasn't ready to talk about it. I wasn't even sure I was going to see her again."

Jen was thoughtful for a moment and Kayla watched the brightness in her eyes dim, the temporary distraction quickly shadowed by the reality of Jen's life.

Kayla put her hand on Jen's knee. "Want to tell me what happened?"

"It doesn't really matter. You've heard it all a thousand times already."

Kayla wrapped her arms around Jen and squeezed. She didn't need to hear the details to know how much Mike had hurt Jen, but Jen still needed to tell her.

"Tell me anyway."

Jen snuggled close to Kayla. Kayla could feel the tremors in Jen's body as she fought the emotions threatening to spill over. Kayla was angry. How could Mike claim to love Jen when he couldn't see her over his love for his drugs? In his world it didn't matter how much Jen was hurting as long as he got what he wanted.

"I don't know how our relationship got so off track. I don't recognize him anymore." Jen wiped at the tears that leaked from her eyes onto Kayla's shirt. "Why do I keep holding on?"

Kayla kissed Jen's hair. "I think you hold on to the dream of who you wanted him to be. It's hard to accept that this is real. You keep hoping he'll change and be the man you thought you married. You love him."

Jen sniffed. "What do I do now, K?"

Kayla sighed, wishing she could conjure the perfect answer to make it all better. "Maybe it's time to start taking care of you. If he won't make a change, maybe you should. You've seen him through his using, and even through more than one treatment program. You've tried everything his way for years and it isn't working."

Kayla held Jen as her body surrendered to the fatigue and grief she had been fighting and she laid her head against Kayla's shoulder.

"He packed a bag this morning. He said he was going to find someone who knew how to have a little fun." Jen sobbed.

Kayla tightened her grip around Jen's shoulders and stroked her hair.

"Can I still stay here with you, K?"

Kayla brushed her fingers through the long strands of Jen's hair that draped across her shoulders. "Of course you can stay. Do you want to talk about it?"

"No. Right now I don't want to have to think about anything."

Kayla's chest tightened. She wanted so much to take the pain away for Jen, but she could only offer support until Jen decided to do something different for herself.

"Have you had dinner?" Kayla asked gently.

"Not really," Jen sniffed. "I couldn't even think about food today."

"Well, I can make us something or we can go out, but you need to eat something."

Jen wrinkled her nose.

Kayla cocked her head and raised her eyebrows. "We could go for Mexican food."

Jen smiled. "You always know how to get to me."

Kayla shrugged. "I pay attention." She grinned. "Come on, it'll be my treat."

❖

Kayla sat on her back deck contemplating the changes occurring in her life as the first light of morning peeked over the ridgeline of the mountains. The past week had been a welcome breath of fresh air to her normally sedate and often lonely life. Work had always been enough to sustain her as she focused on her career and professional growth. Since her grandmother's death, Kayla had withdrawn even further into the safety of her structured routines. She felt lost and alone.

Then she met Jackie and Jackie had stirred something within her, something she hadn't known she needed. A warm smile began to blossom across her face as she thought of Jackie. She was undeniably attracted to Jackie, but she wanted *more*. Was more an option? Was she setting herself up to be hurt again? Jackie had been clear that she wasn't looking for a relationship, but the more time they spent together, Kayla was having trouble keeping her head and her heart on the same track.

She thought back to their conversation that first night in Jackie's apartment when she had been so disarmed by Jackie's kisses that she was ready to go to bed with her, but Jackie had refrained.

You had me just now. I would have gone to bed with you.

I know.

Why did you stop?

You said you didn't want tonight to be about sex. I have to respect that.

Sex would have been easy then. The way Jackie had come on to her that first night at the bar still lingered in her mind. Could this all just be a game Jackie was playing? The thought made Kayla's stomach ache. She didn't want to play games.

The door opened slowly and Jen stuck her head outside. "Hey, there you are. Mind if I join you?"

Kayla smiled at her friend. "Sure, come on out." The sun was up now and it was beginning to get a little warm. Kayla enjoyed the heat that seeped into her body, warming her bones.

Jen leaned back into the chair next to Kayla's. "You're up early."

Kayla shrugged. "Habit, I guess. My body doesn't seem to get the concept of sleeping in on the weekends."

Jen cradled a cup of coffee in her hands. "I can't imagine what it's like being in this house all by yourself all the time. Everything is so quiet and peaceful here. How do you fill all that time? Don't you want to have someone around to talk to, share meals with, watch movies, and all that stuff?"

Kayla thought about her answer. "Of course, but after a while the quiet is comforting. I've gotten used to it. Most of the time I don't feel lonely at all, and when I do, I just call you."

Jen smiled and sipped her coffee in silence for a while, apparently thinking about the answer.

"K?"

"Hmm?" Kayla answered, vaguely aware of Jen as she continued her contemplations.

"Do you think you'll ever find someone…you know…someone you want to share your life with?"

Kayla furrowed her brow and sighed. "I don't know. Sometimes I think about it. But mostly I'm used to things the way they are. It would be nice to have someone like that in my life, but I'm not sure that's in the cards for me." Kayla looked at Jen. "Why do you ask?"

Jen took a deep breath and sighed. "I was just wondering. It just seems so quiet."

Kayla chuckled. "Believe it or not I kind of like it that way, most of the time anyway."

Jen bit her lower lip and shifted uncomfortably in her chair. "Does it bother you that I'm here?"

Kayla was surprised by the question. "Oh, Jen. You don't bother me at all. I like having you here. I might like my space, but I'm no hermit. It's nice to have company. To be honest I've been lonelier lately than I'd like to admit."

This seemed to settle Jen a bit and she relaxed back into her chair with a sigh.

"Thanks, K. And thanks for getting me out of the house last night. I really needed that."

"It was fun. Don't worry about it."

Jen cleared her throat before changing the subject. "So, when are you seeing Jackie again?"

Kayla's eyes shot to Jen at the mention of Jackie's name. "I don't know," she said a bit too forcefully.

Jen raised an eyebrow. "What's wrong? I thought you were really into her by the way you talked about her last night."

Kayla looked off into the sunlit sky and thought about the waves of emotion she had been riding. "That might be the problem."

"What's that supposed to mean?"

"It means that I don't know what she's doing or what she's looking for. I don't want to be toyed with."

Jen wrinkled her brow telegraphing her confusion. "Okay. What's happened that makes you not trust her?"

Letting out a deep sigh, Kayla tried to explain how she'd been feeling about her first impression of Jackie the night they all met, and how different Jackie had been since then.

"At first she seemed to be a real player, only out to have a good time. She didn't seem to take anything seriously. But when she was helping me with my neck, she was so caring, and when we go out, she's considerate and attentive, and she didn't disappear when I put on the brakes. I just don't want her to play with me. The way things are going, I'm afraid I'll get too invested and get hurt."

"So you don't know which is real, the playful, good-time Jackie, or the serious, caring Jackie."

"Exactly."

"Well, isn't that what dating is all about? Isn't this how you really get to know someone and find out if it's just a fling or something more serious?"

Kayla chuckled. "Yeah, but she's made it pretty clear she's just looking for a good time. I already look forward to the next time I see her, and I think about her all the time. I'm afraid *I'm* getting too serious."

"Why don't you ask her?"

That was a novel thought—she could just ask her. Yeah, right. How would that go? *Hey, Jackie, are you really interested in me, or are you just trying to get laid?* No. That wouldn't work at all. Besides if she started asking questions, she would have to be ready to answer them herself and she definitely wasn't ready.

"You're right. I guess I'm just out of practice. I should just slow down and see what happens."

Jen placed a cool hand on Kayla's arm. "I know it's hard, K, but she seems worth a try."

Kayla leaned her head back against her chair and closed her eyes. Did she really have a choice anymore?

CHAPTER EIGHT

Jackie blinked rapidly to clear the sting of sweat from her eyes. She held her arms extended above her chest as she strained against the weight balanced above her. Her arms trembled from fatigue but she pressed the bar upward again. After two more repetitions, she slid the bar back against the rack with a loud clank of metal on metal. She folded her arms across her breasts and focused on the rise and fall of her chest with each heavy breath.

She closed her eyes, enjoying the rush of blood flowing through her arms and hands. As soon as her eyes closed, visions of Kayla flooded her thoughts. She sat up suddenly and quickly moved to the next station to work her shoulders. She pushed her body, using the physical exertion to quell the growing tension distracting her. She couldn't explain the undeniable pull she had felt with Kayla since the first time she had looked into her eyes that first night in the bar, but she wasn't sure what to do with these new feelings.

Her relationships had always been about physical attraction, brief couplings that satisfied her physically with no demands on her emotionally. Her relationship with Cindy had been that way. They had been pretty hot for about a year, but they didn't share anything but sex. It had been months now since they had even spoken, and Jackie rarely thought of her. She liked Cindy. Their physical connection had been intense, but they had rarely spent time together outside the bedroom. Jackie had never felt the need to share her personal thoughts or dreams, and Cindy had preferred it that way too.

She thought of the night she had spent with Heather, the last woman she had bedded. She shivered, remembering the ache she had felt that sent her out looking for company, and then the emptiness she felt after being with Heather. The sex should have left her without a want or a care in the world, but she had felt even more restless afterward. What had changed? And what was it about Kayla that settled that inner storm? When she was with Kayla, all the restlessness faded and they hadn't even slept together. What did that mean?

She shook her head and grasped the metal bar tightly with both hands. She pulled and brought the bar down to her chest, just above her breasts. Her breath puffed out with each pull and she grimaced with the exertion, but no matter how hard she worked she couldn't shake Kayla from her thoughts.

She had wanted Kayla but had said no to sex. That was a first. Then she had Kayla come to the regatta. Since when did she share her life like that? Why did she want Kayla to be a part of the things that made her happy? If they did sleep together, would her feelings change? Would her infatuation with Kayla melt away like fog against the heat of a rising sun? Would Kayla become just another woman in her bed?

Near muscle failure, Jackie leaned forward, resting her elbows on her knees to give her quivering muscles a rest before hitting the shower. She ran a shaky hand through her sweat-drenched hair and pulled the neck of her shirt up to wipe the sweat from her face. Her mind was still a mess, but some of the physical tension that had been thundering through her body had quieted.

She showered and dressed quickly, going through the motions in a daze. On her way out of the gym she pulled her phone from her bag and saw she had a message from Kayla. Calm skimmed through her body like a caress at the sound of Kayla's smooth, rich voice.

Whatever was happening between her and Kayla, it looked like she had another chance to figure it out.

Hurriedly, she tossed her things into her truck and settled in the seat. She took a deep breath and dialed Kayla's number. Her heart beat so hard she could feel the vibration in her throat. She held her breath and her mouth went dry at the anticipation of talking to Kayla. After the third ring Kayla's rich voice filtered through the line.

"Hello, this is Kayla."

Jackie paused. She couldn't seem to get her words in order. She wanted to tell Kayla she had been thinking about her all morning but suddenly felt vulnerable and exposed. This was all new to her and her confidence evaporated.

"Hello, gorgeous. I was just thinking about you." Jackie rolled her eyes at the sound of her own voice. She couldn't think of what to say next.

Luckily Kayla rescued her. "Hey. It's beautiful outside and I'm planning a day in the mountains. Would you like to come with me?"

Jackie forced calm into her voice. "Hmm, a chance to spend the day with a beautiful woman, how could I say no?"

"Always the smooth talker. Is it okay if I pick you up in an hour?"

"I'll be ready."

Jackie ran her hand across her face. She had one hour. She smiled as she looked at the clock. Just knowing she was going to see Kayla had her all keyed up again. Maybe Kayla was just what she needed.

Kayla rang the bell to Jackie's apartment exactly one hour later.

"Hey, right on time, as usual." Jackie pulled Kayla inside.

Jackie's brilliant smile and warm welcome melted Kayla's apprehension. The warmth from Jackie's hand was comforting. How was it that a simple touch could undo her so completely?

Jackie kissed Kayla's cheek. "You look beautiful. It's good to see you." She stepped back and looked at Kayla, her smile deepening the dimple in her left cheek. "So, what's the plan for the day?"

Kayla stared at Jackie as if she had fallen into a deep trance. She studied Jackie's face, looked beyond the glinting surface of her eyes, and tried to peer into her soul, searching for the substance of Jackie's heart.

Jackie shuddered under the scrutiny.

Kayla read her vulnerability and stepped closer.

"Kayla?" Jackie whispered. Her voice strained.

Hesitantly Kayla raised her fingers to Jackie's mouth and pressed two fingers lightly to her lips. She brushed a delicate kiss against

Jackie's mouth, following the path her fingers had traced. The touch of Jackie's lips was like the faint brush of butterfly wings against a flower petal. The physical connection, although brief, lulled Kayla deeper into her trance until her desire sparked.

Their lips met tenderly, moving slowly, stoking the flow of excitement, intrigue, and pure pleasure.

Kayla pulled away, biting her lower lip as she swayed on her feet, her fingers still resting against Jackie's cheek.

"That was nice." Kayla gave a slight shake of her head and closed her eyes. "I don't know what came over me."

Jackie trembled, shifting her eyes from Kayla's lips to peer into her eyes. "That's okay. I really didn't mind." She creased her brow in a curious frown. "You know, you have very unusual eyes."

Kayla smiled, taking a step away, her fingers slipping from Jackie's face. She dropped her gaze, embarrassed by her boldness. "Thank you…I think."

Jackie chuckled. "Trust me, it's a compliment." She wrapped her fingers lightly around Kayla's waist and drew her close. "Would you like to tell me what just happened here?"

Kayla was silent a moment as if considering her answer. "I was looking for something and then I guess I just went with my feelings."

"Hmm, I like the sound of that. What were you feeling?" Jackie asked with her usual flirtatious tone.

Kayla smiled. "I don't think I want to tell you, at least not yet. We should get going."

"So that's how it's going to be." Jackie chuckled and followed Kayla back to the door.

Kayla kept walking, allowing the few steps between them to clear her head of the intoxicating kiss. She wasn't sure what she had hoped to see in Jackie's eyes, but what she found left her needing and wanting. She had been pulled into Jackie as if she was her only source of water in the scouring heat of the desert. For those brief moments, she had forgotten everything. She had seen Jackie's vulnerability, her desire, her uncertainty, and her daring. But she could not read her heart.

"I thought we'd ride through the mountains and have lunch in the park. Does that sound okay with you?"

Jackie grabbed her keys and a light backpack. "Sounds good to me."

Kayla pulled the Z onto the highway while Jackie flipped through Kayla's playlist. She had put the top down before leaving home and the wind was a cool and refreshing contrast to the heat of the midday sun.

Jackie shuffled through song after song.

"What? You don't like my music?" Kayla asked when Jackie changed the music for the third time.

Jackie smiled. "The music is great. We have a lot of the same stuff. I just don't know what mood I'm in. What else do you have in here?"

"I pretty much stick with my playlist and audiobooks."

"Audiobooks?"

"Sure. I can't think of a better way to spend my drive time. I get lost in a story, and before I know it, the drive is over. It's a good way to clear my head of the chaos of work."

"Huh. Maybe I'll have to try it."

Jackie flipped through the list of books in Kayla's phone.

"Jesus, Kayla, there's an entire library in here."

Kayla laughed.

"Isn't that a little dangerous while driving?"

"No," Kayla smiled. "I stay pretty focused, but I do have to warn you about some of the lesbian romance novels. They can really get you going and that can be...distracting."

Jackie laughed. "Are you serious?"

Kayla cut a look at Jackie that said she was dead serious.

"Hmm. Maybe we should listen to one now," Jackie said with a mischievous grin.

Kayla smacked Jackie's thigh playfully. "Don't you dare."

Jackie looked around at the view. "I've never seen anything as beautiful as the Smoky Mountains."

Kayla sighed. "I know what you mean. I can't imagine living anywhere without mountains."

"I never thought I'd be the mountain type. I was a beach girl growing up, but there's something magical about this place."

Kayla took Jackie's hand. "I'm glad you came today."

Jackie smiled and laced her fingers through Kayla's. "So am I. A little sunshine, fresh air, and who knows what could happen."

❖

Jackie lay back on the blanket with her hands behind her head and looked up into the canopy of trees. "This is perfect."

Kayla had led them away from the main path to a small stream in the woods. They could still hear people close by but couldn't be seen for the lush summer foliage. They shared the picnic as they watched squirrels chase each other through the trees and listened to the sound of the flowing water of the creek.

"Look." Kayla leaned close to Jackie, carefully resting her arm against Jackie's back when she sat up and pointed across the water.

Jackie gasped. A black bear meandered along the edge of the stream on the opposite side of the water from where they were sitting. It didn't seem to pay them any attention as it scavenged the ground for nuts and other tasty morsels.

Jackie looked at Kayla, her eyes round with surprise and a hint of fear. "Do you think we should go?"

Kayla smiled. "No. We're fine. It doesn't seem too interested in us."

"I've never seen a real bear before, at least not outside a zoo. It's amazing."

Kayla smiled at the wonder in Jackie's voice. She didn't want to leave this spot as long as Jackie kept looking at her that way. And although she needed to keep an eye on the bear, she knew as long as they respected it and didn't get in its space it wouldn't bother them.

Jackie fell back against the blanket again once the bear had moved out of sight. They could hear excited voices as other hikers spotted the bear farther downstream.

Kayla smiled down at Jackie. She liked the almost childlike glint in Jackie's eyes and was happy to be showing her new things. Kayla ran a finger along the underside of Jackie's arm tickling her skin.

Jackie laughed and wiggled away.

"Ticklish?"

"Very."

"Hmm," Kayla said grinning. She ran her fingers along the sensitive skin again, feeling Jackie shudder beneath her touch.

Jackie laughed and pulled her arms from behind her head and wrapped them around Kayla's waist, quickly playing her fingers along Kayla's ribs.

Kayla shrieked and squirmed, trying to escape the assault of tickling. She fell into Jackie's arms laughing, her heart lighter than she could ever remember. She stared down at Jackie. Jackie's lips were so close Kayla could feel the warmth of her breath against her skin. She wanted to feel those lips against her. The sound of a branch snapping behind her drew her attention and she turned to see what had caused the noise. Less than thirty feet away the black bear was making its way toward them. It held its nose in the air sniffing as its head swayed from side to side seeking out dinner. It was following the scent of their food.

"Holy shit!" Jackie exclaimed an instant before she scrambled from the blanket, leapt to her feet, and ran. She had gone a good ten yards before realizing Kayla wasn't with her. She stopped and looked back.

Kayla patiently gathered up their things and put them back into the cooler.

"Come on, Kayla," Jackie called desperately. "That's a bear!"

Kayla laughed and casually continued to gather the detritus of their meal and stored it securely in her pack. She then gathered up the blanket, and after checking that there was no further debris, she strolled casually over to Jackie.

Jackie shifted from foot to foot, anxious to get moving. She didn't want to hang around and get to know this bear any better. This was a little too up close and personal for her taste. She was all about adventure, but she drew the line at wild animals that weighed more than she did and had very big teeth.

Kayla sauntered up beside Jackie and pointed back to the bear, which was just at that moment reaching the spot where they had been only moments before. "She's only following the scent of the food. She must have gone downstream, crossed the water, and followed the scent back to us."

The bear was very thoroughly sniffing the ground where they had just been sitting, obviously searching for the food.

"I can't believe you were so calm about all that. Weren't you afraid?"

Kayla shrugged. "No, not really, but I don't want to try our luck. Come on. Let's go see what else we can get into today."

Jackie stared at Kayla amazed, and then glanced nervously back at the bear. "Good idea, let's go." She didn't waste any time getting back to the car. Once inside the car, she was still a little shaken by the experience.

"Are you okay?" Kayla asked.

Jackie blew out her breath. "I'm fine, but I never thought I'd be so happy to see a car in my life."

Kayla laughed. "We don't really have a roof, you know."

Jackie grimaced. "Yeah, but at least there are other cars and people around."

"True," Kayla agreed. "But the animals around here don't seem to mind the people so much." Kayla pointed to a herd of deer in a field just ahead of them.

Jackie paled and then laughed at herself.

"I guess I'm really blowing the macho image right now, huh?"

Kayla chuckled. "Maybe a little, but for what it's worth, I think it's cute."

It was true. Kayla loved this side of Jackie and felt privileged to see her playfulness and vulnerability. This was the real Jackie. Kayla smiled as more of her reticence melted away.

"What's next?" Jackie asked as they pulled back onto the narrow winding road that meandered through the park.

"Let's just see where we end up."

They drove deeper into the mountains, watching the Little Pigeon River meander through the hills as the road twisted through the narrow path cut through stone and forest.

Kayla drew in a deep breath, taking in the aroma of wildflowers, water, earth, and sunshine. She relished the feel of the wind blowing through her hair and the smooth touch of Jackie's hand in hers. The faint brush of Jackie's fingers along her arm sent a thrill of pleasure across her skin. Everything was perfect and she wished this day would never end.

Kayla slowed the car, deftly maneuvering it around the tight turns of the road. She had an idea where they would go next and hoped the area wouldn't be too crowded. Her luck held. Only two other cars were parked in the area Kayla had wanted to show Jackie. She pulled off the road and found a spot in the shade. The so-called parking lot was not much more than packed earth with some well-worn gravel.

The roar of rushing water could be heard from the car and Kayla felt a surge of excitement. "You have to see this."

Kayla led Jackie along a path that edged the water until they emerged on a series of boulders. Water gushed in violent torrents over the rocks, twisting and battering its way through the immovable obstacles until finally settling into a large pool of blue.

"Isn't it amazing?" Kayla exclaimed, watching Jackie take in the view.

Jackie's gaze followed the flow of the water, settling on the large pool at the base of the cliff. She watched a young man swim to the base of the rocks.

"You swim in this?" Jackie asked sounding astonished.

"Oh yeah, just watch." She pointed to a mass of giant rocks. "See that boulder there at the head of the pool?"

Jackie nodded.

"That guy will climb back up that path there." She watched Jackie's eyes follow the path. "At the top he'll jump from that rock. People do it all the time."

Jackie's eyes widened. "Are you serious?"

Kayla smiled. "Just watch."

The young man did just as Kayla had predicted. But when he got to the top of the boulder he didn't just jump, he spread his arms out over his head and with a step and a slight push of his foot he sprang off the edge in a dive. He seemed to hang suspended in the air as if falling in slow motion, his arms outstretched in flight. An instant later the momentum and gravity took over and in a flash he pierced the water and disappeared.

Jackie gasped. She could hear the rush of her heartbeat in her ears echoing the roar of the water below. Her eyes were glued to the surface of the water, searching, waiting for the young man to resurface. She was getting a little nervous when his head broke free of the surface of the water. His arms moved in half circles, keeping him afloat, as he shook the water from his face and hair and let out a whoop of glee.

Jackie's body vibrated with excitement and she tightened her grip on Kayla's hand. "That's insane," she said. A thrill ran through her, pulling her to the danger. "I've got to do it."

Kayla's brow furrowed in concern. "Are you serious?"

Jackie smiled and began pulling her cell phone and wallet from her pockets. "That was the craziest thing I think I have ever seen anyone do," Jackie said, her eyes wide with wonder. "I have to try it."

Kayla frowned. "But he could have hit anything in that water— just look at the size of those rocks," Kayla said, gesturing to the boulders below. "You know they don't just end at the pool."

"I know, but the water is obviously very deep here, and like you said, people do it all the time."

"I don't care, it's still crazy."

"I'll be fine. Just watch."

Jackie ran up the path to the top of the cliff.

Kayla held her breath as she watched Jackie step to the edge and peer over at the water below. She turned toward Kayla and waved. She almost glowed with excitement. All Kayla felt was fear.

Jackie squared her shoulders, then took two quick steps, propelling herself over the edge.

Kayla gasped as Jackie tucked her arms and legs, rolling in midair, twisting and turning her body until finally unfolding her long elegant limbs into a perfect straight line a second before piercing the water. Kayla's heart was in her throat. She should have known better than to bring Jackie here. It was just the sort of stupid thing she would do.

Jackie broke the surface and whooped with excitement. "*Hell*, yes."

Kayla took a long deep breath of relief and watched Jackie swim back to the bank.

Jackie plopped down beside Kayla with a flourish. "That was amazing. You should try it."

"Oh no. There's no way I'm doing that. People get hurt all the time doing stupid things like this. You're out of your mind."

Jackie frowned. Kayla was upset. She hadn't considered how Kayla would feel about the jump. She stroked Kayla's forearm. "I'm sorry if I upset you. That wasn't my intention."

Kayla sighed. "I know that people cliff dive all the time, but this pool is so small. It just blows my mind. I can't help but think of all the injuries that could result from a situation like this. You could have been killed."

"I know. But people get hurt everyday falling out of the shower. How do you know you're alive if you never take any chances?"

Kayla didn't answer.

"I really am sorry. We can go if you want."

Kayla shook her head trying to get a grip on her emotions. "No. I'm okay. It was just a surprise. But could we not do anything dangerous for the rest of the day? Besides, there's no way I'm letting you in my car all wet."

Jackie pushed playfully at Kayla's arm, trying to restore the jovial mood to the day. "Come on, let's go down and test the water."

Kayla smiled and pushed back against Jackie's arm.

They watched the jumpers from one of the rock ledges for a while before wading out into one of the shallow pools.

Kayla shuddered. "Oh my God, this is the coldest water I have ever felt in my life."

Jackie couldn't help herself. She scooped a handful of water and tossed it toward Kayla, showering her with drops of cold water.

"Hey." Kayla yelped.

Jackie laughed.

"You are so going to pay for that." Kayla tried to splash Jackie back but lost her balance and toppled forward into Jackie.

Jackie laughed as she wrapped her arms around Kayla a little tighter than necessary. "Hmm, I like this game."

Kayla placed her hands on Jackie's chest and gave a little push as she stepped away. Jackie slipped on the rocks and went down. She sat up, submerged in water up to her breasts, as Kayla scrambled to stand.

After a quick assessment, Kayla laughed. "Are you okay?"

Jackie looked up indignantly, before a smile spread from the corners of her mouth. She laughed.

Kayla reached out a hand to help her up. "Truce?"

Jackie took Kayla's hand and gave a sharp tug, pulling Kayla off balance and into the water beside her. The battle was on.

Chapter Nine

Kayla stirred. The sun was warm on her skin as she lay across the blanket watching Jackie sleep. They had stretched out to dry and had been lulled into sleep by the warm rays of the sun. She studied the still sleeping woman lying next to her and imagined her hands exploring the soft contours of Jackie's body. She had to admit that she liked Jackie. They were easy and playful together, but she still didn't know where she wanted things to go. The way Jackie touched her and looked at her made her hope there was something special growing between them, but the cliff-diving stunt reminded her just how different they were. Kayla cringed at the thought of risking her heart again. She was in serious danger of falling in love with Jackie and she didn't think there was anything she could do about it.

Kayla reached out and brushed her fingers lightly down Jackie's arm, watching Jackie's fingers twitch in response. She raised her hand again and brushed featherlight touches across Jackie's cheek.

Jackie's eyes fluttered open. "Hi."

"Hi." Kayla smiled at the greeting.

"Sorry I fell asleep."

"Don't worry, I did too. I didn't want to wake you, but I couldn't resist."

Jackie took Kayla's fingers into her hand and kissed each tip, allowing the softness of her lips to linger on the smooth skin. Kayla shivered at her touch.

"So this is what it's like to wake up with you," Jackie said, taking Kayla's finger into her mouth and sucking lightly, playing her tongue sensuously across the tip of the digit.

Kayla gasped and closed her eyes against the rush of desire that pulsed between her legs as Jackie slid a hand through her hair and caressed her face. Kayla moaned again as Jackie let go of her finger and claimed her lips with her mouth. She melted into Jackie's arms, her body molding to Jackie as if she belonged to her. Kayla swooned as she took in the sweet taste of Jackie's mouth.

Oh yeah, she was in trouble. Jackie made her want to throw caution to the wind and take chances with her heart.

Jackie slid her arm around Kayla's waist, brushed her fingers just above the soft swell of Kayla's hips into the curve of her back, and played with the sensitive skin along her side, trailing tender touches around to the taut skin of her abdomen.

Kayla whimpered. The flood of desire threatened to brush all reason from her thoughts. All that mattered was the feel of Jackie's mouth and searching hands. With the slightest shift of her hips she slid her thigh between Jackie's legs and pressed into her.

Jackie squeezed her thighs together, trapping Kayla against her. She tightened her embrace and gently rocked their bodies together as she continued to explore Kayla's mouth with her tongue.

Kayla wanted Jackie to touch her. She wanted her more than she had ever wanted a woman. She was on fire with the sweet painful need of her.

It was Jackie who broke the kiss. Her breath came in ragged bursts as she tried to catch her breath. "I've wanted to do this all day."

Kayla couldn't stop the subtle thrust of her hips in response to the sultry rasp of Jackie's voice. She dug her fingers into the skin of Jackie's shoulders, bit down on her lip, and opened her eyes. Another jolt of want hit her when she saw her desire mirrored in Jackie's eyes. Beyond the hunger, beyond the physical desire, Kayla saw a flash of vulnerability.

It was more than she could resist. Kayla abandoned her resistance. "I'm so afraid of how you make me feel, but I think I'll die if you don't touch me soon."

There in the sun surrounded by trees and the sound of flowing water, Jackie pulled Kayla into her arms and explored her body with her hands as she kissed Kayla's neck.

Kayla felt Jackie's nipple harden under her touch as she brushed her fingers across the small mound of breast.

"We were supposed to be drying out, not getting all wet again," Kayla whispered playfully.

"Are you wet?" Jackie rasped.

"Oh yes. I think I'm melting."

Kayla had her fingers looped around the waistband of Jackie's shorts when the piercing sound of a car alarm startled them both. Kayla sat up looking around, frantically trying to regain her bearings.

Jackie laughed and fell back onto the blanket. "Seriously?"

Kayla frowned. "Maybe we should go see about the car. This probably isn't the most private place to—"

"Have mind-blowing sex?" Jackie broke in.

Kayla grinned. "Is that what you had in mind?"

"Oh yeah. The way you feel in my arms, I have no doubt."

Kayla's face burned as heat flooded her cheeks.

Jackie smiled and kissed the scorched flesh. "Maybe we'll have to test my theory later."

Kayla kept her voice steady but her body was screaming for more. "You're dangerous," she said, taking Jackie's hand.

She couldn't believe she'd been so close to having sex out in the open where anyone could have stumbled upon them. It wasn't like her to take such a risk. But she wasn't sure she would have stopped if they hadn't been interrupted. She had to slow things down but she wasn't sure how much longer she could say no to what she knew they both wanted.

Jackie watched the flickering sunlight dance across Kayla's face as they drove. She barely noticed that Kayla drove a little faster than necessary, hugging the tiny sports car into the curves as she raced down the mountain. Jackie's only thought was the feel of Kayla's thigh beneath her fingers as she imagined more intimate touches.

"What are you thinking?" Kayla asked.

Jackie smiled. "I was thinking about the way you feel."

A muscle at the side of Kayla's jaw twitched but she kept her focus on the road ahead.

Jackie was curious about something. "Earlier, you said you were afraid of how I make you feel. What are you afraid of?"

Kayla chewed at her lip. "The same thing everyone always fears. I don't want to get hurt."

"And?" Jackie persisted.

Kayla glanced at Jackie. "And it would be easy to get carried away. In case you hadn't noticed, I'm very attracted to you."

Jackie frowned. "I don't want to hurt you. You were right about me before. I've never had a serious relationship. I've had a series of women in my life who shared my bed, but there was never anyone who made me want more. I don't think I'm that person."

Jackie wasn't sure where she was going with this, but she was always honest about her feelings and her intentions, as much as she could be anyway. In this case she wasn't really sure what she wanted or felt.

Kayla slowed the car. "Jackie, you don't have to tell me—"

"Don't I? It's the only way you're going to trust me. I enjoy being with you. I want to get to know you, and in order to do that, I have to be honest. I want things to be clear between us. I don't want to hurt you." Jackie pulled Kayla's hand into her lap. "I don't have any promises."

Kayla forced a smile, but her insides felt like a tornado had just blown through. Jackie was very clear about where things stood between them. She wasn't interested in a relationship. "I know."

"Good." Jackie smiled. "I have an idea."

Kayla raised one eyebrow, suspicious of the sudden change of topic. "What?"

"Let's order pizza and sit on my deck and talk. I'm starving and I don't want to go out."

Kayla liked the idea. She could still feel the traces of Jackie's hands on her body and she wasn't ready to let her go. But she wasn't sure it was such a good idea to go back to Jackie's apartment in such an aroused state, especially since Jackie was clearly setting some boundaries between them.

Jackie pushed a little harder. "I promise nothing will happen that you don't want. I'll behave."

It wasn't Jackie Kayla was worried about. It was her ability to control her own desires. She didn't trust herself. But what message would she send if she said yes? She had wanted to believe more was going on between them, but Jackie had been clear about her feelings. What did she do now? Could she walk away? Could she give in to her desire and worry about picking up the pieces later?

"Okay," Kayla answered. She had to make her decision soon, for both their sakes.

As soon as they were back in the city, Jackie pulled out her phone and dialed in the number for Stefano's Pizza. "Mind if we do a pickup?"

Kayla shrugged. "Sure."

"Great. I know just the place. Anything you don't want?"

"Anchovies, and I'm not a fan of meat on my pizza. Sorry."

"Not a problem. How do you feel about broccoli and fresh sliced tomatoes?"

Kayla's stomach growled. "Fantastic."

They picked up the pizza and were at Jackie's apartment within the hour. The sky was taking on a pink hue signaling the first moments of the setting sun, and the air was beginning to chill just as Kayla parked the car outside Jackie's apartment.

Kayla's stomach rumbled with both hunger and anxiety. *How can I be so nervous? Only a couple of hours ago I was ready to rip Jackie's clothes off in broad daylight in a very public park.* She was overthinking things again and tried to calm the rush of nerves while Jackie prepared their plates.

Jackie handed Kayla the drinks. "You can go outside and get comfortable. I'll bring the food out."

"Okay."

Kayla stared out over the city, letting the setting sun and crisp air seduce her. She wasn't sure how her predictable structured life had gotten so off course, but at that moment she didn't care. She was already too far gone to turn back.

❖

Jackie was on her best behavior, as promised. She found Kayla easy to talk to and was surprised by how much she enjoyed getting to know her without the goal of sex. It was as if a light was being shined on the empty space in her soul. Kayla looked relaxed sitting in the deck chair with her drink resting on her thigh. Her hair was windblown and her skin glowed from the kiss of the sun. Jackie watched Kayla, listening to the rise and fall of her voice as she spoke. She liked the way Kayla gestured with her hands when she talked and the curve of her lips when she smiled. The best was when Kayla laughed. It was like listening to a songbird after a long cold winter.

"What were you like growing up?" Kayla asked.

Jackie frowned. She hadn't expected the change in topic. "There's not really much to tell. I was a bit of a jock and a closet bookworm."

Kayla smiled. "Hmm, not much has changed then."

Jackie wanted to change the subject. She didn't like to talk about her family or her childhood. "What about you?"

Kayla laughed. "I was a pleaser. My parents died when I was a baby. I don't remember them. But I resented their absence and didn't want to be anything like them. My grandmother was my world and I tried my best to make her happy. She died last year."

"I'm sorry to hear that," Jackie said. She heard the pain in Kayla's voice but there was reverence there too. "Your grandmother sounds very special."

Kayla smiled. "She was."

"Why didn't you want to be like your parents?"

Kayla took a sip of her beer. "They were big on adventure, always seeking the next thrill, until eventually they made a deadly mistake."

"What happened?"

Kayla peeled the label off her beer bottle as she talked. "They were hang gliding. I don't know exactly how it happened, but they crashed into the side of a mountain."

"That sucks. I'm sorry." Jackie could relate to the distance between Kayla and her parents, but she'd never had anyone step up for her the way Kayla's grandmother had. She didn't even know her grandparents.

"I think it would be worse if I could remember them. I grew up with stories about people I didn't know. My grandmother didn't approve of their lifestyle, so anytime I got out of line she would say things like, *You don't want to end up like your parents, do you?* She was everything to me and I never wanted to disappoint her. I miss her every day."

Jackie was quiet. Her thoughts turned to her mother and her own dysfunctional family.

"I'm sorry," Kayla said. "I didn't mean to ramble on about all that."

Jackie shook her head. "It's okay."

Kayla brushed her fingers along Jackie's arm. "What about you? I know you said there were problems between you and your dad, but what about your mother?"

Jackie looked out over the river. "We were close, but she disappeared when I was twelve. I have no idea where she is or what happened to her."

"Oh, Jackie, I'm so sorry."

Jackie shrugged. "Like I said, it was a long time ago."

Kayla frowned. "What do you mean she disappeared?"

"It's not a very good story. I don't like to talk about it."

"So you don't know what happened to her?" Kayla pushed.

Jackie shook her head. "Nope. My old man liked to get drunk and insinuate that he'd done something to her. I don't know if that's true or just part of his sick torture. For all I know she just got tired of the abuse and left. She'd tried it before but couldn't make it with me in tow. It's possible she had to cut us both loose to get out."

"You don't believe that, do you?"

Kayla closed her hand around Jackie's, but Jackie had grown numb and the touch seemed foreign and distant. "What kid wants to believe their mom walked out and left them in hell? But I don't want to think the other either."

Kayla rubbed her thumb across Jackie's hand. She couldn't imagine the pain Jackie had carried all these years. There had to be more to this story. Someone had to know something about what happened to her mother. People didn't just disappear without someone asking questions.

"I can't imagine. I'm sorry."

Jackie didn't answer.

"Was there no one else? No one to care for you?"

"Me," Jackie said sharply. "I take care of myself. That's how it works."

A cool breeze blew through the night air chilling Kayla's skin as the cold note in Jackie's tone signaled a shift in her mood and a growing distance between them. Jackie was shutting down.

Jackie pulled away. "It's getting late and we both have to work tomorrow."

Jackie sounded tired, but Kayla knew it was hurt, not fatigue that drained her.

"I'm sorry if I upset you with my questions. I know this was hard for you to talk about." Kayla brushed her fingers along Jackie's cheek. Jackie's jaw twitched beneath her touch. "I'd like to help."

Jackie didn't answer.

"Thank you for telling me about your mother. I can't imagine what that was like," Kayla said.

Jackie sighed. "I moved here to find her. I thought I would just run into her on the street or someone from our old town would know what happened to her. But I've found nothing. Everyone I talked to thought she just left my old man. That was the story he gave them anyway."

"What do you remember about when she disappeared?"

Jackie shook her head. "Nothing. I wasn't even there. I was away at a swim camp. When I came home, she was gone."

"What about the house? Do you remember anything missing, her clothes, anything? Anything out of place?"

Jackie's brow wrinkled as she searched her memories. She sighed. "I don't know. My dad had her things packed up in trash bags. I managed to steal a few photographs from a pile when he wasn't looking. I have no idea if it was all of her things or just what she left behind."

Kayla had an idea, but she wasn't sure Jackie would go for it. She was already pushing Jackie beyond her comfort zone, and she might not want her meddling in her past.

"Have you contacted the police?"

"Yeah. I did that as soon as I got here. There were some records of domestic issues between my mom and old man, but no missing person's report or anything to suggest she was missing. I looked for death records too. Nothing. It's like she just vanished."

"Would you mind if I have a friend of mine do some digging around? She's a detective and really good at this kind of thing. She locates missing parents for children at my center all the time when they've been removed from the custodial parent and are brought into state care."

Jackie stared at her wide-eyed. "Seriously? Why would you do that?"

Kayla frowned. "It just seems like the right thing to do. You can think about it if you want. It's up to you."

"I think I would do anything at this point. I've given up on ever finding anything about her. If you think your friend can help, I'd appreciate it."

"Good." Kayla smiled, happy she could do something to help Jackie. "I'll call her first thing tomorrow."

Chapter Ten

Kayla bit her lip. She was sure Jackie could feel the tremor in her hands. Something had shifted between them, and Kayla was struggling not to let her nerves give her away. "Could I use your restroom?"

Jackie laughed. "Of course. Come on, I'll show you where it is."

Jackie took her hand for the first time since they had come into the apartment. She led her down the hallway and flipped the light on in the bathroom.

Kayla glanced into the bedroom as they passed.

Jackie did a quick survey of the bathroom before letting Kayla enter. "Here you go. Let me know if you need anything. I'll just go change my shirt." She pointed to a blob of pizza sauce that had dribbled down her shirt over her right breast.

Kayla stared at Jackie's breast, heat flooding her cheeks. She diverted her eyes and hurriedly stepped into the bathroom and closed the door.

Jackie shuddered when the door closed, cutting her off from Kayla. She took a deep breath, and went into her room to change. She was glad they had talked. Kayla had a way of pulling information out of her. No one had ever fought for her that way before. She still felt a little vulnerable, but it was like she had broken a spell and stepped through the illusion of her life into a world of new possibilities. What if Kayla could find out what happened to her mother? She pulled the clean shirt over her head and stepped back into the hall at the same instant Kayla came out of the bathroom. The moment she met Kayla's gaze she felt the connection between them ignite.

Jackie reached for Kayla's hand soothed by the feel of Kayla's fingers laced around hers. She tugged Kayla's hand to lead them back outside, but Kayla didn't move. Jackie looked back at Kayla, puzzled. "What?"

"You shouldn't be the only one willing to take risks."

Kayla stepped closer and brought her hand to Jackie's chest, brushing her fingers across her breast. Her eyes were unfocused and followed the trace of her fingers as they moved across Jackie's chest. She took another step closer.

Jackie's heart pounded in her chest as she watched Kayla's eyes grow glassy with desire. She gasped when hot wetness seeped between her thighs. Her control shattered. "Kayla?" Jackie rasped.

Their lips almost touched, separated by a breath. Jackie breathed in the scent of Kayla and closed her eyes as Kayla slid her hand beneath Jackie's loose T-shirt.

Kayla's eyes flicked up to meet Jackie's. "Is it wrong that I just want to be close to you right now?" she whispered and pressed her mouth against Jackie's. Her hands traced circles along Jackie's stomach, causing the muscles to tighten and roll beneath her fingers.

Jackie shuddered. Every stroke of Kayla's fingers sent ripples of desire coursing through her until her body was rigid with tension and need. "It feels good to me."

When Kayla's hand cupped her breast beneath her shirt, her knees threatened to buckle. She was usually the one in charge, but Kayla controlled her with the slightest touch.

Jackie moaned when Kayla's fingers brushed across her nipple and the last shred of her control broke. "That feels really good."

Jackie grasped Kayla's hips firmly, pulling Kayla against her. She claimed Kayla's mouth, parting her lips with her tongue. The world spun and she was falling, soaring, spinning. With each stroke of Kayla's tongue against hers, she was reborn.

She had been with a lot of women, but something was different this time. She was lost in this kiss. She couldn't think of a time when she had felt so alive. Kayla felt right in her arms. If kissing Kayla felt this good, she had to have more. Her hands never stilled. She wanted to trace every inch of Kayla's body, wanted to know the intimate places that would make Kayla cry out in pleasure. She nipped at Kayla's lips, then slid her tongue into Kayla's mouth, claiming her, possessing her, consuming her.

Kayla dug her fingers into Jackie's skin, searching for an anchor that would hold her to Jackie through the storm that raged in her body. She was completely lost in a whirlwind of sensation, every fiber in her being screaming to be touched. The hunger she felt in Jackie's kiss fueled her desire and she answered Jackie's possessive strokes by pressing her body down on Jackie's thigh, pushing herself into a frenzy of desire. Her legs went weak and she trembled with want. She had to have Jackie. She wanted her inside her. She wanted to feel her mouth on her. She wanted it all. She needed to connect, be a part of someone real, someone alive.

"Take me to bed," Kayla gasped.

When Jackie met her gaze, Kayla felt a pull that went beyond her physical need. Something deep inside her stirred, making her insides tremble.

"Are you sure?"

Kayla peered into Jackie's eyes telegraphing her need. "I don't want to think about that now. Just this once I don't want to think."

Jackie didn't hesitate. She led Kayla into the bedroom stopping beside the bed. She slid her hands beneath Kayla's shirt and slowly lifted it over her head. Her lips immediately claimed the delicate skin of Kayla's neck just above her shoulder. She danced her fingertips along Kayla's back and released the clasp of her bra and slowly slid the straps down her arms.

The time Jackie took to explore Kayla's breasts with her eyes before claiming them in her mouth was pleasant torture to Kayla. Her whole body cried out to be touched.

"Oh God." Kayla moaned as Jackie's lips found her nipple and began to suck, flicking the swollen flesh with the tip of her tongue. Kayla threw her head back and arched into Jackie. Jackie's hands were at her waist and she heard her zipper slide open. Tender hands brushed her sensitive skin as her shorts were pulled down her hips and fell to the floor.

Kayla stood mostly naked, trembling with need. She was mesmerized as she watched Jackie shed her own shirt and shorts.

Jackie pressed their bodies together, blanketing Kayla with warmth. She claimed Kayla's mouth and backed up until her legs were touching the bed.

"Sit down," Kayla said, guiding Jackie with a hand against her chest.

Jackie hesitated. Kayla seemed to sense her reservation. She kissed her tenderly and ran her tongue along her ear, sucking on her earlobe and whispering hot breath into her ear. Jackie's resistance melted. Kayla could have whatever she wanted.

Kayla felt Jackie surrender. Kayla followed Jackie down onto the bed, savoring the feel of cool fabric and hot flesh against her skin. She couldn't believe she was doing this, but she had had enough waiting. Her want for Jackie was fierce and she didn't have the strength to fight anymore. In that moment being with Jackie was her only thought, her only desire, her only need. Damn the consequences.

Kayla couldn't take her eyes off Jackie's perfect body. Her long lean arms and legs were sculpted muscle that framed perfect breasts and a firm flat stomach that rippled with tension as the muscles flexed beneath her skin. Kayla reached out a hand to trace a small tattoo of flying birds that wrapped from Jackie's hip, up her side, and around to her back.

Kayla leaned down to kiss Jackie lightly before kneeling in front of her beside the bed. She wrapped her fingers beneath the delicate lace of Jackie's panties and pulled the fabric free, exposing Jackie's wetness. Kayla ran her hands along Jackie's inner thighs and felt her shudder. She brushed her fingers along Jackie's center, gently parting her swollen flesh, exposing her fully. Jackie gasped and her body tensed.

"Perfect," Kayla murmured and blew a hot breath against the exposed flesh. She marveled at the sweet smell of Jackie's arousal, the perfect pink lips, and the slight tremble in Jackie's legs. She loved seeing what she was doing to Jackie.

After several teasing breaths and faint passes with the tip of her tongue, she felt Jackie's fingers slide through her hair, encouraging more. Obediently Kayla slid her tongue into the wet folds, enveloping Jackie with her mouth.

Jackie whimpered as Kayla's tongue slid against her swollen clitoris. Ecstasy flooded through her veins, melting her, filling her to the point of oblivion. Kayla's teasing had her ready to beg for release. She had never wanted anything so badly. When Kayla's mouth surrounded her, she became intoxicated with pleasure. The storm was gathering, winding into a tight mass in the center of her soul, each stroke of Kayla's tongue pushing her closer to surrender.

Kayla's hands were like silk as she stroked her fingers across Jackie's skin, stroking her stomach, cupping her breasts, and rubbing her fingers across the hard points of Jackie's nipples. Jackie was out of her mind with pleasure. Her thighs trembled and her hips writhed in time with Kayla's momentum, intensifying each stroke. Her body tensed as all her strength gathered into an explosion of sensation that spilled out through her body, down her arms and legs, making her fingers and toes tingle. She grasped Kayla's hair in her hands and pressed against her lips, intensifying the pressure against her clitoris. Jackie cried out as her orgasm erupted sending colossal waves of pleasure crashing through her. The pleasure was beyond belief and she was far from having enough. She wanted Kayla's body to envelop her. She wanted to touch her. She wanted everything that was Kayla.

"Come here."

Kayla kissed her way up Jackie's abdomen to her breasts. She slid an arm beneath Jackie's shoulders and lifted, helping Jackie slide farther up onto the bed.

Jackie drew in a slow, deep breath as Kayla's breasts pressed against her own, sending another wave of pleasure rippling through her. She held Kayla as her body pulsed with the aftershocks of orgasm. Kayla's touch was heaven.

"More," Jackie rasped against Kayla's ear before sliding her tongue along its edge.

Kayla moaned. "Oh God, yes. Anything."

Jackie shuddered as Kayla's fingers slid through the wet folds where her mouth had been only moments before. She opened herself to Kayla's touch, her hips rising to encourage Kayla inside.

Jackie wanted to feel Kayla, she needed to touch her. She slid her hand between Kayla's thighs, feeling the silky wetness of Kayla's arousal. Kayla moaned and trembled beneath her touch. Jackie pushed inside and felt the delicate muscles close around her fingers, joining them together. She pressed her thumb against Kayla's clitoris and thrust into her as another orgasm gathered in her depths, filling her, shattering her. Kayla clenched her thighs together riding Jackie's hand until she shuddered and cried out, signaling her own release. Jackie held on to Kayla as if she might slip away, praying the familiar emptiness wouldn't follow.

❖

Kayla stirred, waking to a soft breast beneath her cheek and the rhythmic thud of Jackie's heartbeat against her ear. Her hand still lay nestled in the soft curls between Jackie's legs. She lifted her head and drew her hand from the warmth of Jackie's sex. Her fingers were still wet from their lovemaking. She drew her hand up Jackie's stomach to cup her breast and Jackie's arm immediately tightened around her. She looked up to see Jackie's eyes on her. Jackie's lips curved into a smile as she began to trace small circles on Kayla's back.

"I'm sorry. I didn't mean to fall asleep," Kayla whispered.

Jackie took Kayla's hand, drawing it to her lips to kiss her fingertips. "I liked it. It was nice just holding you. You are very beautiful when you sleep."

Kayla smiled shyly. She was a little embarrassed now as she remembered the way she had thrown herself at Jackie. But that embarrassment was quickly extinguished when Jackie placed her fingers under Kayla's chin and lifted her head to kiss her.

Kayla was sure she had never been so thoroughly undone by any kiss before. Jackie's lips were tender, yet molten as they molded to her. Excitement flooded Kayla's brain, hijacked her reasoning, and her body responded with an urgent need to have Jackie claim her again.

She whimpered as Jackie rolled her onto her back and the weight of Jackie's body pressed along the length of hers. Soft breasts brushed across her nipples until they were painfully hard. Jackie pressed her pelvis into Kayla and pushed her legs apart with her knees.

Kayla's heart raced. The tenderness in Jackie's touch had Kayla ready to beg for mercy. She knew what was coming and she desperately wanted Jackie to claim her.

Fully exposed, Kayla stared up into Jackie's soft, hungry eyes. She slid her heels behind Jackie's thighs, pulling her against her. She could feel Jackie's heat engulfing her exposed flesh. Jackie slid farther down as her strong hands pushed against Kayla's thighs, opening her farther. When Jackie's mouth closed around her, Kayla closed her eyes in bliss.

What had taken her so long? What had she been waiting for? Kayla surrendered. This time she let her body lead the way. There was no holding back, no hesitation, no fear, nothing but the exquisite pleasure of Jackie's hands and mouth claiming her.

Chapter Eleven

Kayla stared at the clock, watching the numbers change over as time slipped away. It was six in the morning, and she had put off the inevitable as long as she could. No matter how hard she tried to stop time, morning had come. She slowly slid free of the arm draped around her waist, instantly missing the contact. She had awakened to the feel of Jackie's body pressed against her, spooning her with an arm thrown possessively around her, with warm breath tickling the back of her neck. It was a feeling she didn't want to end, but she had to go. She had to be at work soon.

Jackie stirred, reflexively reaching for her as she slid off the bed. As she searched for her clothes, Kayla considered leaving without waking Jackie so she wouldn't disturb her rest, but that was too much like slinking out as if she had done something wrong. She wasn't ashamed of her night with Jackie. She had wanted the night to go on forever. She felt right in Jackie's arms, against her mouth, and inside her body.

Kayla looked down at Jackie's serene face and smiled. She eased onto the edge of the bed and trailed her fingers along Jackie's cheek. She brushed the hair away from her face and relished Jackie's beauty as she lay sleeping.

A faint smile played at the corner of Jackie's lips as Kayla's fingertips brushed her skin. After a minute or so of the caresses, Jackie's eyes fluttered open. She immediately reached for Kayla.

"Good morning," Kayla whispered as she leaned down and kissed Jackie's cheek.

"Good morning." Jackie squinted, her eyes still unfocused from sleep. "Why are you dressed? It's still so early."

"I have to go. I have to get ready for work."

Jackie circled her arms around Kayla's waist and curled against her. "Stay here with me. Take the day."

Kayla cradled Jackie's head against her stomach and stroked her hair. "I have clients today and I'm sure you do too."

Jackie moaned and pulled up the hem of Kayla's shirt, buried her face against her stomach, and began playing her tongue along the rim of Kayla's belly button.

Kayla laughed when she felt the muscles of her stomach twitch with arousal.

"See, you aren't ready to leave," Jackie said dreamily.

Kayla wanted to throw herself back onto the bed and wrap herself around Jackie. "I admit it would be very pleasurable to stay here in bed with you, but I really have to go." She managed to extricate herself from Jackie's embrace and gave her a soft kiss before stepping away from the bed.

Jackie sat up, the sheet falling to her waist exposing her beautiful round breasts.

Kayla sighed. "Not fair."

"What?" Jackie replied innocently.

Kayla bit her bottom lip and shook her head. The cocky grin on Jackie's face mocked Kayla's resolve. It was the perfect display of cocky self-confidence that she found so threatening but so irresistible.

"Call me later?" Kayla asked, suddenly vulnerable and uncertain about what would happen next.

Jackie threw the covers aside, stepped out of bed, and crossed the room in two long strides, the muscles in her legs flexing with each step. "Of course I will. Better yet, why don't you just stay?"

Kayla wanted to stay. She wanted that more than anything at that moment, but she was already in dangerous waters. "I can't," she said breathlessly, her hands pressed against Jackie's bare chest. Kayla couldn't resist the silky feel of Jackie's skin and the sight of her naked body. How was she supposed to leave now?

"At least have coffee with me or let me make you breakfast."

Kayla smiled, feeling slightly reassured by Jackie's reluctance to let her go. Perhaps their night together had been more than just sex. Jackie didn't seem to want their time together to end either.

Kayla glanced at the clock, and then back to Jackie's pleading eyes. She sighed. "Okay…coffee. But you have to put on some clothes first."

Jackie laughed. "Anything you want."

❖

Kayla was thankful for her full schedule to keep her mind focused on her work. But despite her best efforts, her mind wandered at the most unsettling times to her night with Jackie. She couldn't help the smile that crept across her face. It was as if she could feel the lingering touch of Jackie's body still pressed against her.

By four that afternoon she had started checking her phone between clients just to see if Jackie had called. By six the happy elation had turned to doubt and by seven into self-recrimination. She was certain Jackie wouldn't call. They had been through so much in one night. Maybe Jackie had changed her mind. The challenge was over. Jackie had been emotional and wanted to walk away and Kayla had practically thrown herself at her. Kayla scolded herself for being so hard on Jackie. She wasn't being fair. She was driving herself crazy.

Mentally drained, Kayla turned off her computer and gathered her things, glad to put an end to her day. Maybe she should call Jackie. She cringed. That seemed desperate. She had been certain Jackie had felt the same way she did about their night together. But with each passing hour her doubt grew.

Kayla pulled up to her house a half an hour later to find Jen's car parked in her drive. She cut off the engine just as her phone rang. Her heart lurched and her stomach did a summersault the instant she recognized Jackie's number. She was torn between relief and dread as she stared at the name on the screen. *Stop being childish.*

"Hello," she answered

"Hi there. Sorry to call so late."

"No, no, this is fine. I'm just getting home. It's been a long day."

"Yeah, same here. Maybe you should have taken me up on that offer to take the day off and just stay in bed."

Kayla smiled. "Maybe I should have."

Jackie groaned. "Now I need a cold shower. I'm going to be here for at least another hour."

Kayla hesitated. "Do you want dinner?"

"What I would like is to be in bed with you. But I can't tonight."

"Tomorrow night then?"

Jackie sighed. "That's not good for me. I have a dinner meeting with people from work."

"Oh...okay," Kayla said, unable to keep the disappointment out of her voice.

"Maybe Wednesday?" Jackie offered.

Kayla smiled. "Wednesday is good."

"Great. How about I call you and we can make more definite plans then."

"Sure."

There was an awkward pause. "How are you today? Are you okay with...everything?" Jackie asked.

Kayla hesitated. "I am now."

"Good. I've been thinking about you all day. I really enjoyed being with you and not just because...you know."

"Me too." Kayla smiled a real smile this time and sank back into the leather seat. "Thank you for saying that."

"I mean it. Who else can say they had lunch by a stream with a beautiful woman, only to be chased away by a bear?"

Kayla chuckled. "You know that's not what I was talking about. And we weren't exactly being chased."

"Ha. That may be how you saw it, but in my story we were definitely being chased. I think we could have been eaten."

This time Kayla laughed out loud. "You're not right."

Jackie's voice sobered. "I really like it when you laugh. Come to think of it, I like other sounds you make too."

"Don't," Kayla warned.

"What? Are you blushing right now? I bet you are," Jackie teased.

"That's not nice."

Jackie relented. "Okay, okay. I'll play nice just this once. I'll talk to you Wednesday."

Kayla sighed. "Good night."

"Good night, Kayla."

Kayla sat in her car gripping her keys in her hand when her phone rang again.

She jumped, startled by the unexpected call, and quickly glanced at the phone. Disappointment washed over her like a cold shower as Jen's number appeared on the screen. Kayla sighed, a little guilty for her reaction to her friend.

"Hey." Jen's voice was low and tinged with concern. "Is there some reason you're just sitting outside in your car? Are you okay? Why didn't you pull into the garage?"

"I'm fine." Kayla chuckled. "I'll be right in. What's for dinner?"

"Mexican?"

Kayla laughed, thankful for the distraction.

❖

"Are you crazy?" Jen asked with her fork halfway to her mouth. "You should go to her."

Kayla had told Jen what happened between her and Jackie when Jen confronted her about not coming home the night before. It felt good to talk about her feelings, but Jen wasn't exactly one to hold back her opinion either.

"What's the problem K? She's beautiful, funny, and fun to be with. And you obviously have amazing chemistry, right?"

"Yes to all counts."

"Then what are you doing here with me? You should go to her."

Kayla shook her head. "It doesn't matter, she's busy tonight. Besides, I didn't mean to sleep with her last night. It was an emotional day and there are some things we still need to work out. She made it pretty clear she only wants a casual relationship, and I'm not sure I can do that."

"You're scared."

Kayla narrowed her eyes and glared at Jen. "I'm not running. I just…" Kayla shifted uncomfortably and let out an exasperated breath.

Jen let up a little. "What is it?"

Kayla sighed. "Waking up with her this morning was…I wanted too much," she stammered.

Jen took Kayla's hand. "You really like her, don't you?"

Kayla nodded, knowing that *like* didn't exactly describe her feelings for Jackie. She couldn't define it to herself, but she knew she wanted to be near Jackie, hear her voice, and touch her, all the time.

"K, if you really like her, I don't think staying away from her is really going to help. You're just going to drive yourself crazy thinking about her."

"I know that, and you know that, but she doesn't have to know that."

Taking advantage of a momentary silence, Kayla changed the subject. "How are you doing? Any word from Mike?"

Jen rolled her eyes. "Oh yes. He's sent me about a hundred text messages today. He's mad because I won't put money in his account and his truck payment is due."

"Ouch. Good for you."

"Yeah, well, I've decided a real break is best for me right now. He'll just have to figure it out."

Kayla smiled at Jen. "I'm proud of you. I know that's hard for you to do."

"You know, it's easier this time. He's been so mean to me lately that even *I* can't feel sorry for him."

Kayla squeezed Jen's hand. "I'm glad you're finally seeing him for what he really is. You've done everything to try to help him. He's the only one who can change this. I'm glad to see you taking care of your needs for a change."

Tears misted across Jen's eyes and she straightened. "I just want to be happy. I'm so tired of fighting, worrying, and feeling like I don't matter."

"You do matter. And you deserve to be happy."

Jen looked into Kayla's eyes and leaned forward. "So do you, K."

Kayla dropped her gaze and reached for her keys.

"Come on, I'm tired. Let's go home." Kayla didn't want to think anymore. Her night with Jackie had been wonderful, but she knew better than to expect more.

❖

Jackie pushed through her run and made it to the office an hour early. She had a long day of patients ahead of her and then she had to get through an office dinner and breaking in a new associate. The moment she entered the office the reality of just how long a day it would be hit like a ton of bricks. Her life had suddenly become very complicated.

Peter smiled like the Cheshire cat. "Jack, I'm glad you're here. Come and meet our newest associate, Heather Collins. Heather, this is Jacqueline Phillips."

Heather greeted her with a smile. Jackie felt Heather's dark eyes train on her as Heather took her hand in a firm grip.

"Nice to meet you, Jack, I'm looking forward to working with you." A wicked grin curved at the corner of her mouth.

Jackie swallowed hard and cautiously shook Heather's hand. "Welcome aboard. And you can call me Jackie."

There was no point in hoping Heather didn't remember her. Heather's grip tightened as Jackie attempted to extract her hand. She couldn't miss the blaze that flared in Heather's eyes as she brazenly trailed her gaze down Jackie's body.

Peter's cheerful voice trilled through the air. "Okay, Jack, Heather can shadow you today. I'm sure you can show her the ropes," he said with an exaggerated wink.

Jackie wanted to throttle him, even if he did mean well. How could he know she already knew too many very intimate details about their new associate?

"Oh, and don't forget we're all meeting at Coco Moon for dinner tonight," Peter called before disappearing into his office.

"Great," she answered. "Sounds great."

Suddenly self-conscious, Jackie pulled at her sweat drenched shirt. The wet fabric clung to her clammy skin and she was certain she smelled like a goat. "I need to hit the shower before we get started. I'll see you in a bit, Heather."

Heather's eyes were fixed on Jackie's breasts. "Looking forward to it," she said with a wink.

Jackie fled to the showers. Only a few weeks ago she would have been doing the happy dance to have a beautiful woman like Heather display such obvious interest in her, but not today. What were the chances that she and Heather would wind up working together? They hadn't exactly talked about much the night they met. Jackie hadn't even known Heather was a physical therapist. What were the chances of that? Jackie groaned. Complicated didn't even begin to describe her life right now.

Jackie braced her hands on the shower wall and let the water cascade across her head and shoulders. It was definitely going to be a long day. She stood there until her skin became tender under the assault of hot water. She shut the water off and ran a towel over her hair and gave the rest of her body a quick swipe before wrapping the towel loosely around her waist. She was halfway to her locker when she heard the door.

Heather rounded the corner a moment later, her tall frame erect, and her jet-black hair pulled back in a ponytail. She stopped abruptly in front of Jackie, feigning surprise. She trailed her eyes across Jackie's half-naked body. She grinned mischievously and cocked her hip against a locker.

"Hmm. I like this job already."

Jackie continued on to her locker, feeling exposed and oddly uncomfortable. She was used to being naked in front of other women, especially in the locker room, but this was no ordinary woman. This was a woman who had intimate knowledge of her body and what she liked to do with it. The situation was all wrong.

"I'll be ready in a few minutes and I'll come show you around," Jackie said over her shoulder, hoping Heather would get the hint and leave her alone.

"Oh, there's no hurry."

Jackie pulled on a sports bra and her company polo shirt. She knew Heather was still watching her, and her discomfort was starting to irritate her. She glanced over at Heather casually. "Can I help you with something?"

"Hmm. Good question. I'm sure I could think of a few things."

Before Jackie could say anything, Heather moved forward and added, "I do enjoy the view, but for now I can wait outside."

Jackie watched Heather glide around the corner and listened for the door. She let her head fall against her locker with a heavy thud.

"Shit."

CHAPTER TWELVE

"Come on Kayla. Let's go out," Jen pleaded. "It's too quiet around here. Besides you don't have a hot date tonight or anything, right? We hardly ever get off work this early—let's enjoy it."

Kayla put the book she had been trying to read down on the table. "Where are we going to go on a Tuesday night? And please don't say Mexican. I can't do that again."

"Don't you worry. I looked up some new places online. We have options."

Kayla could see Jen was going stir-crazy and needed a break from the constant barrage of texts and threatening voicemails she had been receiving from Mike all evening.

"Okay. You're right. After this crazy day, we should have a little fun."

Jen beamed and bounced up and down on the balls of her feet and let out a delighted squeal.

Kayla laughed.

The place Jen chose had only been in operation for a couple of months. "So, what's the scoop on this place? Is it another gay club?"

"Well it is gay owned, but I think it's mostly a restaurant until midnight and then it turns into a dance club in the back." Jen stopped just inside the door. "Wow."

The room was filled with leather-upholstered booths that were really more like small sofas with a table in the middle. A stained concrete bar top stretched three-quarters of the length of the room, and the front wall was all glass with silk string drapes that allowed in light, while obscuring the view into the club from the outside. The waitstaff were mostly men dressed in black slacks, dress shirts with colorful ties, and suit vests.

Jen's mouth was agape. "I think I've died and gone to heaven."

Kayla laughed at Jen's new infatuation with gay men. Kayla stepped up when the hostess came to seat them. "Two, please."

They sank into the luscious leather booth, both sighing in pleasure.

Kayla ran her hand along the sofa and relaxed into the plush throw cushions that added a spot of color to the warm décor. "This place is incredible."

"Incredible is right." Jen purred as a tall, handsome man approached their table. He had beautiful mocha skin and a trim muscular body. He was dressed in the same black slacks and vest as the others, but his tie was an electric baby blue that set off his eyes. His curly dark hair was cut close to his scalp, leaving just enough hair for brushing fingers through. Kayla was one hundred percent lesbian, but even she admired his beauty.

After much gushing, stammering, and flirting, Jen learned that the waiter's name was Damian and he was from the Dominican Republic. He was an Iraq war veteran and was—to Kayla's surprise— straight and, to Jen's dismay, married.

Dinner was fabulous. Kayla was relaxed and having fun. Maybe having Jen around was good for her. She was at least leaving the house now and was learning to enjoy being around other gay people on a regular basis. Kayla often craved the feeling of sameness and security that came from being with other lesbians and gays, but there were few places for the local LGBT community to gather that weren't dance clubs or smoke filled bars. Kayla wasn't much of a fan of either. This was nice and she looked forward to coming here more often.

As the night went on, the lights dimmed and a moving projector scattered multicolored pin lights in rhythmic patterns on the walls. The techno music that had always been present rose in volume as the room began to fill up. Kayla's attention was drawn to a back room that was sectioned off from the dining area by a wall of glass. A group of people lounged in the many sofas lining the walls surrounding a dance floor. People mingled as they swayed and moved to the beat, succumbing to the intoxicating lure of the music enticing them to move their bodies.

Jen drew Kayla's attention by waving a hand in front of her face. "I have to go to the little girls' room—I'll be right back."

Kayla nodded. She was happy to take advantage of the few minutes alone to people watch. A burst of laughter from the front of the room drew her attention to a large table near the bar. A tall woman with long jet-black hair stood next to a group of men and women. Her head was thrown back in laughter, allowing her lustrous black hair to cascade down her back and shoulders. Her laughter was hearty and she was obviously very comfortable with the attention she commanded. She was very attractive and she knew it.

She watched the woman's self-assured movements, listened to her bold laughter, and observed the way the rest of the group seemed to hang on her every word. What would it be like to have such a commanding presence? A waiter carrying a tray of drinks made his way through the throng of people and they parted to give him room. Kayla's heart froze the instant she saw the tall slim figure step from beside the laughing woman. There was no mistaking the warm brown hair that curled slightly along the pale blue collar, or the perfect curve of jaw framing kissable lips. Kayla's palms itched as the memory of Jackie's strong body pulsed beneath the skin of her hands.

Kayla flinched when the dark-haired woman reached out a hand and brushed Jackie's hair back and draped her arm around Jackie's shoulders.

The sound of Jen's voice pulled Kayla out of her stunned shock.

"Oh my God, I can't believe there are so many gorgeous men here. You won't believe what I saw on the way to the bathroom." Jen froze the instant she registered the change in Kayla. "What's wrong, K? Are you all right?" Jen turned her head and looked around the room.

"I think I need to go now, Jen."

Jen turned back to Kayla. "What did I miss? What's going on?"

"Nothing, I just had some questions answered, that's all."

Jen frowned. "Well, that's vague. Come on, tell me what happened."

Kayla knew Jen wouldn't let it go, so she gave in. "Look to the table at the front near the bar."

Jen followed Kayla's instructions and studied the mixed group of men and women gathered at the long high-top table.

"Okay, that guy looks familiar, but I don't remember from where." Her gaze continued to move across the group until her eyes landed on the tall woman holding court.

"Damn, she's hot."

Kayla glared at Jen. "Keep looking."

Jen studied the group a bit longer. "Hey, there's Jackie," she said, then frowned. "Oh, shit," she said as the tall brunette brushed her hand across Jackie's chest along her collarbone before looping her arm around Jackie's. Jen looked back at Kayla, her eyes wide with concern. "K, this doesn't mean anything. Don't jump to conclusions. Maybe you should go say hello."

Kayla took a deep breath and tried to calm the storm of emotions that thundered around in her brain. Her head throbbed. It was difficult to breathe and she thought she might be sick. She drew a steadying breath and thought about the evidence. Jackie had told her she was going out with her work group and she *was* with a large group of people. They were not in a relationship and Jackie had the right to be wherever, with whomever she wanted. Kayla gave herself a mental kick for being so impulsive and for jumping to conclusions. But the sight of another woman touching Jackie had upset her more than she expected or wanted to admit.

"You're right. She did say she was going out with people from work tonight, and those are the same guys she was with at the bar the night we met."

"See. There you go. This is a work thing. Kind of like us."

Kayla wasn't convinced, but she wanted to believe it was true.

"Let's get the check and we'll say hello on the way out," Jen offered.

Kayla nodded. "Okay."

Heather proved to be very good at her job and to Jackie's relief had been totally focused on her work. There had been no more of the flirtations that had started the day. Maybe she had overreacted to Heather. Maybe she had read more into things than were really there.

That thought was shattered when Jackie strolled into the restaurant. Heather and Peter were already seated at the table having drinks when she arrived. Jackie cautiously made her way over, purposefully sitting next to Peter and across from Heather.

"Hey. About time you showed up," Peter said giving her shoulder a shove.

"Sorry." Jackie glanced up at Heather briefly before looking away. She could feel Heather staring at her, and when their eyes met, Heather was looking at her like she was the main course.

"Everything okay?" Peter asked.

Jackie shrugged, thankful to talk about work. "I had a few things to follow up on, nothing to worry about."

"Good." Peter lifted his glass. "What are you drinking?"

Jackie shrugged. "I'm not sure yet." She looked at her watch, then the door, wondering where the rest of the group was.

"Well, everyone else is running a little late too," Peter said as if reading her mind. "But that just gives us more time to get to know each other better."

Jackie knew by the sharp pinch at the back of her arm that Peter was referring to her and Heather. Jackie smiled and nodded, resisting the urge to strangle Peter.

"So, Heather, how was your first day? Did Jackie take good care of you?"

A spark glinted in Heather's eyes as she flashed a bright smile that should have had Jackie's heart racing.

"Oh, I definitely like what I've seen so far." Heather reached across the table and placed her hand over Jackie's. "I'm sure I can learn a thing or two from Jackie."

Jackie's face was on fire. She pulled her hand away and pushed out of her chair. "I'm going to get a drink. Can I bring either of you anything?"

Heather pursed her lips in what could have been either a pout or acknowledgment of a challenge. Jackie wasn't sure which, but both made her uneasy.

"The waiter has our drink order already," Peter said. "You can give him your order when he gets back."

"That's okay. I want to say hello to Antwon at the bar. Please excuse me for a moment."

Jackie leaned on the bar to get Antwon's attention.

"Hello, gorgeous. What are you drinking tonight?"

Jackie smiled, letting some of the tension slip from her shoulders. "Hendrick's and tonic."

"Hmm, going for the good stuff tonight?" He glanced over his shoulder toward Jackie's table and waggled his eyebrows.

Jackie laughed. "Any other time, I'd agree with you, but—" Her words were cut short as a long slender hand cupped her arm and she felt firm breasts press against her back. Jackie stiffened. Warm breath brushed across her ear as Heather spoke. She replayed the memory of tasting Heather's lips and warning bells clanged loudly in her head. *Don't go there. This is supposed to be a work thing not a get-laid thing.*

Heather set her glass of wine down on the bar top. "This wine is not to my taste. Do you think I could have another glass?"

Jackie was trapped between Heather and the bar and was acutely aware of Heather's breasts pressed against her.

"What would you like instead?" Antwon asked.

Heather brushed her finger down Jackie's glass. "I'll have what she's having."

"Sure thing. Coming right up." Antwon swept the glass away and was gone, leaving Jackie to deal with Heather.

Jackie shifted, trying to put a little distance between them. "That's a big switch."

Heather smiled. "I know what I like." She leaned close to Jackie until her lips brushed the edge of Jackie's ear. "I like my wine dry and my women wet."

Jackie shivered as the faintest brush of tongue slid over her ear. Uncomfortable with where this was going, she pushed back from the bar and stepped away. "Look, Heather, I think you're beautiful, but I don't mix business with pleasure."

Heather smirked. "There's a first time for everything," she said, running a finger along Jackie's jaw.

To Jackie's relief, Antwon sat the fresh drink down on the bar in front of them, interrupting the exchange.

"Anything else, ladies?"

Heather picked up the glass and stepped away. She looked at Jackie over the rim of her glass as she took a drink. "This will do... for now."

Jackie watched her walk away and let out an exasperated breath before downing half her drink. "Maybe you should pour me another glass, Antwon."

"Okay, Jack, but you might want to go easy. It looks like you're going to need your wits about you tonight. She might be a little more than you can handle."

"I think you're right about that," Jackie said finishing her drink and reaching for the fresh glass.

By the time she made her way back to the table, the rest of the group had arrived and were engaged in conversation. Jackie was glad she could stand since the high-top was full. When she scanned the group, she realized with some relief that Heather was missing. Restroom maybe.

Jackie wanted to excuse herself and go home, but Peter would kill her if she bailed on him this early. She was even more flustered when Heather returned and made some joke that made everyone laugh. She had been so preoccupied with trying to figure a way out of the evening that she didn't hear what was said.

When she didn't laugh, Heather reached over and brushed Jackie's hair off her collar and then wrapped her arm around Jackie's shoulders. "Hmm, looks like someone's not keeping up. I wonder what's on that mind of yours?"

Jackie cleared her throat. "Nothing, just tired."

Heather leaned closer to Jackie and brushed her hand along her chest, tracing the ridge of collarbone through the thin fabric of her shirt. "I know just the thing to help you relax."

An awareness permeated Jackie's senses. The tiny hairs at the back of her neck tingled and she had the undeniable feeling that she was missing something.

Heather looped her arm around Jackie's and squeezed possessively.

Jackie lifted her head and scanned the room, searching for the source of this strange sensation. Her eyes fell on the vague figure of a woman in the crowd. Although she couldn't see the woman's face, her body cried out with knowing. Her lips parted as the name slipped out on her breath. "Kayla."

At that moment the throng of people parted and she saw the one person she longed to see. She felt the smile blossom at the corners of her mouth and reach her eyes as Kayla and Jen stepped up to their group.

"Hello, Jackie," Jen said standing close behind Kayla.

Jackie felt a sudden flood of tension rise in her belly as she registered the cold note in Jen's voice.

"Hi, Jen, good to see you again," Jackie said meeting Jen's eyes momentarily before turning her gaze to Kayla. She smiled at Kayla. "I didn't expect to see you here."

Kayla held Jackie's gaze believing the sincerity she heard in Jackie's voice. "I'm sure you didn't."

Jackie frowned. "Would you like to join us for dinner or a drink? I could introduce you to the team."

"We don't want to intrude," Kayla said, her voice sounding soft and wounded to her own ears. She tried to hide the prickle of pain that pierced her chest. She wanted to be wrong about Jackie. "We had dinner already, and we're just on our way out. I wouldn't want to interrupt." Kayla couldn't help but glance toward the woman who had been pawing at Jackie earlier.

"You wouldn't be interrupting anything," Jackie answered quickly.

Kayla studied Jackie's face trying to read beyond her expression. Was Jackie nervous that she had seen her with the other woman? Or did she really want her to stay?

Jackie smiled and reached out a hand to Kayla, her fingers brushing lightly along Kayla's arm before closing around her hand. Kayla felt warmth spread through her fingertips.

Jackie opened her mouth as if to speak but stopped when a hand snaked around her waist. The woman with the long black hair draped her arms around Jackie as if she owned her.

"Hmm, who are your friends?"

Kayla flinched.

The woman extended a hand to Kayla. "I'm Heather."

Kayla took Heather's hand calmly. "Hello, Heather. I'm Kayla and this is my friend Jen. Don't let us keep you from your evening, we were just leaving. It's nice meeting you."

Kayla dropped Heather's hand and stepped around the group without another word to Jackie. She felt Jen close behind her as they reached the door.

❖

Kayla sat in the porch swing allowing the gentle rocking motion to soothe her. She wouldn't cry. Jackie had tried to tell her she wasn't ready. She should have listened. It was better to know things now than waiting till she had deeper feelings for Jackie.

Jen leaned against the porch railing watching her.

"I'm okay, Jen. You can go on to bed."

"Sweetie, I don't know what happened tonight. I don't even know how to make out what I saw with my own eyes. But I think there's more to this story than we know. Jackie didn't seem to be into that woman. Maybe they're just good friends. Like you and me."

"Yeah, I'm sure you're right."

Jen sighed. "Can I get you anything?"

"No. I'm fine. Really, you should go to bed."

Kayla's phone buzzed. She didn't have to look to know the message waiting for her was from Jackie.

"Why don't you talk to her and get some answers about what happened tonight."

"You're right. I need to put this to rest. I'm being childish."

Jen leaned down and kissed Kayla's cheek. "I'll be inside if you need me."

"Thanks."

She played the message. *Kayla, give me a call. This wasn't what it looked like. We should talk.*

Kayla knew she was wrong for judging Jackie without hearing her out, but she had been hurt and wanted to be home. She was sure Jackie hadn't meant to hurt her, but she couldn't bring herself to talk to her just yet. The one thing she knew without a doubt was that Jackie and Heather had slept together. She could see it in the way Heather touched Jackie. But she hadn't once seen Jackie touch Heather back.

Kayla rubbed her temples. Jealousy was a new emotion for her and she didn't like it. After listening to Jackie's message for the fourth time she scolded herself for being so pathetic. Since when did she play the victim?

She wiped her face with her hands and sat up. She took a long shaky breath and dialed Jackie's number. It was getting late, but she had to face this. Besides, this way she would know if Jackie had gone home alone. If so, they could talk. If not, then Kayla would have her answer and there wouldn't be anything left to talk about. It was as simple as that.

Jackie answered the phone on the half ring. "Kayla?"

"Hey." Kayla's voice was tight and flat.

"Thanks for calling me back. I'm sorry. I know how bad things looked, but it wasn't what it seemed."

"Really?" Kayla cut Jackie off. "Explain it to me then. Because what I saw looked a lot like another woman's hands on your body. And I realize I don't have any right to be upset about that, but humor me."

"I just want to explain. I've been honest with you about everything. Just hear me out."

Kayla sighed. "I'm listening."

She heard Jackie expel a breath.

"I met Heather a couple of months ago. Today was the first time I've seen her since then but she seemed to have the idea that we could be more than work partners. I had no idea she was the new associate Pete brought on board until I walked in the door this morning."

"When you say you met her a couple of months ago, you mean you slept together."

Jackie sighed. "Yes. I'm sorry you had to see that. I didn't know how to handle the situation because tonight was a work thing."

"So why aren't you still there?"

Jackie hesitated. "It didn't seem so important anymore." There was a long silence on the line. "Look, I don't know what this is between us, but you should know that I haven't been out with anyone else since we met. I've been honest with you about everything from day one."

Kayla didn't have any reason not to believe Jackie. She wanted to believe her. "I know I don't even have the right to be upset about this. It isn't like we're together or anything. But seeing that woman's hands on you was too much for me. How do I know you won't change your mind next week and decide she's what you want, or some other woman?"

"You don't. I told you I don't have any promises. I just didn't want you to think I had been dishonest."

Kayla thought of the tenderness in Jackie's touch, the lingering of her eyes on her body as if she was memorizing every detail. She had felt how carefully Jackie trailed her lips across her skin, savoring the feel, the taste of her. But more than that, she had felt Jackie open herself to her. She had shown her vulnerability and she had slept in Kayla's arms.

"Kayla?"

Kayla closed her eyes and let her heart guide her. "123 Sea Brook Lane."

"What?"

"That's where I live."

She heard the catch in Jackie's breath when she realized the significance of that simple statement.

"Is that an invitation?"

Kayla considered for a moment. She was about to risk everything. "Yes."

"Why?"

Kayla sighed. "Because I'm tired. I don't know what I'm doing, but I want to feel alive. And that's how you make me feel."

CHAPTER THIRTEEN

The warm glow of lights flickered into view as Jackie made her way down the quiet residential street to Kayla's house. She swallowed hard but couldn't calm the butterflies swimming in her stomach. No matter how this turned out, she didn't want Kayla to believe she had lied to her. As soon as she killed the engine she pushed the door open and jogged around the car. She was about to ring the bell when she heard Kayla's soft voice say her name. She peered into the dim light and shadows to the end of the porch, trying to see beyond the darkness to the silhouette of a woman.

"I'm here," Kayla said, sitting forward until the soft light illuminated her face.

Jackie didn't know what to do. She stared hopelessly at the angelic face, not daring to try to claim it.

"It's okay. Come here."

Jackie took a tentative step forward. Kayla was sitting on an old-fashioned porch swing. The image was perfect and a smile edged into her lips.

As if sensing her hesitation, Kayla took her hand, leading her down on the swing next to her. Kayla's thin fingers seemed fragile as they linked with hers, like holding a wren in the palm of her hand.

Jackie took a deep breath to prepare for what she needed to say.

"You were right," Kayla whispered. "I got scared. It was wrong of me to push and I had no right to be angry with you."

Kayla sat back against the swing and pushed off with her feet, rocking them gently back and forth. Jackie was afraid to move or speak. Kayla was working through something of her own and it was important to them both.

"Neither of us knows where this is going," Kayla said as she brushed her thumb across Jackie's hand. "I have to trust you to tell me if you want something else." She stilled the swing and met Jackie's eyes. "Just promise you'll tell me."

Jackie kissed Kayla's cheek. "I promise, as long as you promise not to push," she whispered, allowing the heat of her breath to brush along Kayla's ear. She sat back in the swing, their shoulders touching.

"Agreed."

Kayla leaned against her shoulder. Until that moment, Kayla had always been in control, she had called all the shots, and Jackie understood this was a simple gesture of surrender. Kayla shuddered against her and Jackie felt something inside her shift.

"I know I didn't make the best first impression and I don't have any experience with dating, but was it really that easy to think I would be out with another woman?"

Kayla sighed. "It was more about what I believe about myself than what I believe about you. My parents didn't want to be tied down with a kid. They wanted the freedom to travel, party, and do whatever they wanted. I got in the way. My romantic relationships haven't turned out any better. I have a hard time believing anyone will ever want to stick around. Despite making it very clear that you don't want a relationship, I've let myself get closer to you than anyone in a long time. I guess I panicked."

"I'm sorry," Jackie said softly.

"No. I'm the one who needs to apologize. I let my insecurities create a problem between us. We have no commitment to each other just because we slept together. I had no right to take my issues out on you. I have no right to expect you to know what you want between us when I don't even know that myself."

"So what do we do now?" Jackie asked.

Kayla wasn't sure what was next. If she continued, she was certain to get hurt. But despite the warnings, despite her fear, she couldn't let Jackie go. She couldn't shake the feeling of rightness she had when she was with Jackie. She had to take this chance.

"Come inside with me," Kayla whispered. She stood, pulling Jackie with her. She brushed her fingers across Jackie's collarbone, tracing the line she'd watched Heather's hand take. Something primal rose inside her, making her want to claim Jackie. She wanted to wipe away any trace of another woman from Jackie's mind, and her own. The fact Jackie was with her now and not with Heather said more than words could.

She led Jackie into the house and down the hall to her bedroom. She had no idea how things would work out between them, but she wasn't about to go out without a fight. She would make sure it would be her hands Jackie would remember touching her.

Kayla shut and locked the door, then turned on the lamp on the bedside table. She wanted to see Jackie and she wanted Jackie to see her. Kayla moved in front of Jackie until they were so close she could feel the heat radiating between them. She leaned close and brushed her lips against Jackie's, increasing the pressure of her kiss until Jackie moaned and gripped Kayla's hip. Kayla pulled away, putting enough distance between them that Jackie couldn't touch. She grabbed the hem of her shirt and pulled it up over her head. She opened the front clasp of her bra and slipped the straps from her shoulders, letting it fall to the floor. She cupped her breasts in her hands and gave her nipples a squeeze.

Jackie stood at the end of the bed watching her. "Are you sure you want to do this?" Her voice was coarse and strained.

"Right now, what I want is you. I don't want to think, I don't want to worry, and I don't want to talk. What I want is your mouth against me and your hand inside me."

Jackie growled and licked her lips, her gaze locked on Kayla's breasts. Kayla's pulse raced, her desire fueled by the feral look in Jackie's eyes. She shed her jeans leaving only the thin layer of silk between her and complete revelation. She ran her hand between her legs, slipping her fingers beneath the thin fabric, and cupped herself. She stroked herself, feeling her clitoris swell beneath her fingers as she watched the storm brewing in Jackie's eyes.

Jackie clenched her teeth, holding back the tidal wave of desire tying her insides in knots. If she didn't touch Kayla soon, she would explode. Kayla's hand dipped beneath the black silk making Jackie's mouth water. She wanted to put her lips against the hot flesh beckoning her. She had to have Kayla. She wanted to feel Kayla's skin against her breasts and the wet folds beneath her tongue. Kayla's hand sank deeper and her breath hitched. Jackie's resistance shattered. She closed the distance between them and fell to her knees, pressing her lips against the back of Kayla's hand, still stroking against her clitoris. Jackie curled her fingers around the thin waistband of Kayla's panties, pulling them down her thighs in one swift motion. She pulled Kayla's hand away, replacing the rhythm of Kayla's fingers with her tongue. The instant her mouth enclosed the treasure, Kayla's legs began to tremble. Jackie cupped Kayla's ass in her hands as she pulled Kayla tighter against her mouth.

Kayla stroked the sides of her face as she rocked her hips in time with the strokes of Jackie's tongue. Jackie brushed her thumb against Kayla's opening, but before she could claim her prize, Kayla stepped away, breaking their connection. Jackie groaned in frustration. Kayla moved to the bed, lifted her knees and spread her legs. Moisture glistened against pink skin. Kayla's clitoris was hard and swollen, nestled between perfect pink lips.

"Take off your clothes," Kayla ordered.

Jackie fumbled with the buttons of her shirt as Kayla slowly moved her hand to stroke herself. Jackie ripped her sports bra and undershirt off in one swift motion, and hurriedly shucked off her jeans. Her skin burned with the heat of her need as her insides fluttered with anticipation of taking Kayla.

Jackie once again pushed Kayla's hand aside. She licked her tongue up the length of Kayla's shaft before tonguing her opening. Kayla whimpered. Jackie framed Kayla's sex with her hands, opening her farther, and sucked Kayla's clitoris into her mouth. She stroked the swollen clitoris with the tip of her tongue until Kayla's legs shook. Jackie's own clitoris throbbed in time with each beat of her heart, each stroke of her tongue. Kayla tasted so sweet. The sounds of her moans were like music to Jackie's ears, urging her into a frenzy.

Kayla pushed against Jackie's head as she squirmed against Jackie's mouth. Kayla gasped when Jackie pulled away, slipping her arm beneath Kayla's back, lifting her farther onto the bed. Jackie pushed Kayla's knees back and settled her shoulders beneath Kayla's legs. She braced herself against the bed as she took the weight and pressure of Kayla's legs against her shoulders. She stroked Kayla with her fingers, feeling the muscles contract against her hand.

"Please," Kayla whimpered. "Take me now."

Jackie slid into Kayla in one swift motion, filling her with one, then two fingers.

"Oh God, yes. More."

Jackie was lost in Kayla. The feel of her, the smell of her, the sound of her voice culminated into the perfect storm. Jackie had the feeling that she was a part of something bigger than her heart could hold. Sweat gathered on her back making the air feel cool against her heated skin. Her muscles burned with each thrust of her hand. Jackie's vision dimmed as her mind was flooded with a burst of color.

Jackie let Kayla's leg slip from her shoulders and moved up Kayla's body until the line between them blurred. Kayla's breath became her breath. Kayla's heartbeat became her own. Her body tensed as her orgasm began to coil in her belly like a firestorm ready to consume her.

Kayla's fingers dug into her back as her body tensed. Jackie felt Kayla's orgasm, as the small muscles contracted around her fingers. She fought to hold on to the rhythm that was Kayla as her own orgasm pulsed to life. Kayla shifted her leg, pressing into Jackie's clitoris. The sudden pressure and the tremors radiating through Kayla pushed Jackie over the edge.

Jackie groaned as her orgasm rocked through her. Her ears rang, her lungs burned, and her body sang with wave after wave of pleasure so pure she thought her heart would explode. Jackie collapsed onto Kayla, her body and soul satisfied.

Jackie's hot breath caressed Kayla's skin. Kayla clung to Jackie, her arms and legs still wrapped possessively around her. She had given everything and hadn't been disappointed in Jackie's response. She shuddered as another aftershock rolled through her belly. She had given herself to Jackie, heart and body, and had never felt more alive than in this moment. Jackie's lips brushed lightly against her neck as she mumbled something incoherent. Kayla brushed her fingers through the damp strands of Jackie's hair, relishing the feel of Jackie's skin on her skin. Jackie rolled to her side clinging tightly to

Kayla, her hand resting on Kayla's hip. Jackie's eyes fluttered closed as Kayla listened to the changes in her breathing. She wanted to watch Jackie sleep but couldn't fight the lure of rest. She placed a kiss to Jackie's lips and drifted into sated slumber.

❖

Jackie startled at the sound of a door slamming inside the house. "Kayla!"

Kayla jumped up, hastily wrapping herself in her robe as she ran to the door.

"Oh God, K, I think he's going to kill me."

Jackie watched with growing confusion as Kayla placed her hands on Jen's shoulders to make her stand still.

"Jen, look at me. What are you talking about?"

"It's Mike. I think he's figured out where I'm staying. He sent me these crazy text messages. At first he was just calling me terrible names and accusing me of cheating on him. But just now he started threatening to kill himself. He sent me a picture of him with a gun to his head with the text that he was going to take me with him."

Jen was shaking and tears streamed down her cheeks.

"Come into the living room and sit down, and let me see the messages," Kayla said reaching for the phone.

Jackie jumped out of bed and grabbed her clothes. The sudden shock of being woken in the middle of the night and the idea that some lunatic might come there with a gun had her heart racing. Her muscles were coiled in tight knots ready to react to the threat. Jackie pushed into her jeans and grabbed her boots as she stumbled down the hall.

"Good God, Jen. How long has he been doing this to you?" Kayla said, holding Jen's cell phone in her hand.

Jen's eyes were wide with fear. "It's never been this bad before."

"Do you recognize where he is in this photo?" Kayla asked.

Jen nodded. "He's at home. That's the bedroom. I can see our wedding picture on the wall behind him."

Kayla reached for the home phone.

"What are you doing?" Jen asked her eyes wide with fear.

"Calling the police."

"You can't. That'll just make him even crazier," Jen cried.

"I have to do this, Jen. He is threatening to kill himself and you. He has a plan and a weapon. I have to call the police."

Jen's knees buckled. She half sat and half fell as she crumpled into a chair.

Jackie was a bit shell-shocked by this sudden change of events, but she had clearly heard Jen say this guy knew where she was, and that meant they were all in danger.

"Look, call me crazy," Jackie said calmly, "but if this guy is coming after you, shouldn't we get out of here?"

Both women stared at her with confused expressions as if she were speaking a foreign language.

"We can call the police on the way to my place. You can both stay there until this blows over."

No one answered. They just continued to stare at her.

Jackie threw her hands in the air palms up and shrugged. "What?"

"That's a good idea," Kayla said as if the information was just beginning to sink in. "Go get your things, Jen."

When Jen didn't move, Kayla grabbed her hand, dragging her to her feet. "Come on, Jen, move."

Jen seemed to get with the program and went to her room to pack.

"Are you sure about this?" Kayla asked Jackie.

"Do you have a better idea?"

Kayla shook her head. "No, but you don't have to do this."

"Well, I don't think we should hang around here arguing about it. I don't want to be anywhere near this place if this nut shows up."

Kayla kissed her. "Thank you."

Jackie's insides were shaking. It was as if every cell in her body had been electrically charged. The hairs on the back of her neck were standing at attention and she had the urge to run. She clenched her jaw. What had she gotten herself into this time?

❖

Jen's phone rang as they were pulling into the apartment complex behind Jackie. Kayla grabbed the phone before Jen had a chance to answer the call.

"What are you doing?" Jen asked.

"You can't answer. It'll only make things worse. He's trying to blackmail you emotionally so you'll do what he wants. If you feed into this behavior, things will only get worse. Let the police handle it."

Kayla hated the fear in Jen's eyes and she hated Mike for putting it there. She took Jen's hand and squeezed. "It's going to be okay. Trust me."

Jen held on to her hand as if her life depended on it. "What if he does it? It'll be my fault. I shouldn't have left."

Kayla wanted to swear. She wanted to throw something, she wanted to kick Mike's ass, but that wouldn't help Jen right now. "Jen, honey, you didn't cause this. He's trying to control you by scaring you. That's exactly what he wants you to think. If he does anything, it's all on him. We called for help. That was the only safe thing you could have done."

Jen let out a ragged breath and Kayla imagined she could hear the tears beating against Jen's heart.

"I'm sorry." Kayla put the car in park and slid her arm around Jen's shoulders. When Jen calmed she pulled away. "Come on, let's go inside."

Kayla and Jackie sat on the sofa with Jen between them as they listened to the belligerent voice messages on speakerphone. Mike was ranting and spewing violent threats. They heard the moment when the police arrived at his house, and he cursed Jen for calling them. The message seemed to go on forever, until he finally played the last card he had. Over the phone they could hear the police at the door and the distinct sound of a gun being cocked. Then came the single shot and the line went dead.

Jen screamed and buried her face in Kayla's shoulder.

"He didn't do it," Jackie said, her voice eerily calm even to her own ears. This was seriously messed up, but she knew the type. She put her hand on Jen's back. "He didn't do it."

Jen turned and faced Jackie, her expression pleading and desperate. "Why do you say that? How do you know?"

Jackie sat ramrod straight on the sofa staring at Jen. "It was a trick to screw with you. If he'd done it, the phone wouldn't have gone dead right away. We would have heard…" Jackie paused. "We would have heard the gun hit the floor, something, but not an immediate end to the call."

Jen sat up a little more and clutched at Jackie's arm. She brushed at her tears with the palm of her hand. "How can you know that?"

Jackie grimaced. "Let's just say, I've met his type before. People who are serious about killing themselves just do it. They don't waste time making tons of phone calls making threats that would get them stopped. This was never about killing himself—it was about screwing with your head."

Kayla didn't miss the look of pain that dulled Jackie's eyes. *Oh, Jackie, what happened to you?* Kayla picked up the phone and called the police station. She knew most of the officers and they knew she had reported the threat. She talked with several people and was transferred from one hold to another until she had some answers.

Jen sat huddled in the corner of the sofa with her knees drawn to her chest. Her eyes were red rimmed from crying and her skin was pale and drawn. Kayla hated Mike for doing this to Jen. She pinched the bridge of her nose between her thumb and forefinger in frustration when she was put on hold yet again. Her mind was racing. No matter what happened now, this incident was going to cause a big mess, and she was right in the middle of it.

Having finally gotten some answers, Kayla ended the call and turned to face Jen and Jackie.

"Okay. Here's what we know." She kneeled in front of Jen. "He's fine. He told the police he was cleaning the gun and it went off as he was putting it away when he heard them at the door. He played innocent, but with the text messages we provided them and the photograph of him holding the gun to his head, they took him into custody and charged him with unlawful discharge of a firearm in the city limits. They want you to come to the station tomorrow to give a statement. I'll meet with the DA and the judge to recommend a psychiatric assessment. He'll be on suicide watch tonight."

Kayla took a deep breath and squeezed Jen's knee. "He's okay, Jen. We'll do what we can to help Mike and keep you safe."

The tears that had dimmed Jen's eyes were now replaced with cold resolve. "I can't believe he made me think he was dead. What kind of person does that?"

Kayla didn't answer.

"A selfish bastard, that's who does that." Jackie's voice was hard and void of compassion. "He doesn't care about anyone but himself."

"What do I do?" Jen pleaded, looking now to Jackie for answers.

"Get out. Get a restraining order, a divorce, change your phone number, or block his calls, whatever it takes for him to get lost."

Kayla saw something flash in Jackie's eyes and wondered if Jackie was still talking to Jen.

"Jen, why don't you get yourself cleaned up and try to get some rest?" Kayla said to defuse the building tension. She took Jen by the hand and pulled her to her feet. "I'm sure a hot shower will help clear your head. We'll know more tomorrow. Right now everyone's safe."

Jen nodded and wrapped her arms around Kayla.

Jackie sighed. "Come on, I'll show you the bathroom."

Kayla watched Jen follow Jackie down the hall. She knew Jackie's reactions were fueled by her experience with her father. This was going to be a very long night.

Chapter Fourteen

Kayla sat next to Jackie on the sofa, gently stroking the back of her hand. "Are you okay?"

"Sure. Why wouldn't I be?"

Kayla knew the evening's events had been hard on Jackie and she didn't know how much she would want to share, but Jackie needed to talk some things out or her rage was going to cause her serious problems.

"It's been an emotional night. I'm sorry we got you in the middle of all this."

Jackie laced their fingers together. "I'm glad you agreed to come here. I don't want to think of what could have happened if he'd come to your house."

Jackie's words were soft and a storm of emotions brewed behind the shifting shades of her hazel eyes. Instinctually Kayla knew she had to be gentle with her questions. She had to let Jackie come to her. She had to let Jackie share her feelings in her own time. Right now she wanted to reassure Jackie, make her feel safe.

"I'm glad I'm here too."

Jackie wanted to run away from the haunting memories flashing through her mind. There was no point pretending she hadn't revealed herself through her reactions to Jen. Kayla was too observant not to see through her. Kayla had to be wondering why. But she hadn't asked and Jackie was both relieved and disappointed. She had the unsettling desire to tell Kayla things she never told anyone.

"You're not going to play therapist on me now, are you?"

"I may ask questions, but it's because I want to help. I can tell this has brought up some things from your past. I know you have to be thinking of your father tonight."

A muscle jumped at the side of Jackie's jaw and she pursed her lips as if holding back her words.

"I got the impression your dad must have pulled stunts like this too."

Jackie sighed. "He did things like this to my mother. He even threatened to kill me a few times if she left him. He knew how to get to her."

"I'm sorry."

"Yeah. If Jen has a brain in her head, she'll get away from this guy."

Kayla nodded. Jackie was right, but Jen was the only one who could make that call.

"I hate that this has brought up hurtful memories for you. This isn't what I had in mind when I asked you to come over. And it certainly isn't how I wanted us to wake up together."

Jackie frowned. "Me either."

Kayla snuggled closer. "Thank you for letting us come here. She's really been through a lot."

"I can imagine." Jackie considered her next question before asking, "So, what's this guy's deal? Is he just the standard drunk who thinks he can come home and take his sorry life out on everyone else, or is he just an abusive bastard?"

With everything that had happened, Kayla didn't think Jen would mind if she told Jackie the truth. When Kayla spoke, her tone was calm and neutral. "Mike has a lot of issues, most of which are due to his prescription drug use. In the beginning Jen didn't know. He works on the road and is gone most of the time, so he was able to hide a lot from her until the physiological and psychological addiction began to change his personality and take over their lives. It's the usual story of trying to find a balance between loving someone and being an enabler. You saw how manipulative he can be, and he knows how to use her emotions to put the blame for everything on her."

"Jesus," Jackie muttered through gritted teeth.

"Maybe with court intervention he can get the help he needs."

"Right," Jackie said trying to fight the bile that was building in her throat.

"You don't think that's the answer?"

Jackie shrugged. "I've seen it before. Guys like him will say what people want to hear until they get what they want, and then they go back to the booze, the drugs, and the violence."

Kayla could almost feel the rage bubbling beneath the surface of Jackie's skin, the old memories pushing her into fight mode.

Jackie stood. "I need to make sure the guest room is ready."

Kayla was surprised by the sudden change and she stood to follow. Kayla heard the pain and anger in Jackie's voice. She was used to this reaction from people who had been hurt by loved ones dealing with the disease of addiction, most often the spouse or child of an addict.

"We could go home now. Mike is in jail for the night. I don't want to create any problems for you."

When Jackie looked back at Kayla, all the rage that had been swarming in her eyes evaporated like a fading mist until nothing was left but pain and fear.

"I'd like you to stay," Jackie said, her voice unusually soft.

Kayla pressed her palms against Jackie's chest and felt a slight tremor ripple beneath her fingertips. Jackie seemed so fragile in that moment, a stark contrast to her usual confidence and strength. The fact that Jackie had asked was telling in itself. There was no way she could leave now.

"There's nowhere else I would rather be tonight." Kayla kissed Jackie with the faintest brush of her lips.

Jackie smiled against Kayla's lips. "Why don't you go get settled in the bedroom? I just heard the shower shut off. Jen will be out in a minute and you can have the bathroom next."

Kayla nodded. Her head swooned at the thought of her body pressed against Jackie's. She quickly tried to push the emotion aside when she remembered Jen would be in the room across the hall. At least she could hold Jackie close while she slept.

Jackie sat on the edge of the bed staring at the floor. So much had happened in this one day that she had difficulty getting her head around it. Maybe Kayla could chase away the emptiness that was slowly swallowing her up.

She raked her fingers through her hair and rubbed her temples, trying to make sense of what was happening in her life. Where did all this drama come from? Things were so much simpler before. She heard a slight rustle and looked up as Kayla stepped into the room. The instant she saw Kayla standing before her all thought slipped out of her mind. Kayla was wrapped in a blue silk robe that fell to midthigh and molded to the curves of her body, hinting of the supple flesh that lay beneath. Jackie's heart ached when she saw the vulnerability and questions in Kayla's eyes. Kayla clutched the robe to her chest.

Jackie's hands fell to her lap and she smiled up at Kayla. "You're beautiful," she said with a hitch in her voice.

Kayla relaxed her grip on the robe and moved slowly across the room. Jackie reached out and pulled her closer until Kayla's knees brushed against the inside of her thighs.

"I wasn't sure I should...I thought maybe you would prefer I stayed with Jen tonight."

The heat of Kayla's body warmed Jackie's hands though the thin layer of silk. She wanted to feel that warmth surround her body. Jackie leaned her head against Kayla's stomach and wrapped her arms around her protectively. Jackie moaned when Kayla ran her hands through her hair and cradled her head against her as she stroked her. There was nothing sexual in the exchange. This tenderness was much deeper.

Jackie's chest swelled as tension vibrated through her muscles. She needed Kayla. She needed her comfort, and Kayla offered to give just that.

After several long moments, Kayla pulled Jackie's head back, framing her face in her hands. Her usually vibrant eyes were dull and unfocused.

"Tell me what's going on with you," Kayla whispered.

"It's nothing. I'm just worried about you."

Kayla shook her head and kissed Jackie lightly. "No, it's more than that. There's something else. I can see the pain swimming behind your eyes like a ghost. You can talk to me."

Jackie buried her face in Kayla's neck and drew in a deep breath. "I don't want to talk. It's been a crazy day and I don't want to think about any of it anymore. I just want to be with you."

Kayla knew Jackie was holding back but respected her request for time. Kayla gently undressed Jackie and encouraged her under the covers. She pulled the silk belt loose and opened the robe allowing it to slip from her shoulders to pool at the floor.

A spark ignited in Jackie's eyes as Kayla undressed. Kayla heard the change in Jackie's breathing and watched the rise and fall of her chest, witnessing the subtle hardening of her nipples through the thin fabric of the sheet. Jackie would share her secrets in her own time. Kayla's own uncertainty faded and was replaced with warmth and need. Perhaps this was exactly what they both needed to put the demons of the day to rest.

Kayla slid beneath the covers, her body brushing against warm skin. She wrapped her arms around Jackie and pulled her head to her chest, cradling her against her breasts.

"You're an angel," Jackie whispered before pressing her cheek against Kayla's neck, brushing her lips against the warm flesh.

Kayla stroked Jackie's hair with her fingers, then along the line of her jaw, along her ear, and the thick line of muscle that ran from below her ear to her shoulder. She continued to stroke and explore Jackie's shoulders, her back, and down the arm that lay possessively around Kayla's waist. The tension in Jackie's body slowly melted as she kneaded each muscle.

Jackie moaned into the soft skin of Kayla's neck and pressed her body closer. Kayla's heart quickened as Jackie's hand slid down her back to the curve at the base of her spine. Kayla surrendered as Jackie coaxed her legs apart, pushing her thigh against Kayla's center. Kayla mirrored the movement, wrapping her legs around Jackie.

Jackie groaned and pressed harder into Kayla, gliding against her until the building pleasure made her want to cry out. Their touches were no longer drawn from the need to comfort, but by the burning need of passion. Kayla dug her fingers into Jackie's back and felt her shudder. In answer, her own orgasm erupted and waves of pleasure surged through her. She held on to Jackie, riding each wave of bliss. Kayla pressed her cheek to Jackie's chest, listening to the thundering of her heart, hoping the tenderness of their connection would be enough to quiet the pain lurking in the shadows.

❖

Jackie was irritable and jumpy, and struggled to get through the workday. The slightest sound or unexpected touch sent her heart racing. She looked at the clock on the wall every two minutes and she had difficulty concentrating on the simplest tasks. She hadn't heard from Kayla all day, and not knowing what was happening was driving her crazy.

It was time for a break. She sat on a bench in the locker room, her elbows on her knees, her hands dangling limp in front of her.

"Are you okay?"

Jackie jumped. She hadn't heard Heather come in.

"My, my, someone's jumpy today. What's got you all wound up, tiger?" Heather stepped around Jackie, gliding her finger across Jackie's shoulder as she walked. "I was hoping we could get"— Heather paused—"reacquainted."

Jackie bit back a retort, not in the mood to deal with Heather at the moment.

"Look, Heather," she finally said holding her hands up palms forward indicating she wanted some distance. "I'm kind of seeing someone right now, and I would really like it if we could keep our contact with each other strictly professional."

Heather pursed her lips in a mock pout. "Too bad," she said after giving Jackie a long appraisal. "You look like you could use a little extracurricular activity to let off a little steam."

Jackie flashed back to her life before meeting Kayla. Only a few short weeks ago what Heather was proposing would have been exactly what she was looking for. Things had seemed so simple then. She never had to worry about anyone, she didn't have to deal with sharing things about her past, and she had always satisfied the dull ache of loneliness with no-strings-attached sex.

She flashed back to the look of hurt she had seen on Kayla's face the night before, and remembered the compassion Kayla had shown despite her own pain. Jackie conjured the image of Kayla lying in her bed and the heart-melting look of desire that seemed so raw Jackie was consumed by it.

Perhaps for the first time in her life she had a chance at something real. A quick tryst with Heather wouldn't satisfy the ache in her soul. Only one person could heal her.

"No thanks."

Jackie grabbed her bag and her cell phone from the locker and pushed past Heather. She could feel Heather's hot gaze on her back as she left the locker room.

"Let me know if you change your mind," Heather called out as Jackie slipped through the door.

Outside Jackie punched in Kayla's number. When the call was directed to voicemail her anxiety ratcheted up another notch. She knew Kayla was meeting with the court officials about Jen's husband and she worried about Kayla's safety if things didn't work out.

She slammed the car door so hard her truck rocked from side to side. Her ears popped from the compression of air trapped in the small space. What was she doing? It was obvious these feelings for Kayla meant nothing but trouble. She didn't need this kind of stress in her life. She couldn't go back to a life of fear and worry. She was torn. Her emotions were all mixed up. When she was with Kayla it was easy to believe things could be different, but the reality was that she was still a scared little girl running from her past.

Stop it, Jackie snapped to herself. She started the truck and made her way to the university gym. She had two hours before her next client and she needed to blow off some steam. Since sex was out of the question, a workout would have to do.

The familiar sound of her phone made her heart jolt. She fumbled with the phone, almost driving onto the curb. Righting the truck, she pulled to the side of the road and managed to answer the call. "Hello."

"Hi," the familiar smooth voice crooned through the phone, "do you have a minute?"

"Yes," Jackie responded quickly, relief rushing through her at the sound of Kayla's voice. "I'm glad you called. I was worried."

"I was afraid of that, but there really is no reason to be. I promise."
Jackie smiled. "Tell me what happened today."

Kayla's sigh was clear even through the phone, and Jackie braced herself for what was to come.

"Well, it's been a little crazy here, but the judge ordered a psychological evaluation and granted the restraining order for both me and Jen."

"I feel a *but* coming."

"Well, Jen is on her way out of town for a while so she should be safe now that Mike has no idea where she is, but the judge let him go. He has a set amount of time to get the evaluation done, but they couldn't hold him since he hadn't made direct contact with anyone and hadn't made any attempt to harm himself. He convinced the judge he was angry with his wife for leaving him and acted irrationally but had no intention of harming anyone."

Jackie gripped the steering wheel until her knuckles turned white. "That's typical."

"It isn't ideal, I agree, but it's a start."

Jackie swore under her breath. "I want you to stay with me for a while. I don't like this."

"It isn't me he's after. I'm okay."

Jackie closed her eyes and tried to keep her voice calm. "Maybe, but he's going to be pissed and he's going to be looking to share the pain, and you'll be the one in his sights if he can't get to her."

"I can't run away every time someone is a little off balance. I can take care of myself."

Jackie bit down on her tongue until she tasted blood. She knew she had to get a grip on her emotions or there was no way Kayla would trust her. When she spoke again, it wasn't anger that caused her voice to crack, it was fear.

"I know you're perfectly capable of taking care of yourself. But please, do this for me."

The silence on the phone seemed interminable and Jackie held her breath waiting for Kayla's answer.

"Well, I guess it would give me an excuse to spend more time with you. And I leave for a conference in a few days anyway."

Jackie gasped. The fear that had been driving her mad all day was finally lifting its grip on her chest. Kayla was safe...for now. "Thank you."

Kayla felt out of place sitting in Jackie's living room alone. Jackie was supposed to meet her an hour ago, but had been called in on a consult for a football injury and wasn't sure when she would be able to leave work.

Kayla considered going home, but she had made a promise to Jackie and she wouldn't break it. Sometimes it was difficult to figure out the right thing to do. She studied the shelves of books. Maybe she could pass the time with a good book. She thumbed through the titles until she came upon a photo album tucked in amongst the volumes. Curiosity pricked at the back of her mind. Should she look through the pages like a voyeur peeking into private moments of Jackie's life? The album *was* in the living room in plain sight. It didn't seem like something Jackie didn't want people to see. Between her boredom and curiosity, it wasn't hard to convince herself to look.

She opened the cover and perused the images. She stopped on a photo of Jackie in a small group. Her head was tossed back in a burst of laughter and her arm was draped casually across the shoulders of two other women who were in equal stages of laughter. Kayla's heart warmed. There were photos of Jackie engaged in various sports, her long lean figure twisted in graceful maneuvers of athletic feats. There was a picture of her holding a mountain bike over her head, covered in mud. Another was of Jackie clinging to the face of a rock like Spider-Man. Some were of Jackie at work. Kayla studied these carefully, mesmerized by the intensity of Jackie's focus on her client frozen in some complicated movement.

As Kayla browsed the images she was struck by the passion and intensity Jackie poured into everything she did. She thought back to the day of the regatta and the pictures she herself had taken of Jackie at the finish line. Jackie's face had glowed with determination and focus. There was a spark in her eyes that was charged with energy and life. It was that intensity that drew Kayla to her like a moth to a flame.

Several pages near the back were empty and Kayla started to put the album away thinking she had come to the end of the picture show. But when she started to close the book, a photo slipped out of the back. This picture was much older and captured the image of a little girl holding hands with a tall thin woman who looked very much like Jackie. Kayla turned the album over and opened the back cover. More photos of Jackie's childhood were tucked loosely in a small envelope. She explored one photo of Jackie as a young girl by a sparse-looking Christmas tree. Her long hair was tangled and she held the front of her nightgown twisted in her fists. Jackie couldn't have been more than seven or eight and Kayla was struck by the forlorn look on Jackie's face. As she studied the images, she realized Jackie's expression was the same in all the others. Her big eyes seemed distrustful and wounded. The pictures suggested Jackie never smiled as a child. Kayla's unease and concern escalated when she came across one photo that made cold chills run up her spine. It was Jackie with a brute of a man. His face was twisted in a drunken smile, his eyes heavy lidded and red. One hand held a bottle of Wild Turkey, the other gripped Jackie's shoulder. Jackie sat on the floor at his feet, her legs curled up against her chest, her chin resting on her knees, and her little fists balled around her ankles.

Kayla was beginning to understand Jackie's reaction to the situation with Jen. *Oh, baby, what happened to you?* Her eyes lingered on the little girl crouched in the photo. She studied Jackie's hands balled into fists as if she was holding back her rage, ready to fight at a moment's notice.

Kayla looked up at the sound of the door as Jackie stepped into the apartment.

"Sorry I'm so late." Jackie stopped in the middle of the room, her eyes falling to the photo album in Kayla's lap.

Kayla smiled up at Jackie, trying to hide the concern and sympathy she felt for the sad little girl in the photographs. "Hey, I was beginning to wonder if you were ever coming home."

Jackie hesitated as if she wasn't sure how to respond. Kayla could tell by the stiffness in her posture that she wasn't happy to find her going through the mementoes of her childhood.

"I didn't mean to pry," Kayla said lifting the album. "I can't believe all the things you've done. You're quite the athlete."

This seemed to give Jackie something to grasp. A smile curved the corners of her mouth but didn't reach her eyes. "Wow, you must have really gotten bored if you've had to entertain yourself with those."

Jackie kissed Kayla on the cheek. As she straightened she lifted the photo album from Kayla's hands, closed it, and placed it back on its shelf.

"I'm sorry if I upset you. Do you want to talk about it?" Kayla asked.

"Not really," Jackie answered.

Jackie's voice was cool and distant as if it was all she could do to speak. Kayla knew Jackie wasn't ready to let her in on her past, but she wasn't used to letting questions go unanswered and she cared enough to want to know about Jackie's past. Had she earned the right to ask?

"Were those photos of your parents?"

Jackie swallowed hard and stepped away from Kayla. These were the questions she'd known were coming, but no matter how much she prepared she wasn't ready to answer.

"Yes."

"You look like your mother."

Jackie smiled. "Thanks."

"Were those taken in Florida?"

Jackie went to the fridge and got a beer and drank half on her way back to the sofa. "No. When those pictures were taken we still lived near here."

"Do you ever see him?"

"No. When I left, I left for good."

She watched Kayla watching her. She could almost read the questions as they formed in Kayla's thoughts and a chill began to creep up her spine.

"I'm sorry," Kayla said.

Jackie shook her head. "No need to be. It's all in the past now."

Kayla sat on the sofa and took her hand. The warmth of Kayla's fingers burned against her cold skin.

"I'm certain we'll find her."

Jackie's heart stopped. She had given up hope she would ever find her mother.

"I looked. She either doesn't want to be found or there isn't anything to find."

"It must be hard, not knowing."

Jackie sighed. "Yeah, it was. Look, I don't want to talk about this stuff anymore. Can you let it go?"

Kayla reached for Jackie's beer and took a drink, her lips slowly lifting into a mischievous smile. "It'll cost you."

Jackie was surprised by the change and more than a little curious. "What?"

"How about some wings to go with the beer?"

Jackie pursed her lips. "Hmm. No more questions?"

Kayla smiled. "For now."

Jackie kissed Kayla's chin. "Deal."

Chapter Fifteen

"Really, you don't have to do this, let me take you out to dinner."

Kayla had arrived at Jackie's apartment with groceries in hand, determined to cook.

"As nice as that sounds, I really want to stay in. It's been a grueling day and I'm going to be eating restaurant food for the next two weeks. Besides, it's the least I can do for imposing on you all week."

Kayla took Jackie's chin between her thumb and fingers and placed a quick kiss on her lips. "Thank you for taking care of Jen and me, that was very sweet. And you have been very considerate despite having me intrude into your space."

Kayla grinned at the blush coloring Jackie's cheeks and lifted her mouth to Jackie's for another kiss.

Jackie grinned. "I think that worked out in my favor. I hate sleeping alone."

"Really? How do you usually remedy that issue?" Kayla regretted the question the moment the words were out of her mouth. "Never mind. I don't want to know the answer."

Jackie laughed. "Actually, I think it's a new affliction. You seem to be the only remedy."

"Hmm." Kayla smiled. "Good answer," she said and stole another kiss.

She moaned as Jackie's hands gripped her hips and pulled her against her, creating a luscious pressure in her center that made her pulse inside.

"You know, I'm really not all that hungry," Jackie murmured as she sucked Kayla's earlobe into her mouth.

"Oh, really?" Kayla leaned back and appraised Jackie. "You look hungry to me."

Jackie shuddered. "God, you have no idea what you do to me."

Kayla laughed. "Wait till you taste dinner."

Jackie flashed a wicked grin and raised a suggestive eyebrow. "What's for dessert?"

Kayla brushed her finger across Jackie's lower lip. "You are."

Jackie groaned as a familiar wetness flooded her middle and soaked her jeans. God, this woman was heaven. She licked her lips imagining the taste of Kayla on her tongue. "Tease."

Kayla smiled and turned her back to the groceries that lay scattered across the counter. She finished the salad and reached to take the marinated chicken from the fridge when her phone buzzed, the vibration amplified by the granite countertop as her phone danced across the surface. She looked at the screen and frowned.

"What is it?" Jackie asked.

Kayla shrugged as she answered the call.

"This is Kayla McCormick."

A stern look of concentration creased Kayla's brow as she listened. She opened her mouth as if to say something but no words came out.

Kayla lowered the phone and punched in several digits before bringing the phone back to her ear.

"Yes, I understand. I'll be right there. Thank you."

By the time Kayla hung up the phone Jackie was about to pounce. She sat rigid against the back of her chair, her fists clenched on her knees like she'd done as a child when things happened that she couldn't control. Something was wrong—she could feel it.

"I'm sorry, but I have to bail on dinner. Someone broke into my house. That was my security company. The police are already there."

"Shit." Jackie stood abruptly. "I'm coming with you."

"You don't have to do that."

"I know I don't have to, but I want to. You shouldn't go there alone."

Relief washed over Kayla when Jackie offered to go. She put the groceries in the fridge and grabbed her keys.

Jackie closed her hand around Kayla's, sliding the keys from her fingers. "I'll drive."

To Kayla's relief, Jackie didn't let go of her hand, instead lacing their fingers together, letting her know she wasn't alone.

❖

Splinters of wood jutted out at odd angles around the frame of Kayla's front door. She stood transfixed as reality arrested her ability to take another step. The door stood open and the lights were on inside the house. Two patrol cars were parked in front of the house, and flashing blue lights made the image in front of her seem like something out of a scene in a movie. But this was no cinematic production, this was her home, and it had been violated.

A knot of fear grew in the pit of Kayla's stomach as she looked into her living room, and a chill ran down her spine as an officer stepped up beside her.

"Ms. McCormick, I'm sorry about all this. I know this isn't easy, but can you think of anyone who would do this?"

Kayla frowned. "What do you mean?"

"Well this wasn't your run-of-the-mill burglary. This guy was clearly sending you a message."

Kayla was in shock but the officer's comment filtered through the fog clouding her thoughts. She looked up at him. He was so young. He couldn't be more than twenty-three. His shoulders were squared and his posture was rigid in an attempt to show authority.

Kayla shook her head. "I'm sorry, could you say that again? I'm having a little trouble taking this all in."

He nodded curtly and gestured toward the room with his palm up. "We need you to take a look around and see if anything is missing."

As if fighting her way out of a dream, Kayla tried to focus on the words, tried to make sense of what was happening. "I'm sorry, but did you say something about a message?"

The officer nodded again and glanced toward the back of the house. "I can show you as soon as we finish in the master. We're still processing that room, so I can't let you in there just yet." He shifted his stance to move directly in front of her line of sight, drawing her attention back to him.

"Is there anyone you can think of who might want to harm you? Any problems with a boyfriend?" He glanced over Kayla's shoulder at Jackie. "Or girlfriend?"

Kayla blinked at the absurdity of the question.

"No. I assure you that isn't the case." She sighed. "But I did have an incident this week involving my work and the husband of a colleague of mine, a friend. I have a restraining order against him. His name is Mike Harris."

The officer wrote down the information and Kayla provided details about the incident.

"Could you tell me about this message you mentioned?"

Before the officer could respond he was called to the back by another officer. He nodded and gestured for Kayla to follow.

Kayla's legs were like rubber. Her heart thundered against her chest so hard her body vibrated. Her hands shook and her skin was cold. She stopped at the door, her gaze falling on the words carved into the wall of her bedroom.

SHE'S MINE.

Kayla gasped. In an instant her emotions ricocheted around in her mind making the room spin. Her fear turned to rage. Why would anyone try to intimidate her this way? Her emotions flipped again and the rage was quickly replaced once again by fear, not for herself, but for Jen.

Mike obviously didn't know where Jen was and Kayla wasn't about to lead him to her.

"It's him. He wants Jen." Kayla glanced first at the officer, then to Jackie, who had moved into the room so silently that Kayla hadn't even felt her move.

Kayla wasn't sure what she saw etched in the lines at the corners of Jackie's eyes or in the set of her jaw, but her eyes were dark, emotionless voids. In the instant it took for Kayla to search Jackie's face, she felt the distance grow as if a giant cavern had opened up between them. She could feel Jackie withdraw, walling herself off.

Part of Kayla wanted to reassure Jackie. She wanted to make her believe everything would be all right, but for the first time in her life, she wasn't sure that was true. How could she convince Jackie everything was okay when she didn't believe it herself? Mike had crossed a line. He had not only harmed her physically, he had invaded her home, her sanctuary. There was no telling how far he would go or what he was capable of doing. As long as he was out there, she wouldn't be safe.

❖

Jackie followed Kayla through the house, surrounded by the methodical movements and chatter of the police officers on the scene. Her limbs were numb and she wasn't sure if what she was seeing was happening now or somewhere in her past. Kayla was the only thing keeping her tethered to reality. She could feel fear radiating off Kayla, her usually confident stride had become hesitant, and there was a faint tremble in Kayla's hand.

Something inside shifted and Jackie closed her left hand, expecting to feel the soft plush ear of the stuffed rabbit she had carried everywhere when she was a little girl. She flinched when her fingernails bit into the palm of her hand. Her father's voice echoed in her mind, laughing at her fear. He always knew how to use fear to control her.

Jackie stared at the words carved into the wall as she stepped past Kayla into the room. The words had been cut into the drywall in jagged fierce strokes. She imagined the rage and insanity behind the act and her mind shut down. She wanted to run away, but she wasn't a little girl anymore.

Jackie jumped at the faint brush of fingertips against her arm. Kayla peered at her, her eyes clouded with fear and worry. She slid her arm around Kayla's shoulders and guided her out of the room and down the hall until they were outside by the porch swing. Jackie was thankful for the comfort she found in the soft sway of the swing and the faint groan of the chain. She took Kayla's hand, hoping to feel something other than fear.

"Are you all right?" Kayla asked shakily.

Jackie forced a smile. "Shouldn't I be the one asking you that question?"

Kayla chuckled. "Maybe, but I asked first."

The playfulness fell away from Jackie's voice. "What are they going to do about this guy?"

Kayla's shoulders slumped and she sighed. "Unless there's some evidence it was him, I don't think there's anything they can do. He has thirty days to get the evaluation for the court, but until then…I don't know."

"He's trying to control you with fear."

Kayla nodded. "So far it's working."

"What are you going to do?"

Kayla thought about her answer and couldn't come up with anything. "I'm not sure. He wants Jen. I think he's trying to get me to lead him to her. I don't think he's really after me."

"You don't know that," Jackie said with an edge of anger in her voice. "He's backed into a corner and he thinks you're the way out. Right now you're the one he thinks stands between him and what he wants. If he removes you from the equation, he thinks he'll have Jen."

"That's a bit extreme, don't you think?"

"No, I don't."

Kayla stiffened and anger once again came to the forefront of her emotional battle. "What do you think I should do then, call him up and tell him where she is?"

Jackie slid her arm around Kayla's shoulders and pulled her close. "No. Of course I don't think that."

"What then? What am I supposed to do?"

"Drop it. Walk away. Don't go back to court. Let someone else take over that he doesn't know. Let him burn himself out."

Kayla felt heat rise in her cheeks and she pushed away from Jackie. She stared at her in disbelief.

"I can't just turn my back. I can't leave Jen to deal with this alone."

"Jen isn't dealing with it," Jackie snapped back. "She left. She's safe. She isn't the one with threats carved into her bedroom wall. She saw her way out and she took it. She left you."

Kayla bit down on her anger. She knew there was something more going on with Jackie, but she didn't know what exactly, and this wasn't the place to discuss it. The last thing she wanted to do was lash out at Jackie when she was obviously carrying so much of her own pain, her own fear.

"Are you sure we're still talking about Jen and me?"

Jackie paled. "Don't."

Kayla bit down on her lip and resolved not to let this come between them. "You're right, I'm sorry. Let's just see what the officers find. Maybe someone saw him here or his truck or anything else that might resolve this. If they can get enough for an arrest, I think the judge would push the order." She placed her hand on Jackie's thigh, needing to feel the warmth of her body to quell the chill that had settled between them. "Right now, let's just finish this so we can get out of here." Uncertainty knotted in her throat as she realized Jackie might not want her to go back to the apartment with her. "Unless you'd rather I didn't."

Jackie jerked as if something had struck her. "What? No. You can't stay here. Of course I want you to come back to my place."

Kayla was relieved. She didn't understand this sudden need for Jackie to want her, this unrealistic fear that Jackie might walk out of her life. She admitted her feelings for Jackie had grown over the weeks since they'd met but something had shifted, and she had feelings stirring that she would have to analyze more closely later.

"Okay." Kayla sighed.

Jackie took Kayla's hand. The urge to protect her was so strong she struggled not to clench her fist. The feel of Kayla's skin against hers was enough to hold her fear at bay, for now. She needed to take Kayla home. She needed to hold her, feel her body next to her, be inside her, and fall asleep with her in her arms. Maybe then she could silence the haunting memories from her past that bit into her skin like a thousand pricks of a knife.

Jackie was quiet on the drive back to her apartment as she tried to sort her thoughts and feelings into past and present. She jerked when Kayla reached across the distance and touched her arm.

"Want to tell me what you're thinking about? You're so tense your muscles are like stone."

Jackie let out a breath. "I can't help but imagine what could have happened if you'd been home when he came looking for you."

Kayla's fingers squeezed lightly against her arm but provided little comfort. She knew Kayla was frightened and she didn't want to add to everything she was already dealing with. Kayla's hand was cold against her skin. She took Kayla's hand in her own and laced their fingers together, lifting Kayla's hand to her lips and brushing a kiss across her knuckles. "Are you cold?"

Kayla's voice was barely a whisper when she answered, "I don't know."

Jackie felt a slight tremble in Kayla's hand. Instinctively she slowed the car and pulled into the parking lot of a convenience store. She stopped the car and looked at Kayla, trying to see her eyes through the dim light.

"Hey. You're safe now. I've got you." She slid her hand around the back of Kayla's neck and worried her fingers across the tense muscles. "I'm sorry I was being a blockhead. I know this isn't easy and I'm not helping with my brooding."

She stroked Kayla's cheek, struck by how fragile her smooth skin was beneath her touch.

"This feels like it's personal to you somehow," Kayla said, pressing her cheek into the palm of Jackie's hand.

Jackie held her breath, not wanting to bring her past into Kayla's world. "You are personal to me."

"No." Kayla shook her head. "It's more than that. This feels like an old pain. What happened to you?"

"It was a long time ago. It's not important now."

"Everything about you is important to me. If we are going to keep doing this, we have to start trusting each other."

Kayla's words were incongruous with everything Jackie had ever known. "It's late. Let's get back to the apartment. We can talk there."

Jackie brushed her thumb across Kayla's lips and forced herself to smile. Before she could put the car in drive Kayla spoke and the words made her heart ache.

"What did he do?"

Jackie gripped the steering wheel so tight it groaned in protest. She clenched her teeth until her jaw ached. She was frozen in that moment, unable to move.

Kayla reached across Jackie and shut off the car. Hesitantly she placed her hand over Jackie's, coaxing her to let go of the wheel. "Whatever happened," Kayla whispered, "I'm right here. I'm not going anywhere."

Jackie loosened her hand on the wheel and let it fall to her lap. It was hard to breathe, as if someone was sitting on her chest. She swallowed, trying to dislodge the lump that had formed in her throat. She tried to speak but her mouth was dry and it felt like her tongue was glued to the roof of her mouth.

"He was more than just the average drunk," she said, hearing her voice as if hearing it from far away. She paused and swallowed again. "Not just a drunk, but an angry drunk, a cruel man."

Jackie took a shuddering breath. "He liked to control people through fear. I learned what set him off most of the time and did everything I could to keep him happy when he was drinking, but it was never enough. Sometimes it was like a sport to him. He liked to beat on my mother, and when she was gone he created sick games to play using me as bait for his dogs. He'd lock me in cages and hoist me into trees and have his dogs tree me. I would spend hours suspended in the air while they growled and barked and leapt into the air trying to get to me. They would hit the cage and bite at me with gnashing teeth. He would sit nearby laughing, sometimes shooting into the air above my head."

Jackie fought to regain control. She couldn't believe she was telling Kayla this. Part of her wanted to tell her, needed to say the words, but the anger was boiling up from the past, spilling over like an overheated pot on a stove.

"So you can say I have a little experience with guys like Mike. I know what he's capable of," Jackie snapped.

"I'm so sorry, Jackie."

"I'm sure it's a story you've heard a thousand times in your practice."

"This is about you, and that's not the same thing."

"Well, I don't want you digging around in my past like I'm one of your clients. I'm tired and hungry and I'm ready to go home."

Kayla winced. Jackie was being harsh because she was too raw to temper her anger. She was glad when Kayla didn't push any further, but guilt quickly began to pick at her brain. She just couldn't handle the questions right now.

"Okay. You don't have to talk about anything if you don't want. I think food is a good idea. Maybe we could do takeout—I'm not much in the mood to cook now."

Jackie started the car, aware of the hurt in Kayla's voice and the cool distance between them.

Chapter Sixteen

Kayla woke to a faint buzzing sound. At first she thought she'd imagined it, but there it was again. She shifted from under Jackie's arm, cradling her possessively around her waist. Trying not to wake Jackie, Kayla slid out of bed and went to the dresser across the room. Her phone lay next to her wallet and her keys. As if on cue, her phone buzzed and Kayla picked it up before the sound of the vibration could wake Jackie. They'd had a tough night and she didn't want to get things stirred up again.

The screen was covered with text messages. Kayla clasped a hand over her mouth to stifle the gasp. The messages were from a number she didn't recognize, but it was clear who they were from.

Kayla pulled on a pair of sweats and a T-shirt and left the room, glancing once at Jackie before closing the door behind her. She read through the messages, her concern growing with each one. Mike was clearly unraveling and she feared he could be a danger to himself and most certainly someone else, and right now that someone else was her.

She considered who to call first. The police? Jen? Thank God, Mike hadn't followed her to Jackie's. She didn't want to imagine Jackie having to deal with any of this mess. She had already been through enough. Kayla listened as the phone rang, waiting for the call to go through. She glanced nervously down the hall, but heard no sound from the bedroom.

"Hello?" A sleepy voice said through the phone.

"Jen. Hey, it's me."

"Kayla? What's up? Uh…what time is it?"

"It's three in the morning, sweetie. We need to talk."

At five thirty, Kayla heard the bedroom door open. She looked up to see Jackie padding down the hall toward her in a pair of boxers and a T-shirt held out in front of her as she fumbled to get the garment on over her head. Kayla's heart warmed with simple adoration at the sight of Jackie so rumpled. When Jackie looked up, Kayla didn't miss the confusion and concern in her eyes.

"Hey," Jackie said as she fell onto the sofa beside Kayla to brush a kiss against her cheek. "What are you doing up?"

"I had some things I needed to settle first thing this morning and I didn't want to wake you."

Kayla ran her fingers across Jackie's cheek, pulled her head down against her chest, and played her hands through the silken strands of Jackie's tousled hair. Jackie was so warm, so strong, so right in her arms. Kayla closed her eyes and drew in the unique scent she had grown to know was purely Jackie, a hint of sunshine and sea air.

"I'm sorry I was such a bear last night. I'm sorry I upset you," Jackie said as she nuzzled against Kayla until she managed to have her head in Kayla's lap. A mischievous grin played at the corners of her mouth as her fingers worked beneath Kayla's T-shirt.

Kayla moaned when Jackie's lips brushed the tender skin of her stomach and played circles around her navel with her tongue. She relished the closeness and feared how much she had to lose. Her muscles tensed when Jackie's thumb rubbed across her nipple.

"Hmm," Jackie mumbled against Kayla's flesh. "What time do you have to go in today?"

Kayla brushed her fingers through Jackie's hair, bracing herself for Jackie's response to what she was about to tell her. "I'm taking the day off. I leave for the conference tomorrow, so I thought I'd use the time to pack and"—Kayla sucked in her breath as Jackie gave her breast a squeeze—"stuff."

Jackie chuckled. "Stuff? Is that a technical term in the psychology world these days?"

"Uh-huh."

Jackie's hands stilled and she pulled away, looking up at Kayla questioningly. "You didn't say anything about this yesterday. What changed? Don't get me wrong—I'm happy you're staying away, considering what happened last night. I just never imagined you would."

Kayla sobered, trying to think of how she should answer the question. She considered not telling Jackie about the text messages or her conversation with one of the detectives she knew, but that wasn't how she worked and Jackie meant too much to her not to tell her the truth.

"I've been on the phone most of the night putting together a safety plan on how to deal with Mike."

Jackie stiffened and Kayla's heart ached for what this was doing to Jackie.

"What kind of safety plan?"

Kayla closed her eyes briefly and took a deep breath. When she opened her eyes she met Jackie's questioning gaze. This wasn't going to be easy and she wasn't sure how Jackie was going to react. She was afraid this might be too much for Jackie. She could lose her.

"I think Mike has escalated into a pattern of classic stalking behavior. So I'm having my cell number transferred to the police department. They'll receive all my calls and any other messages I might get from Mike. I considered changing the number, but that sort of thing typically causes further escalation. As long as he thinks I'm receiving the messages and he can contact me when he wants, there's less risk he'll escalate further for now. This way we can monitor his behavior and not give away the distance I'm putting between him and me."

Jackie took Kayla's hand and stared at her palm as if it would reveal her secrets. When Jackie didn't say anything, Kayla continued.

"When Jen left, she shut off the only phone number he had for her. Not being able to reach her pushed him to go after me." Kayla sighed and picked up her phone. "I discovered these after you were asleep last night." Kayla handed Jackie the phone.

Jackie studied the screen, scrolling through the myriad of messages. By the time she finished reading, her hand was shaking. She tossed the phone onto the table. The explosive clatter might as well have been a gun going off.

"Son of a bitch!"

Jackie stood and paced across the floor, pushing her fingers roughly through her hair. Halfway across the room she stopped abruptly. "Why is this guy still out there? Why hasn't he been arrested? Surely this is enough for the police to pick him up."

"They don't know where he is. He's off the grid for now. The police have been looking for him all night."

"Fuck!" Jackie resumed pacing. "So you're telling me this guy's out there waiting to get his hands on you and there's nothing we can do?"

Kayla shook her head. "For now I'm going to keep a low profile. I won't go anywhere he would expect me to be. I've notified my work and they're taking their own precautions. Jen knows too."

Jackie clenched and unclenched her fists several times. At last she seemed to settle on one thought and froze. "Are you still going to the conference?" Jackie said in a trembling voice.

Kayla sighed heavily. Her lungs were tight as if they were filling with sand. The fatigue and stress weighed heavily on her. "I'm hoping they catch him before then."

"And if they don't?" Jackie pushed.

"I don't know. I need to go."

"Kayla, that's not much time. You can't go. You'll be a target. Did he know about the conference? Was Jen supposed to go too?"

"Yes," Kayla answered, bracing for the verdict that would seal her fate.

The roar in Jackie's ears made it difficult to think. How could this be happening? "Please don't go. Promise me you won't put yourself in this guy's path."

Jackie wasn't afraid to beg. She had begged her mother all those years ago to leave, to get them both away from her father, but her mother hadn't listened, and it might have cost her her life. Jackie cringed at the memory.

"I promise to do what I can to make sure everyone is safe," Kayla answered.

Jackie heard the conditions in Kayla's words. Then she heard her mother's voice making her own excuses for her decisions. *He doesn't mean it. I just have to do better. I'll make sure I don't make him angry anymore. I can make it better.*

Jackie let all her defenses fall. "My dad used to threaten to kill my mother if I didn't do what he said, or if I told anyone about the things he did. For years he would come home drunk and throw our dinner out the back door, yelling that it wasn't what he wanted or the temperature wasn't right, any excuse he could think of to be angry. At first he only hit my mother. As I got older he would come after me if she wasn't around. When I was eight, I came home from a friend's house and found him beating my mother on the living room floor. She was crying, begging him to stop. Blood covered her face. I screamed at him to stop. I hit him with my fists. I finally kicked him in the face and he rolled off her cursing and holding his bloody nose."

Jackie rubbed her face. "I tried to get her to leave him. We did once, for a while, but he wouldn't stop. He'd show up at her work until her manager finally let her go because he was scaring the customers. She tried to have him arrested, but by the time the police would show up, he'd be gone, or he'd act all nice so the police would let him go. With no job we couldn't afford a place to live, so she ended up going back to him. He told us we had nowhere to go, that no one cared about us, that we better shape up or he wouldn't be so nice the next time."

Kayla moved closer and took her hand. Jackie stared at Kayla's hand caressing hers. Would she be strong enough to hold it together now that the dam had broken, now that her past was exposed?

Jackie trembled. She closed her eyes against the memories playing out in her mind. "When I was twelve, my mother disappeared. I thought she'd finally had enough and left me to get away from my father. I don't know if she did or not. I can't be sure, but I don't believe she did. I believe she stayed too long. I believe things got out of hand while I was away at camp, and he killed her."

Kayla's grip on her hand tightened.

"He used to tell me I was next. That if I didn't act right, I'd get what my mother got. He'd laugh at me when I'd ask him what happened to her. He'd just say if he told me, he'd have to kill me."

Kayla was about to be sick. She couldn't imagine what Jackie's childhood had been like. She didn't want to think of Jackie enduring such pain. "Oh, sweetheart, I'm so sorry."

"I can't do it again, Kayla. Don't do this."

"I can't run away from this. This is different."

"How can you be such a hypocrite? You make a big deal of me jumping into a pool of water or putting myself out there to feel an adrenaline rush, things that make me feel alive, but then you won't even take yourself out of a situation that could get you killed. Do you think this makes you some kind of hero or martyr? Well, I think it makes you a fool. I can't be a part of this."

Kayla swallowed. Jackie's words stung. She understood what Jackie was telling her. She couldn't imagine what Jackie had gone through as a child and she didn't want to be the reason Jackie was reliving that pain now. But how could she make the nightmare stop? She reached for Jackie. Jackie pulled away. Kayla wanted to reassure her, she wanted to take her pain inside herself, and she wanted to protect her so she would never hurt again. But she couldn't do any of those things.

"Look, we still have time. They might find him."

"And if they don't?" Jackie's words were like ice.

Kayla chewed her lip. She didn't have the answer Jackie wanted to hear. "I need to go to my house and get some things today. I know you're upset with me, but will you come with me?"

Jackie shook her head. "That's the last place you need to be right now."

"It's my home. I can't stay away forever. I just need a few minutes."

Jackie sighed. "Fine, I'll go. I'm sure you'd just do it anyway."

The sun was just pushing above the horizon when Kayla pulled into her drive. The house was still and looked as it did on the day she and her grandmother had discovered it five years earlier. She'd loved it from the moment she saw it. She smiled. It was good to be home.

The house was silent when Kayla opened the door and dropped her bag into the laundry room. She realized how quiet everything was and considered how empty the house felt. Maybe she should get a cat. It would be nice to have someone waiting to greet her at the door, someone to come home to at the end of the day.

Kayla pushed open the bathroom door and flipped on the light. An uneasy feeling pricked at the back of her brain as she looked around the room, evaluating the small space. Nothing was out of place, but the discomfort was still there, the smell was wrong. She fumbled with her keys until she grasped the pepper spray in her hand like a grenade, her thumb poised over the trigger.

"What is it?" Jackie asked.

"I don't know. It just doesn't feel right."

She inched her way down the hall stopping to peer into the bedroom as she passed. Nothing seemed out of place, but she knew something was wrong, she could feel it. She swallowed hard and pushed on toward the living room. The first sign of trouble was the scattering of beer cans across the living room floor. Kayla's heart lurched as she scanned the trash littering the floor, realizing they were not alone in the house. Her brain screamed for her to run, to get out of there as fast as she could, but something held her in place. She was done running.

Jackie slid a hand around Kayla's arm and squeezed. "Let's get out of here and call the police," she whispered.

Kayla shook her head and crept around the furniture to peer over the sofa. She stifled a scream when she saw Mike sprawled on the couch. He didn't move as she stepped closer. Considering the number of beer cans littering the room, he must be passed out.

Jackie picked up a bookend off a shelf and held it in her hand like a shot put.

Kayla crept to the side table and picked up the phone, her eyes landing on the pill bottles lying among the cans. A new fear crept over her. "Oh my God, no."

Jackie frowned and looked around to see what else there could be. She jumped when Kayla kicked the side of the sofa.

"Mike, wake up. Mike!"

Mike didn't move.

"Shit," Kayla said as she quickly dialed 911. She had no idea how long Mike had been in her house or how long he'd been unconscious—for all she knew, he could be dead. Great. The last thing she needed was to have her best friend's husband die on her sofa.

She felt Mike's wrist for a pulse. His hand was cold to the touch, but she felt the faint beat of his heart. "He's alive." Kayla leaned down and shook Mike. "Come on, Mike. You can be a prick if you want to, but don't you dare die in my living room."

The ambulance and police arrived at her house within minutes of the call. Kayla answered the questions she could, but she didn't know much.

An officer picked up the pill bottles and looked at her. "Are these yours?"

They were obviously hers—her name was printed as clear as day on the label. "Yes, it appears so. He must have found them in my medicine cabinet."

"I understand you have a restraining order against Mr. Harris. Can you tell me what he's doing here?"

Jackie stood close by, watching the EMTs hurriedly place Mike on a stretcher and wheel him out. She had a distant resolved look on her face that made Kayla's blood chill.

"He broke in here a few days ago. I've been staying with a friend since then. I had no idea he was here until I came in and found him like this," Kayla explained.

The officer nodded. "Pretty clever of him to hide out here while you were gone. I guess that's why he hasn't been picked up on the warrant. Looks like he's pretty lucky you came home when you did."

Kayla nodded, but she didn't think lucky was exactly how she would describe Mike's situation. Things didn't look good for him.

"I'd like to go to the hospital with him. I know his wife and I don't feel right leaving him alone like this."

The officer shrugged. "Suit yourself, but an officer will be there with him. We'll contact his family, so there's really no reason for you to be there."

"Let his family handle this, Kayla. You've done all you can do," Jackie said coolly.

Kayla sighed. There really wasn't anything else she could do, but she didn't feel right sending Mike off alone when she wasn't sure he would even survive. No matter what he'd done, he didn't deserve that. "Okay, but I have to at least call Jen and let her know."

"Suit yourself," the officer repeated, then walked away speaking into a radio clipped to his shirt at the shoulder.

Kayla sighed. "I hate this. How am I going to explain to Jen that her husband overdosed in my house?"

"Do you need me to do it? Other than the fact that he had the nerve to break into your house again, it can't be that big of a surprise."

Kayla shook her head. She didn't miss the anger seething in Jackie's voice. "No. It should be me, and I don't think anyone ever expects this to happen to someone they love," Kayla said, putting a little bite of her own in the words.

Jen answered with her usual chipper voice. "Hey, you, what's up?"

"Hey, Jen. I'm sorry I don't have good news. There's a problem."

"What's wrong?" Jen's tone went somber.

"I just found Mike unconscious on my couch. The ambulance just took him to the hospital. It doesn't look good, Jen. There were beer cans all over the place and he'd taken the pain pills and muscle relaxers that were in my medicine cabinet, and God knows what else."

"Oh my God."

Kayla closed her eyes and sighed. "Is there anything I can do? Anyone I can call for him?"

"No. I'll call his mother. It will be hours before I can get there. I'm sorry you had to find him, but thank you, K."

"I'm sorry too."

The call disconnected and Kayla was left feeling empty.

She watched an officer walk through her living room taking photos of the mess Mike had made of her house. She wanted to order them all to get out. She wanted her life back. She was tired of answering questions and feeling like she'd done something wrong. She hadn't asked for any of this.

Kayla did everything the officer asked. She was relieved when he finally had all the information he needed and was on his way out the door.

"Thank you, Officer."

"No problem, ma'am. You have a good evening."

Kayla turned back to Jackie and the mess scattering her living room. She hoped Mike would be okay and that this would put an end to his drama. It was time to get her life back together.

She looked at Jackie. "I can't believe it's really over."

"Is it?"

Kayla frowned. "Of course. I just hope he pulls through this."

Jackie looked at her emotionless.

Kayla held her hands out in front of her. "Don't you see, if he does pull through this, he'll have a chance to get the help he needs."

"Right," Jackie said sarcastically.

Kayla didn't know what else to say.

Jackie sighed. "Look, you obviously have a lot to do here and I need to get to work."

"Okay." Kayla hesitated. "Jackie, everything's going to be okay now."

"I know, I'll see you tonight," Jackie agreed. But somehow Kayla didn't believe her.

The first thing Jackie noticed as she came through the door was the silence. It was well after midnight and she should have been home hours ago. She didn't have to look through the apartment to know Kayla was gone. They hadn't talked since their argument at Kayla's house. She didn't have anything to say.

Jackie dropped her keys on the table by the door and made her way through the apartment. Her skin grew cold as she drew nearer to her bedroom. With each step the coldness crept inside her until all the warmth was drained from her body.

The bedroom was exactly as she always kept it, but it felt empty. There was no sign that Kayla had ever been there. She turned away and as she did she noticed a new picture frame sitting on her dresser. It was a black-and-white photograph of her at the regatta. Kayla had captured the moment of triumph as she crossed the finish line. In that moment she thought she caught a glimpse of the woman Kayla wanted—*needed*—her to be.

Jackie felt something inside her break. She hadn't come home to Kayla as promised. She'd put up a barrier between them. Through her absence and her silence she'd essentially asked Kayla to walk out of her life, and just like her mother, that was exactly what Kayla had done. Once again Jackie found herself alone, wishing someone would come and save her. But this time the only person she needed was the very person she had sent away.

She ground her teeth and punched her fist against the wall. The old emptiness crept through her like a poison. She had to get out of this room. On the way to the balcony she grabbed a beer from the fridge and fell into her favorite lounge chair. She watched the night-life slowly emerge from the growing darkness that mirrored her soul.

It was the chill that finally drew her from sleep. She shivered and pulled her arms and legs close to her chest. Despite the cold, she couldn't bring herself to go inside. She shivered again. She craved the feel of Kayla's body against hers. She missed her. But how could she go on like this? She couldn't deal with the fear and worry of someone lurking in the shadows to hurt Kayla. She'd finally broken free of that life. It was just too much.

Jackie shifted on the chair and felt something hard burrow into her thigh. She reached beneath her and retrieved her cell phone. It was six in the morning. She had two hours to decide what to do before Kayla boarded a plane.

Jackie pushed herself up. On her way to the door she grabbed her keys. She wanted to push the pain and the memories out of her head. The past was roaring through her mind like a speeding train filled with faded images from a nightmare. Jackie ran until sweat mingled with the tears streaming down her cheeks and she had to stop to throw up. She gasped for air, desperate to regain control. She looked at her watch. Damn it. She might have just enough time to catch Kayla if she hustled.

Jackie raced into the airport and searched the lines of people and rows of ticket counters. She pushed through the crowd toward the security check. Kayla stood in line, anxiously checking her phone each time she took a step closer to the counter.

All Jackie had to do was call her name. It was so simple. Kayla was within reach. Jackie stood silent and watched Kayla, trying to sort through the cyclone of emotions tearing her apart. Her heart melted when Kayla looked up and smiled at the attendant. Her smile was warm to anyone who didn't know her, but the smile didn't reach Kayla's eyes, as if it was being weighed down.

"Kayla," Jen called from the other side of the security barrier. Jackie looked past Kayla and saw Jen waving on the other side. When Kayla reached her, Jen pulled Kayla into a warm hug.

Jackie swallowed. Mike must have pulled through. Would he come after Kayla again? Kayla had known the risks she was taking with Mike, and here she was, throwing her life in the air as if it didn't matter. Jackie clenched her teeth against the bile boiling in her stomach as her past and present collided. She closed her eyes and tried to put everything in its place. But her nerves were raw with fear, and the anger from her past blinded her to what was right in front of her.

"Oh my God, it's good to see you." Jen squealed, wrapping her arms around Kayla.

Kayla hugged her. She was surprised Jen had decided to attend the conference with everything that had happened, but she was glad she was there.

"It's good to see you too. Are you sure about this?"

Jen sighed. "There isn't anything I can do sitting around here. He's going to be fine. They were able to wake him up. I'm happy to say the process of doing so was not a pleasant one, and I hope Mike remembers every second of it, though I doubt it. He's stable and once the hospital releases him, I'm sure he's headed to jail."

Kayla took Jen's arm as they walked to their gate. "How are you doing with all of this?"

Jen sighed. "I'm mad as hell." Jen glanced at Kayla apologetically. "Don't get me wrong, I'm very relieved he's okay, but I'm still mad at him for doing all of this to both of us. And I can't forgive him for what he's put you through, K."

"What are you going to do?" Kayla asked.

"I don't know yet. I thought this week would give me time to figure that out. I don't know about you, but I'm looking forward to getting away from everything."

Kayla nodded.

"What about you? How are you doing? I know all of this has been hard on you too."

Kayla looked away, remembering the cold tone in Jackie's voice and the distance between them the day before.

"Kayla. What is it?"

"This has been pretty hard on Jackie. I don't know if we're going to see each other anymore."

"This wasn't your fault. She'll understand that."

Kayla shook her head. "No. This whole thing has brought up some pretty nasty stuff from her past. I don't think she can handle it. I don't think she wants to."

"I'm sure she just needs some time, like we need some time."

Kayla forced a weak smile. "Yeah, maybe you're right. But we were supposed to have dinner last night and she didn't show and she didn't call. I haven't heard from her since she left my house after Mike was taken to the hospital. She didn't want me to go today. Maybe I should have listened."

Jen squeezed Kayla's arm. "I'm really sorry, K."

"It isn't your fault."

"Thanks for saying that, but if I hadn't enabled Mike for so long, none of this would have happened."

"Well, there's no need to beat ourselves up over this. It is what it is, and we can't change any of it." Kayla didn't want to talk about it anymore. She'd already spent the night waiting for Jackie to call, feeling the thread between them fray with each passing hour. She hugged Jen's arm against her side, trying to believe her own words.

Kayla fell into her chair, exhaustion propelling her into gravity's embrace. She had been going from session to session all day and felt as if her brain would explode.

Jen sat down across the table in front of her and handed her a drink.

"Here, try this, it makes everything better."

"I doubt that," Kayla said, taking a sip. She groaned as the cool liquid coated her tongue and sent the soothing flavor of coconut cascading across her taste buds. "Hmm. You might be onto something here."

Jen giggled. "You know it." She waved off the glass as Kayla offered it back to her. "No, go ahead. You need it more than I do." Kayla didn't respond, but took another sip of the tantalizing drink. She didn't know what was in it, but it was delicious.

"So, how are you doing?"

Kayla licked her lips, her mouth suddenly dry. "I'm okay. Any news about Mike?"

Jen shrugged. "He's going to be fine. Of course as soon as he was stable at the hospital, they took him to jail. He agreed to a year-long drug rehab program somewhere in Texas so he wouldn't have to do his time in jail. I hope it works."

"What are you going to do?"

"I'm going to file for the divorce. I love him. I will always love him. But we are broken, and I don't think I can ever trust him again."

Kayla placed her hand over Jen's. "I'm sorry."

"Me too." Jen picked up the drink she'd handed Kayla earlier. "Maybe we both need another one of these."

Kayla smiled. "You might be right."

"Have you talked to Jackie?" Jen asked.

"No."

"Why not?"

"I think I need to give her some time. She's been through a lot and I'm not sure she'll want to see me again once I get back."

"All the more reason you should call. You don't want her to think you don't care."

"I know. Maybe tomorrow."

Kayla stared into her drink, musing about her life and Jackie. What had it been like for her parents, always living one thrill to the next, chasing whatever adventure they could find?

"Hey, where'd you go?" Jen asked.

Kayla blinked to clear the tears that pricked at her eyes, unsettled by a sudden rush of emotion. "Sorry. I was thinking about my parents. I know what happened to them. I spent most of my life resenting them for not being there for me growing up. I didn't want to be anything like them. But now I'm not so sure about things."

"What do you mean?"

"I don't know. Jackie was everything my grandmother warned me about, but she made me feel alive. I miss her so bad it hurts to breathe, but I don't regret anything with her."

"That's good, right?" Jen leaned forward, resting her elbows on the table. "Maybe it's time to do things your way and stop trying to live by someone else's rules."

Kayla pushed away from the table. "Thanks." She had spent her life analyzing her parents. Jackie had called her a hypocrite. Maybe she was right. "It's another long day tomorrow. I think I'll turn in early. Will you be okay?"

Jen smiled. "I'm fine. Go on and do what you need to do. I'll be up later."

Kayla was grateful Jen let the issue drop. "Thanks."

Kayla stepped onto the elevator, warring with her conflicted emotions. Maybe the thing that drew her and Jackie together was their shared abandonment issues. At least she'd had her grandmother. Kayla sighed. Her heart ached for all that Jackie had lost, all she had endured. It was more than just the pain she knew Jackie's father had inflicted. There was the self-imposed guilt about her mother that Jackie shouldn't have to shoulder.

The elevator dinged and Kayla walked to her room. She had left the bedside lamp on and the faint glow bathed the room in muted light. She dropped onto the bed pulling one of the pillows to her chest. It was time she stopped trying to answer the questions about Jackie's life. Jackie had to make her own decisions.

Was it over between them? She just didn't know.

Chapter Seventeen

Kayla walked into the bar with a confidence she didn't feel. She wasn't sure why she was going out, but she knew she couldn't sit alone in her hotel room another night. Jen had been gone for two days, and the walls were beginning to close in on her. The conference was over, and this was supposed to be her big vacation. She laughed at the memory of her plan to meet a woman and live on the wild side for a few days. It turned out her walk on the wild side had been much different than she'd planned. At least the emptiness she felt now was better than the half-life she'd been living, playing it safe.

She settled in at the bar, noting the small groups of women and the sound of laughter that scratched away at her melancholy. She smiled, warmed by the cheerful banter of strangers.

"Hi. What can I get you?"

Kayla looked up at the bartender, a tall thirtysomething woman with sun-bleached unruly hair and a golden tan. Her eyes were the calming blue of the ocean. Faint lines were creased into the corners of her eyes from squinting into the sun, and her smile was playful, if not slightly seductive. Charming didn't begin to describe her.

Kayla sat up a little straighter and took in a deep breath. "What do you recommend?"

"Hmm, that depends on what you like. Are you up for something sweet and fruity, bold and creamy, or something with a little hop?"

Kayla suppressed a laugh but couldn't help the smile that curled at the corner of her mouth. "Nothing fruity. How about something with coconut?"

"You've got it."

The piña colada was pure sin. Kayla savored the rich taste of the coconut as the rum seeped into her like a warm breeze. Some of the tension she'd been carrying eased from her shoulders and she exhaled a long breath, hoping to expel the hurt and disappointment that were her constant companions.

She should be thankful to have this time to clear her head. Going home to her empty house would have been unbearable.

"How's the drink treating you?" the bartender asked, drawing Kayla out of her reverie.

Kayla smiled as the bartender leaned over the bar top, her elbows resting on the smooth wooden surface. She roamed her eyes across Kayla's face, lingering on her lips.

"It's perfect, just what I needed."

The bartender shot Kayla a dazzling smile that exposed faint dimples in her already perfect cheeks. "Glad to hear it." She held out her hand. "I'm Brace."

Kayla enjoyed the flirtation. She shook Brace's hand, enjoying the feel of the warm fingers grasping her own. The touch was friendly and Kayla felt a little less alone.

"I'm Kayla," she responded warmly.

Brace smiled. "How long are you in town?"

Kayla frowned and cocked her head to the side questioningly. "Am I that out of place? How did you know I'm from out of town?"

Brace shrugged. "I've worked here for three years. I know all the locals and I'm certain I would remember if I'd seen you before."

Kayla looked away this time, a little uncomfortable with the compliment. "Thanks. I'll be here for a few more days."

"That's good. I hope to see you around more this week."

Kayla didn't answer, choosing instead to study her drink.

Brace didn't go away though. Instead she studied Kayla with a crooked grin. "So, what's so heavy that you need Ms. Piña's company tonight?"

Kayla looked up. "I don't know what you mean."

"When most people come to the beach, it's all about fun and sun. Why the gloomy face?"

Kayla sipped her drink. "That obvious, huh?"

"Well, I am a professional."

Kayla chuckled at the irony in the joke. "It's complicated."

"Ah, that means it's a woman."

Kayla sighed. Her throat tightened and she was surprised by the sudden rush of pain that twisted in her heart.

"It's a slow night and I have the extra time. Want to talk about it?"

Kayla shook her head. "Thanks, but no." She appreciated Brace's attempts to cheer her up, but the last thing she wanted was to openly analyze and expose her feelings to a stranger.

"Well, if you do want to talk, this is the place." Brace straightened and opened her hands palms up in a show of supplication. "Like I said, I'm a professional."

Kayla smiled weakly, quickly losing interest in the banter.

"Hey," Brace said softly, "if you decide you want or need anything, let me know."

Kayla looked into Brace's eyes, preparing her brush-off, but was surprised by the genuine look of compassion she saw in her gaze. Kayla faltered, again feeling some of her defensiveness deflate.

"Thank you, Brace. I will."

"Good enough," Brace said, snapping her towel and moving down the bar to check on a group of women playing darts.

Kayla didn't know how long she'd been sitting there. She'd had more to drink than usual and it was time to head back to the hotel. When she turned to ask for the check, she was surprised to find a different woman behind the bar. She felt a sliver of disappointment that Brace was not there with her disarming smile.

"Excuse me. Can I get my check, please?"

The new bartender was an imposing woman with a shaved head, broad shoulders, and biceps Kayla doubted she could wrap her hands around.

"You're good. Your tab's already been cleared. Brace took care of it when she checked out."

Kayla was surprised. "But she shouldn't have done that—she doesn't even know me."

The bartender shrugged. "Take that up with her, she's in the back kicking it with her girls." She nodded toward a group of women around a large table in the back of the bar.

Kayla frowned and peered through the bar to see what the group was doing. Cheers erupted and she saw Brace and several of the women toss their heads back as they downed shots of liquor.

"What are they doing?" she asked.

The bartender glanced at the group and smirked. "Just a stupid drinking game."

Kayla felt her resolve settle. She was tired of playing it safe, and this was the perfect opportunity to do something outside her comfort zone. What did she have to lose?

"I'd like to buy a round for the table and one for me too," she said with more fortitude than she felt.

The bartender looked at her for a long moment, as if giving her a chance to change her mind. She shrugged. "Okay, coming up."

Kayla followed the bartender to the table where Brace sat. Brace looked up and grinned as the tray of shots was placed on the table in front of her.

"You're a lucky ass, Brace," the bartender said as she leaned forward.

Brace leaned back in her chair and smiled when she saw Kayla. "Yes. Yes, I am."

Brace pushed back her chair and stood as she held out her hand to Kayla. "Would you like to join us?"

Kayla considered each woman at the table, aware that the game being played now had nothing to do with drinking. *What am I doing? I should turn around and walk away right now before I do something stupid.* Kayla considered her options. She was tired of always playing it safe. What had safe gotten her? Nothing. Nothing but endless nights sleeping alone nursing her bruised ego and battered heart. Doing the right thing had cost her everything. She was tired of always doing the right thing. What had Jackie said? *If you don't take any risks, how do you know you're alive?* Well, it was something like that.

Kayla picked up a shot glass and handed it to Brace before taking one for herself. She touched her glass gently against the one Brace held, the faint clink punctuating her point. Kayla threw back her shot in one swift motion.

The women at the table erupted in cheers as Brace studied Kayla quizzically before tossing back her shot in one practiced swallow.

Kayla felt the burn of the alcohol travel all the way to her heart, where it died, impotent against the pain and emptiness there. She knew alcohol wouldn't take away her pain, but for one night she didn't want to think about the mess her life was in or what was or wasn't happening with her and Jackie. Wasn't that what Jackie would do?

Brace pulled out a chair and motioned for Kayla to sit.

Kayla took the offered seat and picked up another shot. She might be able to trick her mind and perhaps even her body, but she would never convince her heart. But tonight her heart was the one she wanted to forget the most.

Jackie was hit by a wall of sound the moment she pushed through the door at Kristtopher's. Music pounded against her eardrums with a consuming ferocity that left little room for the chaotic sounds of voices as people fought to be heard over the driving beat. She didn't know why she had promised Peter she would come out, but after the week she'd had, the last thing she wanted was to be alone in her apartment surrounded by memories.

She hadn't slept more than a few hours in days. She couldn't even bring herself to lie down in her bed. Instead she chose to stare at the television most of the night, only to wake, exhausted, from the restless cramped night on her sofa.

Jackie spotted Peter and the rest of the group already in full party mode at a table by the dance floor. She stopped at the bar and ordered a beer and a double shot of Fireball. She would need the double if she planned on being human tonight.

A firm hand landed on her shoulder just as the empty shot glass hit the bar top. She fought down the ice-cold whiskey that instantly transformed into liquid fire burning its way to her gut. The heat was still creeping through her cheeks when she turned to see Peter grinning at her. She took a cooling drink of her beer and motioned to the bartender for two more.

"Ready to rumble, champ?" Peter joked.

Jackie shrugged. "Just catching up with you." She grinned and handed him a glass.

"I like the way you think. Let's see what other good ideas you can come up with tonight."

Jackie glanced around the room. Women crowded the bar. There would be no shortage of opportunities to fill the empty hours of the night. Her stomach churned. Maybe that was just the Fireball hitting bottom. She pushed aside her unease and followed Peter across the room to a crowded table.

Heather turned her head, laughter bursting from her lips as she put her arm around the petite blonde beside her. She fixed her gaze on Jackie like a predator that had spotted its next meal.

Jackie downed the shot in her hand hoping the spicy liquid would burn away the disquiet that sat at the back of her throat like a broken scream.

"Come on, tiger," Peter said taking Jackie's hand. She didn't hesitate to follow. She was thankful for the distraction and hoped dancing would burn off some of her restlessness.

She was surrounded by writhing bodies but felt like a ghost walking among the living. It was like being invisible, unable to touch or feel what was real. The heat and the booze were taking effect, causing a numbness to seep through her body. She closed her eyes, letting the rhythm of the music and the frenzy of movement carry her away.

She didn't open her eyes when a hand snaked around her waist to caress her stomach. A lean firm body pressed seductively against her back, matching her movements. Jackie slid her hand over the fingers that were dangerously close to sliding beneath the waistband of her jeans, stopping them from delving any farther. When she didn't pull away, hot lips played along her throat and toyed with the lobe of her ear.

She wanted to believe the lips against her skin belonged to someone else. Kayla was the only one she wanted to touch her. She held Kayla's image in her mind as the room began to spin, and she swayed clumsily into the body pressed against her. Before she could regain her balance the woman slid around her and licked her tongue up the length of Jackie's neck.

Jackie wanted it to be enough. She wanted to lose herself in a woman the way she always had. But no matter how much she drank, and no matter how hard she tried, she could feel the ache bleeding into her consciousness. She pulled away, but firm lips claimed hers and an insistent tongue plundered her mouth with confidence and unfettered passion. With each stroke of tongues, Jackie was falling deeper into the swarm of drink and loss and misplaced desire.

"Come with me," Heather's raspy voice crooned, barely registering in Jackie's thoughts. Not Kayla. Through the haze, Jackie began to fight her way back out of the lies she had been telling herself that allowed her to let another woman touch her. This was wrong.

Jackie pulled away.

"What is it?" Heather stepped closer and slid her hand into the collar of Jackie's shirt and traced her fingers along the edge of her breast. Jackie was drowning in a war of emotions that threatened to destroy the barriers created by her heart. Just as she was about to let go and fall back into the black abyss of meaningless sex, a voice penetrated the darkness, enveloping her as clearly as if it had been real.

Jackie.

Jackie jerked, certain she had heard Kayla call out her name. She looked around the room expecting to see Kayla standing beside her. She clasped Heather's hands and pushed her away.

"No." She held Heather at arm's length and looked into her eyes for the first time that night. "I'm sorry. I can't do this."

"Hmm. That's not what I remember. You were very capable the last time."

Jackie moved away when Heather tried to kiss her again. She wouldn't hide her feelings behind alcohol anymore. It was Kayla's voice she wanted to hear. Kayla's voice she had heard call her name. It was Kayla she wanted.

"I'm not that person anymore," Jackie said before walking out of the bar.

She didn't know what she was going to do about her feelings for Kayla. But if she was ever going to have a chance to find out, she had to stop lying to herself. She had to stop running.

"Where are you staying?" Brace whispered.

Kayla shivered at the brush of warm breath across her cheek. She hesitated, still not certain what she was doing.

"You really shouldn't walk alone. You've had a lot to drink and I'd feel better if I could see you home."

"I'm just across the street at the Hilton. I think I can make it."

Brace slipped a hand around Kayla's waist. "Great. Let's walk." Standing proved more difficult than expected and Kayla was suddenly thankful for the firm hand that steadied her. She let Brace lead her to the hotel and didn't pull away when Brace's hand tightened around her waist as the elevator climbed. Kayla's heart raced, and it was difficult to think through her alcohol-induced haze.

"What number?" Brace asked, when the elevator door opened.

Kayla stepped off the elevator and stopped in the middle of the hall unable to take another step. Could she really allow this woman into her room, into her bed?

"Hey, what is it?" Brace asked.

"Thank you for making sure I got in okay. I enjoyed the company tonight, but I can't ask you in."

Kayla held her breath as Brace studied her. Her tender gaze was inquisitive, not challenging or seductive. She raised Kayla's hand to her lips. "Okay, if that's what you want, but I thought you might want to talk."

Kayla was confused. Did she want to talk? It really didn't matter. She knew what would happen if she let this go any further. And as much as she wanted to pretend she could push away her hurt and move on, she just wasn't wired that way.

"Thank you, Brace, really. You've been very sweet, but…"

"But there's someone else." Brace brushed the backs of her fingers along Kayla's jaw. "I get that. You know where to find me." Brace grinned mischievously. "You know, just in case you change your mind."

Kayla stepped back, breaking the contact. "I'll keep that in mind. Good night."

She was certain she could feel Brace's eyes on her as she turned the corner. She locked the door to her room and let out a long breath as disappointment seeped into her bones. She was so tired. She made it to the bed and collapsed onto her back. She wanted to lose herself in the plush bedcovers and mounds of pillows, desperate for the smallest comfort. Images of Jackie flooded her mind and longing crept through her veins like a river of ice, leaving her lost and barren.

Kayla shivered as she imagined Jackie's hands on her. She grasped for the image, wanting it to be real. Where was Jackie? What was she doing? Who was she with? The last thought proved too much and it pushed her loneliness into misery, and the days of pent-up emotions erupted, unleashing a flood of pain, anger, and disappointment. "Jackie," Kayla cried out in anguish burying her face in the pillow.

Kayla woke in the morning, surprised she'd been asleep. She opened her eyes and groaned as the light hit her like a knife stabbing through her forehead, igniting a persistent pounding headache. She pressed her palms against her temples, pushing against the pressure threatening to make her head explode. How much did she drink last night? Good grief, she didn't get hangovers. Kayla sighed. She must have had more than she thought. She had the sudden memory of doing shots with Brace, and Brace walking her to her hotel.

Squinting, Kayla looked around the room to make sure she was alone. She let out a relieved sigh when she didn't find any sign that anyone else had been there. She was further relieved when she realized she was still wearing her clothes from the night before. Maybe getting drunk was the worst thing she'd done. At least she hadn't slept with Brace.

Kayla pushed out of the covers and made her way to the small coffeemaker. One pitiful cup of coffee, a hot shower, and three Advil later, she stepped onto the beach hoping the ocean waves would wash away the dull ache in her head and the emptiness in her heart.

She strolled along the beach remembering the first time her grandmother had brought her to the ocean. She was afraid of the water, but her grandmother held her hand and led her along the water's edge until step-by-step she waded into the water. Her grandmother had shown her that most of the time the ground was just under her feet, and all she had to do was stand and she could right herself again. When the water was too deep and she struggled, her grandmother would wrap her arms around her and lift her up until she could stand on her own again.

She missed her grandmother and wished she were there now to pick her up and help her find her way. Her grandmother had always been the one person who could always make her feel better. What would she say to her now?

Kayla laughed to herself. She had no idea what her grandmother would say, but she was certain she wouldn't approve of her sitting around feeling sorry for herself. Her grandmother never would have approved of the way she'd behaved with Jackie. Perhaps she should consider that her grandmother was wrong. Even though she was hurt, she didn't regret being with Jackie. Jackie had opened her eyes to things she hadn't realized she needed. Missing Jackie wasn't something that would change anytime soon. So they had some things to work out, and maybe Jackie would end things between them. But that didn't mean what they shared didn't matter. Jackie did matter, and when Kayla wasn't wallowing in self-pity, she had no doubt that she mattered to Jackie too.

It was easy to let disappointment write stories in her head about not being loved enough, not being good enough, not being wanted. Hadn't that been what she had done with her parents? But she had been wanted. Her grandmother had always made her feel wanted, loved, and cherished. Her feelings about her parents were designed around her expectations of who they were supposed to be in her life, how they were supposed to have lived.

Kayla smiled. It was time to change her story. Her happiness was up to her. It was time to go home.

Jackie pushed her way out of the bar desperate to find her way out of the mess she had made with Kayla. She leaned against the cold stone of the building trying to figure out how she was ever going to make things right. The sounds from the bar intensified and then were slowly muffled as the door opened and closed when someone walked out. She groaned as footsteps approached her. She didn't want to deal with Heather anymore.

"What's up, Jack?" Peter said as he approached.

Jackie was relieved it was him. She could use a friend right now.

"Hey, Pete. I'm sorry to run out like that, but I don't think I'm up for this tonight."

"Want to tell me what's going on?"

Jackie raked her hand across her face. "I screwed up. I screwed up big."

Peter clasped her shoulder. "How about we go somewhere for a cup of coffee and you can tell me all about it."

Jackie nodded. "I'd like that."

Peter put his arm around Jackie. "Come on, there's a Waffle House down the street."

Kayla waited as Peter stirred sugar into his coffee. He took a sip, sighed, and put the spoon down. Once the coffee was to his liking he settled his gaze on her.

"Let's have it. You've been half crazy for days. What's the story?"

Jackie took a deep breath and told Peter everything. When she finished, Peter folded his arms across his chest and stared at her.

"Well? Are you going to say anything?" she asked.

"Do you love her?"

Jackie frowned. "Weren't you listening? I just told you."

"No, you didn't. You told me you met a woman who made you realize what an ass you are. I want to know if you love her."

"Why does it matter?"

Peter sighed. "Because I know what it's like to be someone's convenience, a toy they use to make themselves feel better. I don't want you to do that to Kayla. If you love her, that's a different story."

Jackie thought about what Peter had told her about Calvin the night they met at his aunt's bar. Peter loved Calvin, but Calvin had other ideas about their relationship. She saw how much that hurt Peter. She didn't want to do that to Kayla.

"I've never been in love before. Kayla makes me believe things are possible that I never even dreamed. I don't want anyone but her. I don't know what to do without her."

Peter smiled. "Have you told her that?"

Jackie sighed. "No."

"I think you should. Right after you apologize for being such an ass."

"I know. I can't believe I left her to deal with that lunatic on her own. I have no idea what happened to him after they took him to the hospital. What if he was okay and found a way to come after her again?" She shook her head. "The bottom line is I wasn't there when she needed me. I was just thinking about myself. I was selfish. It's been days now. I don't even know if she's okay. Anything could have happened."

"Call her."

"I already thought of that. But by the time I got my head out of my ass it was too late—she was already gone. What am I supposed to say now? It isn't exactly something I want to explain over the phone."

"You did screw up."

"Tell me something I don't know."

"Does she love you?"

Jackie sighed. "I don't know. I know there's something special between us. I know she feels that too."

"When does she get back in town?"

"Day after tomorrow."

"Well, I suggest you get your act together before then. If you're serious about her, you have to start acting like it. If not, you need to figure out how to satisfy that itch some other way. She doesn't need you jerking her feelings around like that."

"I know. Maybe she's better off without me."

"All the more reason to have this shit figured out before you do talk to her. Make up your mind and stick with it."

Jackie studied Peter. He was a good friend and the closest thing to family she had. "I'd like you to meet her. You'd like her. I don't have any family for her to meet besides you."

Peter smiled. "Now you're talking."

CHAPTER EIGHTEEN

Kayla rubbed sleep from her eyes and sank into a booth at Pete's Coffee Shop.

"Hey, Trish."

"Good morning, sunshine." Trish eyed her, taking in her lack of sleep and overall weariness. "Damn, how long has it been since you slept?"

Kayla grimaced. "Gee, thanks, you're making me feel so much better. I just flew in last night and, as you mentioned, haven't had much sleep. Someone called and woke me up before dawn."

"Sorry." Trish smirked. "I just thought you'd want this as soon as possible."

Kayla stared at the file Trish tossed on the table. She opened the file and began to read, her eyes widening with each revelation.

"I don't know what to say. I can't believe you found her."

Trish sat back in her chair with a smug grin. "I can't believe you doubted me."

Kayla smiled. "It's not that. I know how good you are at your job, but this was a special case."

Trish nodded. "Yeah, there was some really shady stuff there to wade through to get to the answers, but it's all there."

"I can see." Kayla sighed. "I just have to figure out what to do with this now."

"What do you mean?"

Kayla shook her head. "Nothing. The situation has changed since I asked you to do this for me, that's all."

"Well, that part is up to you." Trish stood, dropping two bucks on the table as she downed the rest of her coffee. "Let me know if there's anything else you need. I've gotta run."

"Thank you, Trish, I owe you one."

"Don't even think of it."

Kayla read through the file again, amazed at the story unfolding before her very eyes. How was she ever going to tell Jackie? They hadn't even talked in the two weeks she'd been away and she wasn't certain Jackie would want to see her at all. This wasn't exactly the kind of thing she could just drop in the mail and wish Jackie luck.

Kayla sighed. It wasn't up to her to decide if Jackie needed the information or not. Jackie deserved to know what happened to her mother. She just wasn't sure she was ready to see Jackie. She wasn't sure her heart could take it. She missed her. She'd fallen in love, and the woman she wanted to spend her life with had walked out of her life. That wasn't something she could get over in a couple of weeks.

Kayla forced herself to drive to Jackie's apartment. She knew the longer she put this off the more she would just torture herself. She needed to get it over with.

She stood outside Jackie's apartment for the longest time, unable to make herself ring the bell. Every time she reached out her hand, her eyes welled up with tears.

She cleared her throat, wiped her eyes, and tried again. She pushed the buzzer before she could chicken out.

She heard movement behind the door but no one answered. She tried again.

"Who is it?"

Kayla's heart skipped at the sound of Jackie's voice.

"It's Kayla. I need to talk to you."

The door opened with a sudden flourish that startled Kayla.

"What are you doing here?"

"Uh, I'm sorry I didn't call first. Is this a bad time?" Kayla tried not to scan the room, afraid Jackie wasn't alone.

Jackie seemed flustered. Her skin was unusually pale and her eyes were red.

"Are you okay?" Kayla asked.

"I'm fine. I'm sorry, come in."

Kayla followed Jackie inside. The room was a mess. An old pizza box sat on the floor next to the sofa and the coffee table was littered with glasses and beer bottles. Jackie wore old sweats and her hair looked like she'd just woken up. And by the looks of the tangled blanket and rumpled pillow on the sofa, Kayla was pretty sure that was exactly what had happened.

"How was your trip?" Jackie asked as she crumpled up the blanket and pillow into a pile on the floor.

Kayla frowned. "It wasn't the trip I had hoped it would be, but I think it was a good time to sort through some things."

Jackie swallowed. She was pretty sure she was one of those things Kayla had needed to sort through. She should have called. She'd wanted to call a million times but didn't know how to get over Kayla's bullheadedness and her own fear.

"Yeah, I know what you mean."

Kayla still hadn't looked at her.

"Look, I didn't come here to give you a hard time." Kayla sighed. "I don't know what's going on between us right now, but I have something I need to talk to you about."

Jackie was confused. What else did they have to talk about?

"A few weeks ago I told you about a friend of mine, the investigator I had look into your mother's disappearance."

Jackie's heart stopped. "You found my mother?"

"Yes. I received the information this morning."

The world was out of sync. Time and Kayla's words seemed slowed and out of proportion. Nothing seemed to make sense. Jackie blinked several times, trying to clear her head.

"What did you find?" Jackie wasn't sure her words came out right. Her voice seemed hollow and distant through the rushing sound of blood pulsing through her ears.

Kayla reached for Jackie's hand. The touch was comforting and made Jackie's heart ache for the loss of every love she had ever known.

"Maybe you should sit down."

Jackie nodded and sat on the edge of the sofa, poised for the news she knew would change her life.

"The first thing you need to know is that your mother is alive."

Jackie's eyes filled with tears of relief. She could finally let go of the greatest fear of her life. The ache in her heart followed when she realized what this meant.

"Okay. That's good." Jackie's words were strained as she spoke. "Is she happy?"

Kayla squeezed Jackie's hand. "I'm afraid it isn't that simple. I know what you're thinking, but your mother didn't leave either."

Jackie was confused. "What do you mean?"

"There was an accident."

Jackie looked ashen, and Kayla was afraid she was about to pass out.

"Sit back and lean your head back." She pushed lightly against Jackie's chest, guiding her back onto the sofa. She moved some of the trash littering the table. "Put your feet up a minute." She lifted Jackie's feet, placing them on the coffee table. She dashed into the kitchen, wetting a dishtowel before returning to Jackie.

"Are you okay?" Kayla asked as she brushed Jackie's hair back from her forehead with the tips of her fingers and dabbed her brow with the towel.

Jackie reached for her hand, wrapping her long fingers around Kayla's. "I'm okay. I just got a little dizzy."

"Can I get you something?" Kayla asked, her voice laced with concern.

Jackie looked up at her, her eyes filled with questions and wonder, and something more.

"I missed you." Jackie said in a whisper.

Kayla drew in a sharp breath. Her heart raced. This was Jackie. How had she let so much time slip between them? "I missed you too." Kayla sat back, breaking their contact. "Do you feel like sitting up?"

Jackie nodded and raised up until she rested her elbows on her knees. Kayla settled onto the sofa next to her.

"Are you ready?"

Jackie nodded.

Kayla pulled out the file and handed it to Jackie.

Tears filled Jackie's eyes as she stared at the pages trying to take in what she read. Her mother was alive.

She'd spent most of her life searching for the answers to what happened to her mother, haunted by fear and hurt. But now that the answers were right in front of her, she was afraid of what she would find. What if she didn't like the answers?

Kayla sighed. "Your mother suffered a traumatic brain injury during a car accident. She didn't come back for you because she couldn't."

Jackie closed her eyes and let the information sink in. She swallowed hard as the words began to filter through her consciousness. Her mother hadn't left her after all.

"Her maiden name was Forrester? I never knew that," Jackie croaked.

Fire scorched through her veins as she realized what had happened. Her father had hidden her mother from her. All those years he had known where she was and hadn't told her she was alive. Jackie hated him even more for making her believe the lies about her mother and keeping her from her.

Kayla was quiet while Jackie read. The warmth of her hand on Jackie's thigh was a comfort linking her to hope.

Jackie let the papers fall to her lap and leaned her head back against her seat. It was all laid out in front of her, the injuries, the rehabilitation her mother had gone through, and the physical and mental deficits her mother had suffered. She saw this kind of injury in her work and it took a lot of time and rehabilitation to bring someone back from that kind of devastation. She didn't have the medical records to explain the details, but she had a pretty good idea what her mother suffered. How had she done it alone?

Jackie looked up at Kayla. "All this time and she was less than a thirty-minute drive from my home. How's that possible?"

Kayla stroked Jackie's hand. "I think your heart led you back to her, you just needed a little help."

"Can I see her?"

Kayla smiled. "When you're ready."

CHAPTER NINETEEN

Meadow View wasn't too bad for an assisted living home. The happy yellow exterior was surrounded by beautiful landscaping that gave it a resort feel. Jackie sat in the car staring up at the windows as she tried to imagine what her mother's life was like. She had imagined seeing her mother a million times, but now that she was here she couldn't muster the courage to face her. She was terrified that her mother wouldn't know her or even remember her. What then? She bit her lip. She was being a coward.

Jackie followed Kayla through the french doors and scanned the room. A few residents sat watching television as she signed in at the front desk.

"Excuse me, can you tell me where I can find Jacqueline Rose Forrester," Jackie said to a passing nurse. Jackie swallowed the lump in her throat and scolded herself for not knowing to look for her mother under her maiden name. No wonder her vain attempts to find her mother had never amounted to anything. She hadn't even been looking for the right name. Jackie was pulled back into the present as the nurse pointed down a broad hallway that led out to a courtyard at the back of the residence.

"Ms. Rose likes to sit in the garden during the day."

"Thank you."

Jackie and Kayla walked along the path toward the gardens. Jackie smiled. Her mother had always loved flowers. The path led to a small fountain surrounded by zinnias, roses, and peonies. A woman sat on a bench facing the pond. A cane rested next to her and she held her left hand at an awkward angle at her side. Jackie froze. The familiar face that resembled her own seemed drawn, and the short cut hair was a stark contrast to the long locks her mother had once been so proud of.

Jackie's heart broke and mended itself in one instance. This was her mother. She was alive.

"You go," Kayla whispered.

"Aren't you coming?" Jackie asked, surprised.

Kayla smiled and patted her hand. "I'll be right here if you need me."

Jackie swallowed against the torrent of emotions bombarding her and nodded. "Thank you."

Jackie stepped closer until she was only a few feet away from the bench.

Her mother turned and smiled at her.

Jackie smiled back. "Hello, Rose," Jackie said softly.

"Hello."

Her mother's voice was soft but stronger than Jackie expected. She waited but there was no sign that her mother recognized her. The disappointment was a sharp stab to her heart.

Her mother gestured to the seat next to her. "Would you like to sit with me?"

Jackie smiled and watched her mother's eyes follow the movement of a cat that was trying to sneak up on a bird.

A frown slowly creased her mother's brow and she turned back to face Jackie again. This time she studied Jackie's face, her warm green eyes clouded with pain and something close to recognition.

"Do I know you? You seem familiar."

Jackie nodded and smiled faintly. "You used to know me. But that was a very long time ago."

Her mother studied her intently. "You remind me of my daughter. You look like her. But I lost her."

Jackie slid her palms against her jeans to hide their trembling. Her mother recognized her. "It's me. I'm Jackie."

The color in Rose's cheeks brightened and her eyes glistened as she searched Jackie's face. Her chin trembled, and with a shaky voice she asked, "Jackie?"

Jackie nodded. She was afraid to speak. She was afraid to even breathe.

Her mother gasped and covered her mouth with her good hand. Her hand shook and her eyes were wide with disbelief and shock.

Jackie studied her mother's face and the long scar that crossed her forehead, fading into her hairline. She recognized the damage that had been done. Her heart ached for her mother and all the time they had lost and all that they had suffered. She hoped she never saw her father again. This betrayal was too much, even for him.

"How can this be?" Rose asked.

Jackie took her mother's hand, drawing it to her lips. Her mother gripped her fingers and stared into her eyes with hope and grief. "It's me, Momma. I'm sorry. I didn't know."

Her mother shook her head and pulled back. She moved her fingers across Jackie's face, stroked her hair, and clutched her shoulder as if she was trying to convince herself Jackie was real.

"How are you here? I lost you."

"A friend found you for me. I'm sorry it took me so long." She thought about what her mother said. "What do you mean you lost me?"

Her mother's chin trembled. "The accident. You died."

Jackie shook her head, confused. "What accident?"

Her mother bit her lip and pointed to her scar. "Martin said I killed you."

Jackie was consumed by rage as she realized what had happened. Her father had convinced them both the other was dead. Of course that was the easiest way to cover his tracks and keep either from asking questions or trying to find the other. He had manipulated them both. She couldn't hate anyone more than she hated her father in that moment.

"Martin lied to us both, Mother. He told me you were dead too. He kept us apart."

Her mother frowned and shook her head. "Oh God. Why? Why would he do that?"

Jackie shook her head. "I don't know." Jackie had the urge to break something. She wanted to scream at her father, to hurt him the way he had hurt her so many times. But she held her anger at bay and focused on her mother. Her father had stolen too much time from them already. She wouldn't allow her hatred of him to steal this moment from her too.

"He doesn't matter anymore," Jackie said in a whisper. "All that matters is that I have you back now."

Rose nodded and clasped her hand around Jackie's wrist. Her fingers were soft but strong as she gripped Jackie's arm. The look in her eyes was desperate. "I don't remember things. I don't remember the accident. But I never forgot about you."

Jackie smiled. The words were like a healing salve on an old wound, mending the pieces of her heart back into place. There were so many things she wanted to know, so many things she needed to say, and now she finally had time for all of them.

Jackie closed the door to her mother's room. They had talked for hours and she was just beginning to believe the dream was real. But it was getting late and her mother needed to rest. She let her hand slip from the smooth wood of the door, comforted by knowing she would see her mother again in a matter of hours.

She found Kayla sitting in the lobby playing chess with one of the residents.

"Hey," Kayla said as Jackie placed her hand on her shoulder.

"Sorry, Ben, looks like my time is up. Maybe we can play again sometime."

The old man clasped Kayla's hand in both of his. "Anytime, young lady. I hope you'll come back soon."

Kayla kissed his cheek. "I will."

Jackie stopped outside and drew in a deep breath of night air. "I don't know how to thank you for giving me back my mother. I feel like I'm in a fairy tale and I've just been released from some evil spell."

"How did things go?" Kayla asked.

"She's amazing." Jackie sighed. "There are a lot of things I may never know, and there seems to be no end to the evil my father could do. But I have her back now, and that changes everything. You have changed everything."

Kayla smiled. "I'm glad."

"I was afraid she wouldn't know me, but she did. She never forgot me. My father convinced her I was in the accident with her and that I was killed. He kept us apart on purpose. What kind of person does that?"

"I don't know," Kayla answered. "Are you ready to go home?"

Jackie nodded.

The flickering lights flashed past the window in a blur as Jackie tried to put together the pieces of her life. There was so much she wanted to say to Kayla, but she didn't know where to begin. As Kayla pulled into the apartment complex, Jackie realized she had to find her courage or Kayla would be gone again.

"I came to the airport the morning you left. I wanted to tell you I was sorry for letting my fear get in the way of us, but I chickened out at the last minute. I'm sorry I let you down."

Kayla was silent so long Jackie was sure she would never speak to her again.

"There were things happening in my life that were too close to your past. I understand how hard that was for you, but I can't understand how you could just walk away from what we had."

Jackie bit her lip. *What we had.* Kayla had used the past tense.

"I was wrong. I was stupid. I didn't realize how important you were to me until you were gone. I didn't want a relationship because I was afraid of losing you the way I lost my mother. I thought if I walked away, I wouldn't get hurt. I didn't realize it was already too late."

Kayla frowned. "What are you saying?"

Jackie sighed. "These past couple of weeks without you have been miserable. I can't sleep, I can't eat, I don't want to do anything without you."

Kayla shook her head. "You made it pretty clear you didn't want a relationship."

Jackie nodded. "There were a lot of things I believed for a long time, but I was wrong. I feel like I'm a different person now. You changed everything, Kayla."

Kayla had tears in her eyes. "How do I know you won't change your mind? What will you do if some idiot decides to turn my life upside down again?"

Jackie took Kayla's hand. "I won't change my mind. I've realized I'm not a kid anymore. I don't have to run away anymore. I never thought I'd want to share my life with anyone, but now I can't imagine my life without you."

Kayla couldn't believe what she was hearing.

"All this time I was afraid to admit that I need you. But I'm not afraid anymore. I don't want to lose you, Kayla."

Kayla let out a sob.

Jackie brushed her fingers across Kayla's cheek. She looked into her eyes and smiled.

Tears streaked Kayla's face now. Jackie hoped they were happy tears.

"Can you forgive me? I know you think it's too risky, but will you give me another chance?" Jackie asked cautiously. "You've given me back my mother, you've shown me how good it feels to share my life with you. Give me a chance."

Kayla buried her face in Jackie's shoulder. She was about to take the biggest risk of her life. She'd promised herself she'd start living and stop being afraid to take risks. Yes, Jackie could change her mind, but how would she know what forever was if she didn't start here? Wasn't this what she'd always wanted?

"Yes," Kayla said firmly.

"Yes, what?" Jackie asked.

Kayla lifted her head and met Jackie's gaze. "Yes to everything." Kayla smiled. "When you walked away, walked out of my life, I felt empty inside. I spent the past two weeks trying to figure out how I was going to put my life back together when I didn't like the pieces anymore. I realized I don't want to just play it safe. I want to feel alive. I want to wake up every day and wonder what will happen next. That's what you give me."

Jackie wrapped Kayla's face in her hands and kissed her. Kayla tasted her own tears as Jackie's tongue parted her lips.

Jackie deepened the kiss, her lips bruising against Kayla's mouth. Kayla clung to Jackie's shoulders and was consumed by the rightness of Jackie's touch. She'd thought she'd lost Jackie. Having her in her arms now was more than she had hoped, but everything she had dreamed. Kayla pulled away, breaking the kiss, her breath ragged bursts fueled by her racing heart.

"Let's go home."

Jackie smiled. "Your place or mine?"

CHAPTER TWENTY

Jackie started picking up trash and empty beer bottles the moment they walked into her apartment.

"Sorry about the mess."

"What happened in here? Did you have a party or something?"

Jackie sighed. "Hardly, I've kind of been a mess the past couple of weeks."

Kayla's heart warmed at the sight of Jackie so out of sorts. They still had a lot to work out, but she had no doubt Jackie was worth it. Kayla reached out and took a bottle from Jackie's hand, placing it back on the table.

"This stuff can wait."

Jackie stilled.

"I don't care about the mess."

Jackie nodded.

"It's been a big day. A lot has happened. Maybe we should just slow down and take it all in."

Jackie looked at her as if she was seeing her for the first time. When Jackie didn't move, or say anything, Kayla began to feel self-conscious. "What?"

"I'm afraid I'll wake up and all of this will be a dream."

Kayla wrapped her arms around Jackie's neck. "I guess I'll just have to make sure I'm there when you wake up."

Jackie smiled, sliding her arms around Kayla's waist. "I like the sound of that."

Kayla pressed her lips to Jackie's, savoring the heat growing between them. She needed to reestablish their connection. She knew

Jackie's body, and she needed Jackie's touch to tell her what words couldn't.

"That doesn't mean I have to sleep on the sofa, does it?" Kayla asked playfully.

"God, I hope not."

Kayla slid her hands down Jackie's chest, brushing her fingers over Jackie's breasts. She felt Jackie shiver beneath her touch.

Jackie slid her hands beneath Kayla's shirt, needing to feel her skin beneath her touch. Her pulse raced, her heart thundering in her chest as if she was back on that rock about to jump into the water below, but this time, she was about to take a much bigger leap.

Kayla slipped her hand in Jackie's, lacing their fingers together. Jackie stepped back, tugging gently on Kayla's hand, leading her to the bedroom. At the edge of the bed, Jackie brushed her fingers along Kayla's jaw, cradling her face in her hand. She kissed along the line of Kayla's jaw until her lips found Kayla's mouth. Her lips were soft and the gentle brush of Kayla's tongue against hers sent a jolt of need coursing straight through to her soul. This kiss was slow and easy, even reverent.

Jackie felt her clitoris swell. She was wet with need and want, but this was one time she didn't want to rush. She wanted to savor every moment, every touch. She brushed her thumb across Kayla's nipple and heard a quiet moan.

Jackie slowly undid the buttons of Kayla's blouse, kissing the newly exposed skin as her fingers slid the garment off Kayla's shoulders. She closed her lips over the hard nipple pressing against the thin fabric of Kayla's bra.

Kayla groaned and leaned into Jackie, intensifying the pressure of Jackie's mouth on her breast. Of all the times they'd made love, nothing had ever felt this intimate. Kayla's legs grew weak as Jackie fell to her knees and pressed her lips to her stomach as she slid her jeans and panties down. She pressed a kiss to the small mound of hair. Kayla's legs were shaking now.

"Are you okay?" Jackie asked glancing up as she moved to brush kisses up each thigh.

"The bed would be good."

Jackie slid her arm around Kayla and lifted her into her arms, guiding her onto the bed. Kayla's head swooned as she met Jackie's gaze. The moment their eyes met, Kayla knew where she belonged. Something shifted and her heart opened. She watched Jackie undress before settling onto the bed beside her, tracing her fingers along the dips and curves of Kayla's body.

Kayla gasped as Jackie parted her, brushing her fingers against her clitoris before slipping into her. Jackie sucked a breast into her mouth as she stroked Kayla. With each tug on her nipple, each stroke filling her, all Kayla's doubts melted away. She wasn't afraid anymore. In that moment, she knew where she belonged.

Jackie held Kayla in her arms, relishing what a gift it was to hold her and feel the aftershocks of her orgasm ripple through her body. Jackie buried her face in Kayla's hair as she nuzzled against Kayla's neck. The past two weeks had been hell without Kayla but had given her time to realize what had been missing in her life. Kayla was like calm water beneath her as her boat skimmed across the surface. Kayla was the wind in her hair as she raced along a country road. Kayla was her hope, her sanctuary, her peace. She had proven she could make it on her own—she knew how to survive. But Kayla had shown her how to open her heart and trust. Kayla had shown her that her life could be so much more.

Jackie brushed a strand of hair from Kayla's cheek, and leaned down and kissed her. This woman had given her her life back. She had saved her.

"Hey"—Kayla lifted her hand and stroked Jackie's face— "what's going on with you?"

Jackie looked at Kayla, trying to memorize every detail of her, every detail of this moment.

"What?" Kayla asked with concern in her voice.

Jackie brushed a kiss against Kayla's lips. She shook her head slightly and let out a long breath. "I love you."

Kayla's eyes misted with tears and for a moment Jackie was afraid Kayla was upset.

"Is that okay?"

Kayla shook her head. "More than okay, it's everything."

Jackie smiled. "I should have told you this weeks ago, but as a good friend pointed out to me, I was being an ass."

Kayla laughed. "Who's this friend? I owe them a huge thank you."

Jackie grinned. "My buddy Pete. And I can't wait for you to meet him."

Kayla stilled. "Are you sure?"

"Yes. I love you, and I plan to spend the rest of my life proving that to you every day, if that's what you want too."

"Oh, I do, sweetheart, I do. I love you too."

Jackie's heart soared. For the first time in her life she knew what love felt like and it was amazing.

"There's still a lot of things we need to work out. Your mother for one. You two have a lot to work through."

Jackie wrapped her arms around Kayla and pulled her close. "Thanks to you, that's true. But that's what families do—they work through things together."

Kayla laid her cheek against Jackie's chest, comforted by the strong steady beat of her heart. A family. She was going to have a real family. She smiled, reassured by Jackie's strong arms enveloping her. She pulled away looking at Jackie seriously. "If we're going to be a family, I want a cat."

Jackie laughed. "A cat, a dog, I'll even get you a bear. Anything you want."

Kayla pulled back, peering into Jackie's eyes. "I love you."

Jackie kissed her. "I love you."

Kayla picked up the little ball of fur currently untying her shoes. She and Jackie had picked out the kitten together but couldn't settle on a name. Jackie wanted to call her Bear and Kayla thought she was sweet and wanted to call her Sugar. Kayla scratched the kitten behind the ear and was rewarded with a calm, steady purr. She stared out the window marveling at how much her life had changed.

Kayla smiled as Jackie pulled into the drive.

"Look, Sugar Bear, Momma's home."

Jackie bounded through the door carrying a new cat bed.

"Hey, beautiful." Jackie kissed Kayla and rubbed the cat's head. "I missed you guys today."

Kayla smiled. "Hmm, how much?"

Jackie slid her hands along Kayla's sides and gripped her hips, pulling her to her.

Kayla groaned. "Don't start something you can't finish. We're having dinner with your mother tonight."

"It's still early."

"Not early enough."

Jackie laughed. "Later, you're mine."

"Sweetie, I'm always yours."

Jackie smiled. "I love you too."

The kitten swatted Jackie on the cheek and bit her nose.

Kayla laughed. "Sugar Bear missed you today."

Jackie raised her eyebrows. "Sugar Bear? Huh, that works. Look what I brought you." Jackie held up the cat bed for Sugar Bear to sniff. The kitten grabbed it with her paws in her own little version of a bear hug.

Jackie laughed. "I think she likes it."

Kayla smiled. "Hey, you need to get a shower and get ready or we're going to be late."

Jackie kissed Kayla again, groaning when Kayla nipped her lower lip. "Maybe we should shower together and save some time," Jackie teased.

Kayla shook her head. "You're insatiable. If we start in the shower, there's no way we'll make dinner. Now go."

Jackie kissed her before jogging down the hall to the shower.

The love in Kayla's heart swelled and she knew she would spend the rest of her life loving this woman. She put the cat down in her new bed and headed for the bathroom. Maybe it wouldn't hurt if they were just a little late.

About the Author

Donna K. Ford is a licensed professional counselor who spends her professional time assisting people in their recovery from substance addictions. She holds an associate degree in criminal justice, a BS in psychology, and an MS in community agency counseling. When not trying to save the world, she spends her time in the mountains of East Tennessee enjoying the lakes, rivers, and hiking trails near her home.

Reading, writing, and enjoying conversation with good friends are the gifts that keep her grounded.

Donna can be contacted at donnakford70@yahoo.com

Books Available from Bold Strokes Books

Forsaken Trust by Meredith Doench. When four women are murdered, Agent Luce Hansen must regain trust in her most valuable investigative tool—herself—to catch the killer. (978-1-62639-737-8)

Her Best Friend's Sister by Meghan O'Brien. For fifteen years, Claire Barker has nursed a massive crush on her best friend's older sister. What happens when all her wildest fantasies come true? (978-1-62639-861-0)

Letter of the Law by Carsen Taite. Will federal prosecutor Bianca Cruz take a chance at love with horse breeder Jade Vargas, whose dark family ties threaten everything Bianca has worked to protect—including her child? (978-1-62639-750-7)

New Life by Jan Gayle. Trigena and Karrie are having a baby, but the stress of becoming a mother and the impact on their relationship might be too much for Trigena. (978-1-62639-878-8)

Royal Rebel by Jenny Frame. Charity director Lennox King sees through the party girl image Princess Roza has cultivated, but will Lennox's past indiscretions and Roza's responsibilities make their love impossible? (978-1-62639-893-1)

Unbroken by Donna K. Ford. When Kayla and Jackie, two women with every reason to reject Happy Ever After, fall in love, will they have the courage to overcome their pasts and rewrite their stories? (978-1-62639-921-1)

Where the Light Glows by Dena Blake. Mel Thomas doesn't realize just how unhappy she is in her marriage until she meets Izzy Calabrese. Will she have the courage to overcome her insecurities and follow her heart? (978-1-62639-958-7)

Escape in Time by Robyn Nyx. Working in the past is hell on your future. (978-1-62639-855-9)

Forget-Me-Not by Kris Bryant. Is love worth walking away from the only life you've ever dreamed of? (978-1-62639-865-8)

Highland Fling by Anna Larner. On vacation in the Scottish Highlands, Eve Eddison falls for the enigmatic forestry officer Moira Burns, despite Eve's best friend's campaign to convince her that Moira will break her heart. (978-1-62639-853-5)

Phoenix Rising by Rebecca Harwell. As Storm's Quarry faces invasion from a powerful neighbor, a mysterious newcomer with powers equal to Nadya's challenges everything she believes about herself and her future (978-1-62639-913-6)

Soul Survivor by I. Beacham. Sam and Joey have given up on hope, but when fate brings them together it gives them a chance to change each other's life and make dreams come true. (978-1-62639-882-5)

Strawberry Summer by Melissa Brayden. When Margaret Beringer's first love Courtney Carrington returns to their small town, she must grapple with their troubled past and fight the temptation for a very delicious future. (978-1-62639-867-2)

The Girl on the Edge of Summer by J.M. Redmann. Micky Knight accepts two cases, but neither is the easy investigation it appears. The past is never past—and young girls lead complicated, even dangerous lives. (978-1-62639-687-6)

Unknown Horizons by CJ Birch. The moment Lieutenant Alison Ash steps aboard the Persephone, she knows her life will never be the same. (978-1-62639-938-9)

Divided Nation, United Hearts by Yolanda Wallace. In a nation torn in two by a most uncivil war, can love conquer the divide? (978-1-62639-847-4)

Fury's Bridge by Brey Willows. What if your life depended on someone who didn't believe in your existence? (978-1-62639-841-2)

Lightning Strikes by Cass Sellars. When Parker Duncan and Sydney Hyatt's one-night stand turns to more, both women must fight demons past and present to cling to the relationship neither of them thought she wanted. (978-1-62639-956-3)

Love in Disaster by Charlotte Greene. A professor and a celebrity chef are drawn together by chance, but can their attraction survive a natural disaster? (978-1-62639-885-6)

Secret Hearts by Radclyffe. Can two women from different worlds find common ground while fighting their secret desires? (978-1-62639-932-7)

Sins of Our Fathers by A. Rose Mathieu. Solving gruesome murder cases is only one of Elizabeth Campbell's challenges; another is her growing attraction to the female detective who is hell-bent on keeping her client in prison. (978-1-62639-873-3)

The Sniper's Kiss by Justine Saracen. The power of a kiss: it can swell your heart with splendor, declare abject submission, and sometimes blow your brains out. (978-1-62639-839-9)

Troop 18 by Jessica L. Webb. Charged with uncovering the destructive secret that a troop of RCMP cadets has been hiding, Andy must put aside her worries about Kate and uncover the conspiracy before it's too late. (978-1-62639-934-1)

Worthy of Trust and Confidence by Kara A. McLeod. Special Agent Ryan O'Connor is about to discover the hard way that when you can only handle one type of answer to a question, it really is better not to ask. (978-1-62639-889-4)

Amounting to Nothing by Karis Walsh. When mounted police officer Billie Mitchell steps in to save beautiful murder witness Merissa

Karr, worlds collide on the rough city streets of Tacoma, Washington. (978-1-62639-728-6)

Becoming You by Michelle Grubb. Airlie Porter has a secret. A deep, dark, destructive secret that threatens to engulf her if she can't find the courage to face who she really is and who she really wants to be with. (978-1-62639-811-5)

Birthright by Missouri Vaun. When spies bring news that a swordswoman imprisoned in a neighboring kingdom bears the Royal mark, Princess Kathryn sets out to rescue Aiden, true heir to the Belstaff throne. (978-1-62639-485-8)

Crescent City Confidential by Aurora Rey. When romance and danger are in the air, writer Sam Torres learns the Big Easy is anything but. (978-1-62639-764-4)

Love Down Under by MJ Williamz. Wylie loves Amarina, but if Amarina isn't out, can their relationship last? (978-1-62639-726-2)

Privacy Glass by Missouri Vaun. Things heat up when Nash Wiley commandeers a limo and her best friend for a late drive out to the beach: Champagne on ice, seat belts optional, and privacy glass a must. (978-1-62639-705-7)

The Impasse by Franci McMahon. A horse packing excursion into the Montana Wilderness becomes an adventure of terrifying proportions for Miles and ten women on an outfitter led trip. (978-1-62639-781-1)

The Right Kind of Wrong by PJ Trebelhorn. Bartender Quinn Burke is happy with her life as a playgirl until she realizes she can't fight her feelings any longer for her best friend, bookstore owner Grace Everett. (978-1-62639-771-2)

Wishing on a Dream by Julie Cannon. Can two women change everything for the chance at love? (978-1-62639-762-0)

boldstrokesbooks.com

Bold Strokes Books

Quality and Diversity in LGBTQ Literature

victory EDITIONS

Drama

MATINEE BOOKS

SCI-FI

E-BOOKS

MYSTERY

erotica

SOLILOQUY

EROTICA

YOUNG ADULT

BOLD STROKES BOOKS

LIBERTY

Romance

W·E·B·S·T·O·R·E

PRINT AND EBOOKS